St. Martin's Paperbacks Titles
by Ronda Thompson

The Dark One

The Untamed One

The
Untamed One

Book Two in the Wild Wulfs of London series

Ronda Thompson

St. Martin's Paperbacks

THE UNTAMED ONE

Copyright © 2006 by Ronda Thompson.

Cover photo © Shirley Green

ISBN: 0-312-93574-9
EAN: 9780312-93574-0

Printed in the United States of America

St. Martin's Paperbacks edition / May 2006

St. Martin's Paperbacks are published by St. Martin's Press, 175 Fifth Avenue, New York, NY 10010.

10 9 8 7 6 5 4 3 2 1

This book is dedicated with love to the "aunts." Georgia, Lola, Nela, Lisa, Rose, Dora, and Myriam, your support over the years has meant more to me than you will ever know. Thank you for always being there for me.

Damn the witch who cursed me.
I thought her heart was pure.
Alas, no woman understands duty,
be it to family, name, or war.
I found no way to break it,
no potion, chant, or deed.
From the day she cast the spell,
it will pass from seed to seed.

Betrayed by love, my own false tongue,
she bade the moon transform me.
The family name, once my pride,
becomes the beast that haunts me.
And in the witch's passing hour
she called me to her side.
Forgiveness lost, of mercy none,
she spoke before she died:

"Seek you and find your worst enemy;
stand brave and do not flee.
Love is the curse that binds you,
but 'tis also the key to set you free."

Her curse and riddle my bane,
this witch I loved yet could not wed.
Battles I have fought and won,
and still defeat I leave in my stead.
To the Wulfs who suffer my sins,
the sons who are neither man nor beast,
solve the conundrum I could not,
and be from this curse released.

Ivan Wulf,
In the year of our Lord
Seventeen hundred and fifteen

Chapter One

The woods of Whit Hurch, England, 1821

The musket ball had passed through his shoulder. Blood seeped from the wound, warm and sticky against Jackson Wulf's skin. The peasants of Whit Hurch were superstitious lunatics, the lot of them. They chased him now, voices raised in anger, eyes filled with bloodlust to kill him. The village folk believed that he was some kind of beast—a man during the daylight hours, a wolf when the moon sat round and plump in the night sky.

Damn the idiots . . . they were right.

"There he is!"

A musket cracked. The ball splintered a tree not an inch from Jackson's face. His fair looks were the one gift he'd been given in his cursed life. "Not the face, you bloody bastards!" he shouted. "Anything but the face!"

Another ball whizzed past, down lower. *Not that, either!* Jackson thought, and took off again. A woman's high-pitched plea sounded behind him.

"Papa, do not kill him! I love him!"

Sweet Hollis, the barmaid at the tavern he'd frequented these past five nights. Her father owned the tavern and the few rooms upstairs, one of which Jackson had occupied this past week. The daughter had slipped Jackson a free tankard or two behind her father's back. She'd also let it be known that she wouldn't mind Jackson slipping her a little something in return. Jackson had been tempted, as women were one of his many weaknesses, but he'd stayed focused upon his quest.

Women were the crux of his troubles and always had been. A year prior when he'd traveled abroad, Jackson had foolishly given his heart to a young society miss. Lady Anne Baldwin had embodied all that a proper gentleman desired in a wife. Beauty, grace, kindness. He'd become smitten with her, and her ready friendship with a man most of society shunned. In the end, the young woman had never known that she had stolen his heart or that she'd brought his family curse down upon his head.

Centuries past, all Wulf males had been cursed by a witch. Cursed by a witch, and perhaps released from the same curse by a witch's death, Jackson was thinking. Rumors had led him to the village of Whit Hurch, where it was said a witch lived among the villagers. Through careful questions, Jackson had learned that the woman had disappeared some months ago but was thought to be hiding in the woods surrounding the village.

Jackson hadn't found her yet, but he had vowed that he would. His future and the future of his brothers might be tied to killing her. A riddle written within a poem left by the first cursed Wulf instructed that future Wulf males seek out their worst enemy, be brave, and do not flee. If Jackson could find the witch he'd heard once lived in the village, killing her might end the curse for him and his brothers. That was if he managed to stay alive long enough.

Shots sounded behind him. Jackson ran until his brow was beaded with sweat. His shoulder stung and the loss of blood made him light-headed. Glancing up, he noted that the night was still a ways off. Normally, he would not wish the full moon upon himself, but now, in order to survive, he needed the wolf that would rise up inside of him.

It was such a transformation, witnessed by one of the village folk last eve when he thought he was alone in the woods, that had brought him to his current predicament. Jackson couldn't control it. Perhaps he might have learned to live with it if he could, but like his fondness for liquor and women, in the end he always surrendered to a force stronger than his will. No more, he had decided.

Jackson's oldest brother, Armond, had married. A marriage of convenience, or so Armond claimed, but Jackson knew better. If Armond wasn't fully in love with his young bride already, it was only a matter of time. Jackson had decided to save them all.

It was important to him to end the curse that robbed him and his brothers of a normal life. The curse that had robbed them of their parents and of their social standing among London society. Jackson had been given nothing of importance to do in his life . . . nothing but this, and he would succeed. He would find the witch and he would kill her if it meant breaking the curse. But the woods were vast, and even his superior tracking skills had yet to lead him to the woman he sought.

Exhausted, Jackson paused, leaning against the trunk of a tree to catch his breath. He wiped the sweat from his brow with the sleeve of his fine coat. The breeze picked up, and turning, he closed his eyes and allowed the cooler air to revive him. A scent suddenly drifted to him on the wind. It was a woman's scent. Even slightly befuddled from blood loss, Jackson knew the scent of a woman when he smelled it. His hearing was much more attuned to sound than that of a normal man. He listened.

He heard a soft moan, a slight feminine grunt, and then

the sound of ragged breathing. Noises a woman might make while entertaining a lover. Was it the witch? Jackson had trouble believing so, for in his mind the woman he sought was old and ugly. With her scraggly hair and wart-ridden face, the only way such a woman could get a man into bed with her would be to cast a spell over him.

Still, her scent drew Jackson. The smell of woman, of sunshine, of earth and rain, and the subtle scent of honeysuckle and, oddly enough, blood. The sounds of heavy footfalls crushing through the brush, of voices raised in excitement for the hunt, drifted away from him, and all he heard was her. All he smelled was her. She filled him with her presence, lulled him with the soft sounds she made, and he went to her willingly, almost as if fate commanded it.

Weaving in and out of the trees, Jackson fought the pain of his injury, ignored the clotted feel of blood beneath his shirt, and pressed onward. The cottage he stumbled upon a while later was little more than a shack, overgrown with vines so that it was almost invisible against the thick forest wall.

He neither smelled a cooking fire nor saw the tattletale rise of smoke from the cottage's crumbling chimney. He heard no sounds of life, not even among the forest animals. Hackles rose on the back of his neck. The silence was eerie.

The woman was inside; he did sense that much. Jackson reached for the knife he kept strapped to his belt. It was not there. No knife, no weapon. Some killer he was. The village folk had surprised him. He'd barely been able to dress and escape his lodgings over the tavern when they had come for him.

If he must, he'd kill her with his bare hands, Jackson decided. If the woman was in fact the witch he sought and her death meant a normal life for him and his brothers, he could do it. His resolve strengthened, Jackson crept to the cottage door and eased it open.

The lighting inside was dim, but his eyesight was superior to that of a normal man. A woman tossed upon a straw mattress thrown down against the dirt floor. Her knees were bent and spread wide, her legs bare. The large mound of her belly moved beneath a soiled frock bunched around the top of her thighs. No lover did she tryst with, but with the burden of labor.

Jackson's gaze traveled up her swollen body, past the tangled mass of red curls hanging over her shoulders, to her face. Their eyes met, held, and it was as if neither could catch a breath.

"So, you've come for me at last," she whispered. "Kill me, but do not harm the babe. He is innocent."

Hackles rose on the back of Jackson's neck again. If she knew why he'd come, this was the woman he sought. The witch. His greatest enemy. But she did not look as he had pictured her in his mind. She was not old and stooped, with warts and facial hair. She was beautiful. Even covered in perspiration, her hair tangled, and her clothing worn and soiled, her beauty could not be disguised.

Her eyes were the deepest shade of green, like the forest that protected her. The tangled curls that hung past her shoulders were as fiery red as a summer sunset. Although her body was now swollen with child, her bones were small and delicate. Jackson could crush her easily.

"Not yet," she said, as if reading his thoughts. "Let me deliver my child. I beg of you, do not harm him. After you've killed me, take him to a village family. Do not tell them where you got him, only that he is alone and in need of someone to watch after him."

Her words unnerved Jackson. She seemed accepting of

his duty. Resigned to her fate but not resigned to the fate
of her child. And still, he had trouble believing this was
the woman he sought.

"Are you a witch?"

Her gaze narrowed. "You know that I am," she said.
"That is why you are here, is it not?"

Pain clouded her eyes before he could answer. She bit
down hard on her full lower lip, bringing blood. Her belly
bunched and moved and she lifted her hips and pushed
but, as his eyes could plainly see, to no avail.

"He's stuck," she finally managed to say as she lay
back against the straw, gasping for breath. "The babe
needs to be turned. Let me see your hands."

Dazed, by either his own blood loss, her knowledge
that he would come for her, or simply having to witness a
woman with spread legs in a circumstance far different
than he was accustomed to, Jackson lifted his hands for
her inspection.

"They will do," she announced. "Your fingers are long
and slender, your hands delicate despite your tall frame.
You must put them inside of me. You must turn the babe
so he will be able to make his journey."

Jackson's fingers had been inside of a woman before,
to be certain, but never for the purpose she suggested. Her
plea held no appeal to him whatsoever. He frowned down
at her and shook his head. "I cannot," he assured her. "I
know nothing of these matters."

When pain gripped her again, she grabbed a stick and
stuck it between her teeth until the pain passed. "Then do
nothing," she panted. "Stand and watch me die, and the
child along with me. It will be easier than having to kill
us later."

What she said was true enough. Jackson had never
raised a violent hand to a woman in his life. That thought
had teased him throughout his quest—destruction of the

enemy he must face and conquer in order to break the curse. He'd known to emerge victorious he must kill her, but the killing, he'd never allowed himself to dwell upon that . . . to question whether he was capable. Had fate played into his hands? But if nature stole her life and he did not, would the curse still be broken?

It suddenly occurred to Jackson that if there was a child, there was a man. Jackson sniffed the air but caught no scent that anyone except the woman had inhabited the cottage.

"Where is the babe's father?" he asked.

Her eyes widened slightly. "You do not know? He did not send you?"

Confused, he shook his head. "No. I've come to kill you for my own reasons. Your foul deeds against my family, or at least the deeds of your kind."

Her labor took whatever response she might have made. Her back arched. Her belly lifted, rippling beneath her gown. A low moan escaped her parted lips. She pushed, pushed, he saw, with all her strength, which wasn't much, and again, nothing happened.

"Have you a weapon?" she panted.

Rather shamefaced, he answered, "No."

The woman frowned. Her pain-filled gaze ran the length of him. "Then it was with your hands you intended to kill me." She struggled up upon her elbows. "Do so now. If you won't put them inside of me, put them around my throat. End this suffering for me. Without your help, the babe and I are doomed anyway."

Mercy killing? To Jackson, it sounded so much better than outright murder. He should end her suffering. Seeing her pain brought him no pleasure, no sense of justice. It sickened him. But to kill her so that her suffering might end . . . he could live with that, couldn't he?

He swayed slightly with dizziness as he approached

her straw mattress. Jackson kept his gaze averted from her lower half, exposed for his eyes, which might have pleased him immensely under different circumstances. He knelt beside her. She stared up at him, pain evident in her eyes but not fear. God, she had more courage than he did.

"Do it," she urged, then tilted her head back, allowing him access to her slim throat. "I have long suspected that my differences would someday lead me to this end. I accept my fate."

The woman's passiveness angered him. Where were her instincts for survival? Where was her rage that she had been given a life different from everyone else's? Why did she offer him her throat when she should be fighting him to the bitter end? Perhaps she deserved to die. If she valued life so little, why not oblige her?

Her skin was soft, warm beneath his fingers when he wrapped them around her neck. The contact caused a spark, like the air fraught with tension before a storm. She felt it, as well, for her eyes, which she had closed against him, suddenly opened.

"You are different, too," she whispered. "You are not a man. But neither are you a beast. You are both."

There was no call to deny her claims, if Jackson was a little unnerved that she saw him for what he was. His face had served him well in the past—a disguise that hid his darker nature.

"I will be a man again," he assured her. "And nothing but a man when you die by my hand."

She moistened her lips, and he noticed how ripe and pink they were despite the abuse she'd put them through. "But what sort of man will you be?" Her unsettling eyes, slanted, almost feline, studied him. "The sort who can live with himself afterward?" She leaned forward and sniffed at him. "The liquor I smell on your breath tells me the answer to my own question. You will drown in it. In the end, it will make you even less of a man than you are now."

Jackson's grip tightened around her throat. Her words stung him. The truth to them, he supposed. He'd had a nip even this morning when he first rose. He'd told himself only to chase the chill from his bones. He told himself a lot of things since his lust for liquor, and for women, had taken over his life.

Beneath him, the woman gasped in pain. Her hands closed over his. She pressed his fingers against her throat. "Please," she whispered.

Women had begged for his mercy before, but always because they thrashed in pleasure, never in pain. Jackson tried to force his fingers to squeeze. They would not oblige. It was the babe, he told himself. The witch was right. The child she carried was innocent of the mother's sins. Jackson eased his hands away from her throat. Through tear-filled eyes, she stared up at him.

"Whatever you are, it is not as bad as what you become in this moment," she said. "Will you sit idly by then and watch us suffer for whatever sin you think I have committed against you?"

"No," he assured her. Jackson moved down between her legs. It was a place not usually unfamiliar to him but a circumstance nearly beyond his comprehension. "Tell me what to do."

Chapter Two

Lucinda had wanted to cry when the man removed his hands from around her throat. His refusal to end her suffering quickly did not come as a surprise to her. Men, people in general, seemed to like her to suffer. She was a witch and did not try to disguise the term politely by calling herself a healer, although she did have a certain skill in that area. She had been paid to cast spells, to read fortunes, to deliver children. Her mother had been a witch and her mother before her and on down the line for centuries past.

People shunned Lucinda in the light of day, but then they crept to her cottage in the village under the cover of darkness. They asked for potions to make them more attractive, they fetched her for a birth going badly, for a number of things, but she knew well enough if a crop failed or if the weather turned bitter, she would be the first to be blamed.

Now, when all had been dark and despair, her heart leaped with hope. He would help her . . . which made little sense if he also still planned to kill her. Lucinda didn't mind dying so much, but the babe, the innocent taken root by a foul deed done to her while she lay unconscious in the great lord's manor, was not to blame for her sins, or his father's.

She thought that Lord Cantley had sent this man to kill her—to dispose of the child lest he one day pose a threat to the crown—but the stranger had his own reasons to want her dead. She would accept his help now and ask questions later.

"Slide your hands inside of me. Find the babe and turn him. I suspect he is trying to come into the world facing the wrong way."

Glancing down between her legs, he shuddered. "My hands will never fit in there."

"They will," she insisted. "You are not to worry about the damage you do to me. If I am to die anyway, there is no point in being gentle. The child. I want him to live."

The man lifted a brow. "Him?"

"A son," she assured him. "In the basket in the corner, there is a bottle of liquor. Use it to cleanse your hands, but do not drink it," she added, as if in afterthought. "At least not until you've delivered the child and murdered me while I lie here too weak to protect myself. Then by all means, celebrate your bravery over killing a defenseless woman."

The man frowned down at her, but then he scrambled to the corner and found the bottle as she'd bade him to do. Lucinda watched him douse his hands in the brandy. She also saw him eye the bottle with longing, almost as lustfully as a man eyed a beautiful woman. He placed the bottle back into the basket and rejoined her. The man removed his coat, a finely made coat, she took time to note, and then rolled back the sleeves of his equally fine linen shirt.

"I thought when I first stumbled upon you that you

were brave," he said. "I see now that you simply suffer from ignorance. Begging so prettily for the life of your child, then demeaning me in the next breath does not aid your current cause."

Lucinda had always had a sharp tongue. She'd never been taught to mince words. She was no highborn lady, schooled in manners and how to blush prettily for a man to get her way. Lucinda usually said what she thought without care to the consequences. It wasn't as if people had to think well of her. People had not thought well of her since the day she was born.

Pain chased her thoughts away. "Now," she panted. "Reach inside of me and turn the babe."

She felt his hand probing her, gently at first, then with more urgency as the pain made her gasp and moan. He was right, though; just the presence of one hand was almost more than she could bear. Two hands would never fit.

"I feel it," he said. "I feel the head, but it is not turned facing up."

The news perplexed Lucinda. She'd delivered many babies, had begun doing so at the tender age of thirteen. She was certain the babe's position inside of her must be the problem. Another thought occurred to her.

"Can you feel around his neck? Is the cord strangling him and keeping him from moving forward?"

"Cord? What the bloody hell does that mean?"

"Just find his neck," she insisted. The awful pain was building again, and if he could untangle the cord from around the babe's neck normal progress could be made. "Do you feel something there?"

"Yes," he finally answered. "Something ropelike, but slimy."

"That's it," she said. "Can you manage to loosen it?"

"I'll try."

His trying nearly killed her. Lucinda grabbed the stick

and stuck it between her teeth to keep from screaming. The man might stop if he knew how badly he hurt her, but then again, why would he? He wanted her dead. She supposed he had never imagined he would kill her quite this way.

"I've done it." His voice held an edge of excitement. "I've loosened the cord from around the babe's neck."

And not a moment too soon. The urge to push was upon her and Lucinda couldn't control her body's natural instincts. She had little strength left, but she lifted herself upon her elbows, and when she could no longer fight her body's response she pushed. The babe moved.

She felt the difference inside of her, and knowing that she now had a fighting chance to save her son gave Lucinda a surge of strength that should have long been used up. Lying back, she rested for a moment, waiting for the next assault of pain. It came quickly, almost too quickly to aid her need for rest.

"Push harder," the man demanded.

If Lucinda had the strength, she would kick out and mar that handsome face of his. It bothered her that she'd noticed his fair looks, considering her circumstances. But then, his handsomeness was hard not to notice. She supposed only a dead woman might remain unmoved by that face.

Then Lucinda had no time to think about the stranger's startling good looks. Not the wheat-ripe streaks in his hair, the warm, tawny hue of his skin, the dark velvet color of his eyes, the length of his lashes, or the deep indentations his dimples slashed into the sides of his cheeks. It was time to push again, and Lucinda tried with what little strength she had left.

"Harder!" the man ordered. "Harder or you'll never live to see the face of your child. Push and I promise you, I will see that he is well taken care of."

Hope tried to rise above the waves of her despair. Could she trust the word of a man who'd admitted he'd come to kill her? Lucinda wanted to. God, how she wanted to. "Promise," she whispered. "Promise me that you will take care of him. Promise me that he will never go hungry, or unclothed, or without shelter."

"I promise," the man said. "Now, push, dammit!"

When the next pain came, she did exactly that. Lucinda pushed with all her might.

"I see the head!" the man nearly shouted. "He's coming!"

Lucinda bore down. The pressure was so intense it felt as if she were being ripped apart. She nearly screamed, but she refused to use the energy. Instead she bore down hard. Two more strong pushes and the child slipped from her body.

"I've got the slimy bugger; what do I do with him now?"

Trying to catch her breath, she instructed, "Hold him up by his feet. Give him a slap on his arse."

A moment later, the sweetest sound that she had ever heard filled the tiny cottage. A cry of outrage. A cry of life. Her son had been born. Resting upon her elbows, Lucinda watched the stranger wrap the child in his fine coat. He stared down at her son as if he'd forgotten Lucinda existed, the handsome lines of his face etched in wonder.

"He's perfect," he whispered.

"Does he have everything he's supposed to have?" she asked, her motherly instincts taking over.

He counted fingers and toes. "Yes. A little over-indulged with his manly parts, though."

An irrational urge to giggle nearly overtook her. Under the circumstances, Lucinda shouldn't find anything he said amusing. "That's normal. With small babes," she specified. "I suppose they grow into their manly parts soon enough. Or I suppose in some cases, they might even outgrow them."

He glanced up at her. "Not in all cases," he assured her.

"You must cut the cord," she said. "I want to hold him."

The man's smooth brow furrowed. "Cut it? With what? I told you that I have no weapon."

It was foolish to trust him, but what choice did Lucinda have? If he really intended to kill her, she vowed to hold her son in her arms before he did. "The basket." She nodded to the corner again. "Inside, there is all we need to tend to my son. The pain caught me off guard and sent me to the floor. I didn't have time to fetch it."

The stranger gently laid her son upon the ground, fetched the basket, and knelt by her side. Lucinda instructed him on what to do, how to tie the cord, cut it so that the babe did not bleed to death. There were clean cloths in the basket, and as he set about cleaning the child Lucinda saw to her own sorry state.

The frock was ruined beyond saving. Lucinda turned her back and had no choice but to strip from her bloody clothes. She reached into the basket for a clean frock, clean drawers, and the thick rags that would staunch her bleeding. While the stranger was focused on cleaning the babe, she saw to her own personal matters. She'd barely had time to pull the clean frock over her head, the front still gaping open where the buttons hadn't been fastened, when he was suddenly there beside her, handing her the child.

The sight of her son made Lucinda forgot all else. He was beautiful. He was perfect in every way. Then Lucinda saw the mark upon his thigh and her blood turned to ice. It was the mark of his father—a small purple dragon. It was also a death toll for her child. The Earl of Cantley had ties to the crown. He was the king's cousin. The lord of the manor would never allow a bastard to one day threaten the throne of England or to threaten all that he would bestow upon his legitimate heirs. That was the reason he'd ordered her death before the babe was born.

Having brought two of Lord Cantley's legitimate sons into the world, Lucinda easily recognized the mark. So would any who saw it. "You poor babe," she whispered, pressing the child close to her breasts. The babe cried, rooted at her breasts, and finally latched onto her nipple. From the first weak pull a bond was formed.

Lucinda stared down at the babe, her eyes awash with tears, her heart swelling with love. Her survival instincts finally rose inside of her. Suddenly fierce protectiveness unfolded within her. Not only for the babe but for herself as well. She glanced at the stranger from beneath her lashes. He wasn't looking at her but seemed fascinated by the sight of the babe suckling at her breast.

"I had forgotten they served any purpose save that of my own pleasure," he said. "Maybe a man's fascination with a woman's breasts begins from the moment he is born."

Her gaze strayed to the sharp knife he had laid on the ground beside her mattress. "Who are you?" she asked.

Still distracted by the babe, he answered, "Lord Jackson Wulf."

Lucinda had heard his name before or, rather, his last name. Even in the villages, gossip about the higher circles of London society was a subject much talked about. She supposed she would have known he was of noble birth even had he not told her his name. The man's clothing, his speech, his mannerisms, all spoke of his higher position in life. Lucinda had heard of the wild Wulfs of London. It was said they were cursed by insanity. Not true, she realized. They were cursed by something much darker. But what did that have to do with her?

"Why do you seek vengeance?" she asked. "I do not know you, nor do you know me."

Perhaps reminding him of his intentions was not the wisest thing to do, she realized, too late. His gaze moved from the babe up to her face. His eyes suddenly had a glow about them they hadn't had moments before. For the first time, Lucinda noticed his injury—the blood that stained the shoulder of his fine shirt, a good amount of blood, she noted.

"I know your kind," he answered, his voice bitter. "There is a riddle. I must face my greatest enemy and emerge the victor. It was a witch who cursed us a century ago. A witch's death that might set us free."

Not all of her kind were evil and would curse men. Lucinda was a white witch, as her mother had called her. She could not cast evil spells or even bring harm with her magic. Still, a bad deed against someone was always easier to remember than a good one. Lucinda tried to put a brave face forward. "I see," she said. "I must look frighteningly dangerous to you, lying here half-dead from blood loss and clutching a wee, innocent babe to my breasts. If you intend to kill me, what are you waiting for?"

He had glanced away from her and didn't appear to be listening. "They're coming."

Confused, for she heard nothing but an eerie silence, she asked, "Who is coming?"

His profile was magnificent. Every feature upon his handsome face was no less than perfect. Even the strong line of his jaw and the sensual shape of his lips were not in contrast but in perfect accord with each other. His brows and lashes were dark compared to his sun-streaked hair. Even the shadow of his beard was dark. Dark and light. He was a man of contrasts and she sensed the trait went deeper than his skin. And yet his was a face that had never known violence. There were no scars to muddy his handsome features.

If he felt her regard, he did not acknowledge it. He sat very still, his attention obviously focused upon something beyond her comprehension. While he was distracted, Lucinda slowly moved her hand toward the knife. She gripped the hilt and pulled the weapon closer.

"The villagers," he finally answered. "They hunt me. Hunt me as if I am an animal."

Lucinda's heart lurched. The villagers were after him? He'd brought them to her door? Lord Cantley had put a price on her head to make certain no one gave her shelter in the village. If Jackson Wulf didn't kill her, one of Lord Cantley's paid henchmen certainly would once she'd been turned in for the reward.

"Night falls." He said the words softly, but his voice sounded different than it had a moment earlier. "You and the babe are in danger from me, and so are they."

From his own admissions, Lucinda had been in danger from the moment he'd stepped inside of the cottage. She had been forced to hide away in the pitiful shack these many months. Conditions here were hard for her. She'd feared she might starve to death and the poor babe inside of her would be born so small he'd not have a fighting chance in life.

"They will be upon us in a moment." Jackson's odd gaze swung back to Lucinda. "The night reaches out to me more quickly than their feet can carry them here. If I kill you now, this can end for my family."

The babe slept nuzzled against her bare breasts. Slowly, Lucinda laid him aside. She clutched the knife tighter in her fist. The sight of Jackson's glowing eyes unnerved her. His eyes and the way they drifted downward to her bare breasts. No wee babe suckled there now. The way he looked at her was different. He lusted for her. It was not an expression Lucinda was unfamiliar with.

She would use his weakness against him if she must, for Lucinda doubted that she could stab him without the element of surprise on her side.

It took nearly more courage than she had, but she whispered, "Touch them. Touch me. If I am to die, give me pleasure with the pain."

Again, his odd glowing eyes lifted to her face. He did not touch her, but he leaned toward her. She was surprised by the spark that ignited when his mouth brushed hers. It made her jump and jerk away, but then Lucinda took a deep breath and leaned forward, pressing her lips against his. The spark was still there, only overshadowed by much darker emotions. He took her chin in hand and gently opened her mouth.

The stroke of his tongue inside her mouth made her pulse leap and spread butterflies to her stomach. He also used it to sooth the bite marks she'd made to her lower lip. She might have resisted his pull had he not done that. Had he not shown that small amount of compassion toward her. Compassion was as new an experience to her as giving a kiss, instead of having one wrested from her. His hand twisted in her hair. He slanted his mouth in a way that brought them closer somehow, allowed him deeper access.

It was too much for her usually dulled senses to handle. He was too much. Too male. Too skilled. Too dangerous. Despite all that she had suffered and all he intended for her to suffer, hunger rose up inside of Lucinda, desire—both things she had never experienced with a man, even though she was now a mother.

Her life was not one of gentle wooing. It was coarse and often vulgar. Any kiss that had been taken from her in

the past had been the same. This man, this beast, her
would-be assassin, knew how to kiss a woman. How
could lips be both firm and gentle? Sweet as apple butter
but potent as apple wine? He'd sucked her down into a
whirlpool with one kiss, and now she spun helplessly
around and around at the water's mercy.

He drowned her in feelings unfamiliar and unwanted,
and like a drowning woman, Lucinda fought to find the
surface and breathe again. Her arms slid up around his
neck. Shyly she touched her tongue to his. He made a
deep sound in his throat that vibrated to the very core of
her. She despised him for forcing emotion from her, despised herself for feeling anything but loathing for a man
who planned to kill her. His eyes were closed so that he
didn't see the knife clutched in her hand. Slowly, Lucinda
raised her arm, steadied the blade, and brought it down
into his back.

Chapter Three

Jackson sensed danger before he could clear his mind enough to react. The blade pierced his skin, but at his sudden intake of breath the woman hesitated. Her hesitation cost her from inflicting any true damage. Jackson struggled from her arms. He twisted the knife from her fingers and flung it across the room.

"You were going to kill me," he accused, surprised that he had trouble catching a normal breath when all he'd done was kiss her.

"You said you were going to kill me," she shot back, and she, too, sounded breathless.

"But to act as if you wanted me, that is low."

Her chin jutted up. "No lower than killing a woman after she has just given birth to her first child!"

She had a valid argument. But there was no time to compare sins. Already Jackson's skin had begun to itch. It was the fur forming beneath his flesh. The fur that would spring forth upon his body, cover him in the pelt of an animal—a wolf. He quickly rose, tugging off his clothing. When claws shot from his fingertips, he would ruin his clothes in the beast's frantic efforts to remove them.

"What are you doing?" the woman whispered.

"Preparing for the change," he answered. "Gather up the babe and go. I'll have to kill you another day."

She said nothing for a moment. Then she made an un-feminine snorting noise. "Gather up the babe and flee? Do you think I have the strength to go racing through the woods? I've just given birth!"

Jackson knelt beside her. He brought his face close to hers. "If you want to live, if you want your child to live, you will find it, and find it quickly!"

She might have been about to argue further, but pain suddenly shot through his stomach and forced him to clutch his middle.

"What's wrong with you?" she asked.

Rocking back and forth with the pain, he answered, "You mean besides the musket ball that tore a hole through my shoulder and now the stab wound to my back? I'm changing," he said more seriously. "Get out while you still can."

In a matter of moments Jackson knew he would fall to the floor because the pain had become so excruciating. He would experience close to what she had just experienced. A birth. The birth of the wolf. While he still had the clarity of thought, he reached down and removed his boots. Since he wasn't modest, he thought nothing of shucking his trousers. If he managed to survive this night, he'd like to have clothes to wear when morning found him naked and dazed.

The woman still lay against the straw pallet, now clutching the babe to her and staring at Jackson, her kiss-swollen mouth slightly ajar.

"Get moving!" he ordered. "And close the door on

your way out. Maybe I can distract them long enough for you to escape."

She blinked up at him. "You want to save me? First you want to kill me, and now you want to save me?"

Carrying on a normal conversation had become difficult. Jackson felt fangs lengthen in his mouth. Perhaps she needed to see them to rouse her from her stupor and send her running. "I cannot let anyone else kill you," he explained. "The duty is mine." Pain ripped through him again, sending him down on all fours. "Go," he growled. "Escape while you still can!"

It was the sight of his teeth, the fangs that flashed in the cottage's dim interior, that sent Lucinda scrambling up and away from him. She had feared that she didn't have the strength to rise from the pallet, but she had done so without thought to her limitations.

Her legs felt shaky beneath her frock. She needed a bath desperately, but now was not the time to think of luxuries. Now was the time to think of survival. Now was the time to think of her son, given to her without choice, without even recollection of receiving him.

She backed away from the man who'd gone to the floor on all fours. Many had forgotten that the world was a place of white miracles and black magic. The villagers still clung to the old superstitions. Lucinda had helped them to do so, being a witch as she was. The sight of a man with fangs and fur sprouting out from beneath his skin surely unnerved her, but it did not surprise her.

Although she was by nature curious and Lucinda would have liked to remain to see the transformation complete, she knew to linger could cost both her life and the life of her child. She bent and grasped the basket that held what little she owned. Cautiously, while Jackson

Wulf continued to struggle from the shape of man into that of an animal, she edged along the rotting walls of the cottage toward the door.

She paused at the doorway. A glance over her shoulder nearly sent a shriek from her throat. He stood now, on all fours, the man completely gone, a wolf in his place. His eyes glowed inside the cottage's dim interior, and they were focused intently upon her. If he killed her while in wolf form, could his curse for a fact be broken?

Or were his claims nonsense? How could she be his greatest enemy when the two of them had never met until today? Lucinda had done him no harm, cast no spells against him. But he had saved her life, the life of her child, so could she in good conscience leave Jackson to the villagers?

The babe in her arms let out a soft cry, which helped with her decision. She had another's life to think about now, not just her own. This man-beast—whatever he was—would come after her if he lived. Men had never been a pleasant part of her life. She'd never known her own father. Lucinda had no last name, nor would her poor babe. In a moment of weakness the stranger had helped her; she could show no weakness in return.

Lucinda quickly slipped from the cottage and pulled the thatched door closed. In the distance, she heard the shouts of men on the hunt. Night had fallen, but she'd learned the woods well during the past months she'd spent hiding here. She hurried in the opposite direction of the village, the direction the hunters would approach from. Her legs still shook. She summoned the will to go on, the strength to put one foot in front of the other and as much distance as she could between herself and the cottage.

Behind her, a howl sounded. Chills raced up her spine. Struggling with the babe in her arms and the basket of what little she owned, she continued onward. Her cottage in the village had been much nicer. She'd owned things, bought with the coin from those who wanted good spells cast and babies delivered. But then her own curse had ruined everything she had worked for. Her fair face had attracted the great lord's attention. When Lucinda refused to be flattered by a married man's interest in her, he had stooped to using her own potions against her.

Lucinda should rightfully hate all men. They had caused her naught but trouble, and still she hesitated in the woods, turning back to stare in the direction of the cottage. She heard the sounds of shouts, then musket fire. The noise made her flinch. Much worse was the sudden smell of smoke on the air. In the distance, flames leaped toward the sky. The village men had set the thatched cottage aflame.

Somewhere deep inside of her, she felt a moment of loss. Almost grief. Why she did not know, nor did she have time to examine it. Jackson Wulf, handsome devil that he was, had meant to kill her, had admitted as much. His death should come as a relief to her. He would not follow. He would not threaten her again.

Blinking back the sting of traitorous tears, Lucinda turned from the sight of the night sky glowing yellow in the distance. It occurred to her that she had nowhere to go, no roof to put over her wee babe's head. Jackson Wulf had promised he'd see to the child. He'd taken responsibility, at least with words; she could not know if he would have stood by them with actions as well.

He had family. The Wulf brothers were legendary. And if outcasts among society, they had wealth. Should she go to them? Tell them of their brother's death? Perhaps they would be beholden to her. Perhaps they would pay her for bringing the news . . . then again, perhaps they would kill her.

Chapter Four

London, three months later

The bed was too large for a lone woman. But it was soft and the bedding was fresh. Lucinda stretched like a cream-fed kitten. She slept in a soft cotton gown. A row of silk ribbons decorated the neckline. Never before had she felt silk against her skin. A fire burned in the grate, casting a warm glow around the large bedchamber. She felt safe and content for the first time in her life.

In the room next to hers, her son wailed softly. Lucinda almost instinctively rose to pad next door, but she remembered that the wet nurse would see to Sebastian's needs. Lucinda's milk had dried up only a scant month into her son's life, aiding the brave decision she'd made once she reached London.

In the bat of a lash, she'd gone from being a poor witch with no last name to a grand lady. Lucinda lay back against the sheets and sighed her contentment once more. Her son was quiet now, no doubt nursing at Martha's big breasts. Hawkins, the household steward, had secured the woman for Lucinda. Now she hadn't a care in the world . . . at least not until the owners of the fine town house returned to London.

But Lucinda didn't want to think about that. The past three months had been heaven on earth. There was a fine roof over her head, food in her belly, and clothing to wear that was far grander than any she'd ever owned before. Hawkins had assured her that Lady Wulf would not mind if Lucinda borrowed anything she might have need of in the woman's absence. Lucinda wondered if the woman was traipsing around the country estate, Wulfglen— where, Lucinda had learned, the lady and lord had gone for an extended honeymoon—naked.

Surely no one woman could require all the clothing Lucinda had found left behind in the woman's wardrobe. All the niceties aside, Lucinda was most grateful that her son was safe from harm and that he wouldn't starve on the streets.

Lord Cantley would never think to look for her here. She supposed there was already gossip floating around London about her, for servants were known to talk, but Lucinda was well used to being the subject of gossip. No, she'd not leave this place a moment before she had to, and she'd not think about what would happen when her so-called relations returned to learn of Jackson Wulf's death and of the dead man's young wife and son.

Lucinda Wulf. For the first time, she had a last name, if it was one she'd stolen rather than one rightly given to her. But she wouldn't feel guilt over what she'd done. What else could she do? Jackson Wulf had admitted that he had planned to kill her—had promised to look after Sebastian. And so he was, in a way.

Lulled by the crackling fire and a sense that for once all was right in her world, Lucinda settled deeper in the covers and drifted off to sleep.

◆ ◆ ◆

The give of the mattress roused her a short time later. She didn't have time to come fully awake before a warm body pressed against her. Lucinda tensed at the same moment the body beside her did. The body was that of a man. A shamelessly naked man. She screamed to high heaven.

"What in the bloody hell?"

The door burst open. Lucinda scrambled from the bed. The night fire had burned down and she had trouble making out the features of the fiend who'd stolen into the house, stolen into her bed.

"Move and you're a dead man!"

"Hawkins." She breathed a sigh of relief and rushed to the servant's side. He held a pistol.

"Slowly get out of the bed and move closer to the light where I can see you," Hawkins instructed.

There was the sound of the sheets rustling; then, as bade to do, the man rose, a dark shadow in the bedchamber's gloomy interior. Slowly, the man moved toward the glow from the small fire that burned in the grate. His face was still hidden in shadows, but the firelight flickered over his naked, tawny-colored skin, and Lucinda couldn't help but stare. Good Lord, whoever he was, he had a fine body.

A memory stirred in the furthest corners of her mind. Had she seen this man's naked body before? The answer came to her only seconds before he stepped closer to the fire and the flimsy light managed to illuminate his handsome features.

"Lord Jackson," Hawkins said in his emotionless voice. "We thought you were dead."

Lucinda had never fainted in her life, but she now came seriously close. Her knees nearly gave way. There before her, standing in all of his naked splendor, stood the man she had left for dead. The man whose name she had

stolen. The man who wanted to kill her. The man who
was more than a man . . . the man who had turned into a
wolf before her very eyes.

"We, Hawkins?"

The servant indicated Lucinda. "Your lovely young
wife and I."

"My wife?"

Lucinda's safe world came crashing down around her.
But if she was a witch and an outcast, she had learned to
fend for herself in the world. She did the only thing she
could think to do given the circumstances. With a feigned
cry of joy, she rushed to Jackson Wulf's side and threw
her arms around him.

"You're alive!" she exclaimed for the benefit of
Hawkins. "I cannot believe it."

The firelight danced in Jackson's eyes as he stared
down at her. "Nor can I believe, after spending three
months searching for you, that I would finally give up and
come home only to find you waiting for me in my bed."

His naked flesh singed her through the thin fabric of
her nightgown. He was terribly intimidating, even if one
didn't know what he truly was. Lucinda tried to step away
from him, but his arm went around her waist and held her
pressed against him.

"You look much better than when last I saw you," he
said, a dryness to his tone that grated upon her already
raw nerves.

Her gaze sought his shoulder, where in the firelight she
saw the puckered skin where he'd been shot. She wondered if he still bore the stab wound she'd inflicted to his
back.

"As do you," she countered. "In fact, you look nothing
like you did when last I saw you."

Their eyes met and clashed.

Hawkins cleared his throat. "I will leave you to your

reunion," he announced. "I am pleased that you are, in fact, alive, Lord Jackson."

If the man was pleased, nothing in his voice or his bland expression gave him away. Lucinda had seen Hawkins come to life only when in the presence of her son. Otherwise, he was terribly droll about everything. The door closed and she had no choice but to face what she had never thought to face. Her husband.

"We need to talk," Jackson Wulf said.

"You cannot kill me," she claimed, staring defiantly up at him. "All of London believes I am your wife."

He rolled his eyes. "They'd expect nothing but for me to kill you, then. Wulfs do not marry. No woman in her right mind would have one of us."

"Your brother Armond is married," she pointed out. "He and his wife, Rosalind, are enjoying their honeymoon at the estate. Hawkins told me so."

He frowned. "Yes, he is married, and if he hasn't given his heart to Rosalind yet, he soon will. Then the curse will be upon him. I had hoped to stop it before it ruined his life, but I may be too late now."

"Why his heart?" She was curious, even if beneath her gown her legs were shaking. Best to keep Jackson talking rather than spur him into any action that might result in her death.

"The curse," he reminded her. "For a Wulf to give his heart, he must sacrifice his humanity. The family name. Wulf. It becomes a beast that haunts us."

Which meant if Jackson Wulf was already cursed, he had given his heart to a woman. She knew he had no wife. Where was this woman whom he loved? Who was she? And why did Lucinda feel a sudden prick of jealousy over the fact?

"I don't believe there is anything amiss at the country estate," she told him. "Rosalind has sent a letter to

Hawkins informing him that the only reason they have not yet returned is because Gabriel seems to be missing, and they suspect if he returns, it will be the first place he will go."

"Then there still may be a chance to save Armond," Jackson considered, and his gaze ran over her. "You've certainly managed to wedge yourself into my life in a short time."

She'd told him too much—had reminded him that he had once planned to kill her and possibly still did. Lucinda hadn't helped him develop any opinion of her except a bad one. Of course, her opinion of him was no better. Except regarding his outward appearance, leastwise.

She had trouble keeping her eyes on his face. He still held her close, and she was uncomfortably aware of his nakedness. "Could you dress?" she asked. "I may not be a highborn lady, but your vulgarity offends me all the same."

"Does it?" He quirked a brow darker than his honey-colored hair. "If it offends you, then I suggest you stop looking every chance you get."

Heat exploded in her cheeks. She struggled from his arms. "I am not looking," she assured him. "And nothing displeases me more than the sight of you. I was certain the villagers had killed you."

"Sorry to disappoint," he said. "An animal fared better in that circumstance than a man, or so it would seem, since as you can see, I am very much alive."

There was nothing the least bit disappointing about Jackson Wulf . . . well, not his outer appearance leastwise. Lucinda had never seen a man more blessed . . . and everywhere. Lest she was tempted to lower her eyes and have another look, she turned her back on him.

"I had no choice but to take this path. I had nowhere to go, nothing. My babe, I had to think of him and of your promise to me where he is concerned. At first, I had simply hoped that your brothers might pay me for bringing them word of your death . . . then, well, no one was here but the servants."

"So you lied to Hawkins. You stole into my family's home like a thief, and all of this after you'd left me for dead."

He did make it sound so much worse than her rationalizing had done when she'd made her decisions. "You said you meant to kill me," she reminded him.

"Yes," he agreed softly. "And I still should."

She spun around to face him. He'd donned a pair of trousers while her back was turned. The shadows of the room now hid his features from her.

"But before I do anything, I plan to get good and foxed." He walked to a corner table where she'd seen a decanter and glasses. "I suggest you use the time to flee. Perhaps I will never find you."

Flee? To where? And what of her child? She could no longer feed him, although she supposed he was at least now old enough to stomach porridge. Still, what kind of life could she give him?

"What of my child?" she asked Jackson.

His broad back was turned to her as he poured his drink. Muscles rippled when he shrugged. "I made you a promise; I will keep it. Leave him here. He will be well looked after."

Her heart felt as if it were being torn in half. Part of her knew that she could never bear to give up Sebastian; the other part, the rational part, said that he would be better off without her. Lucinda suddenly wished Jackson Wulf were dead. Her life would be much less complicated without him.

Perhaps he would meet with an accident this very

night. Perhaps in a drunken stupor he would fall down the darkened stairs and break his neck.

"Do you plan to share my bed tonight?"

His question startled her. She glanced across the room at him. He now lounged with his hips propped against the table, sipping his drink and staring at her with his strange eyes.

"I hardly think so," she answered coldly.

"It might be awkward," he agreed. "Both of us planning to kill one another and all. At the same time, it might be titillating. The danger. The uncertainty. Not knowing if the other means to caress or strangle. To kiss or kill."

Had he read her thoughts? Did he have greater powers than the gift of shape-shifting?

"I shall sleep next door with my child," she said, and started toward the door. Jackson moved so swiftly he was across the room in an instant, barring her escape.

"If you are smart, you will not sleep this night," he said. "You will run while you can." His strange eyes softened upon her for a moment. "If it makes a difference, I do not enjoy the thought of killing you. I do so only for my own self-preservation and for my brothers and their future."

"And what if you are wrong?" she asked. "What if killing me changes nothing for you?"

He frowned and took a drink. "There's the rub. I won't know until after I've done it." He suddenly wheeled away from her and strode back to the table to pour another drink. "I suggest that you leave in all haste. Good-bye . . . I don't even know your name."

"Lucinda," she provided.

"Lucinda," he repeated, and she liked the sound of it on his tongue. "Good-bye, Lucinda. I hope our paths do not cross again. It would be to your continued good health if that were the case."

"And perhaps to yours, as well," she felt inclined to add. He wasn't dealing with a lady, and Lucinda, although she liked the role well enough, refused to show him any weakness, any fear. It was how she'd managed to survive for the past twenty years. Her mother, now passed, had once told her that she was an old woman by the age of ten.

Jackson raised his glass to her. "We have both been warned. I'll never trust my back to you again. Although the taste of your sweet lips was almost worth it."

She hated him for reminding her of the kiss they had once shared. She hated herself more because during the months that had followed their dramatic first meeting she had thought often about that kiss. Her cheeks blazed again, and unwilling to have him see his effect upon her, she opened the door and hurried into the hallway.

The wet nurse, Martha, had fallen asleep in a chair by the fire. Lucinda walked quietly to the large cradle Hawkins had pulled from the attic. She stared down at her son. His little cheeks were plump and pink. He made a sucking motion with his mouth while he slept. At times, she still couldn't believe that he was hers. Such a gift to receive from something so horrible ... horrible in thought, leastwise, for Lucinda couldn't remember the attack on her person at all.

She'd gone to Lord Cantley's country manor to aid his wife in the birth of their third child. The countess had labored long, and he worried that his wife might die before giving him another heir; the earl had sent someone to fetch Lucinda. He'd nearly waited too long, but Lucinda had prepared the woman a strengthening draught, and the child, a daughter, was born late in the evening.

Lady Cantley had been exhausted, and out of concern Lucinda had sought the earl's permission to give her a sleeping draught, one that would ensure the lady slept

even through having the child put upon her breast to
suckle. Lord Cantley agreed, and Lucinda had fetched the
special potion from her things. After she'd given the lady
the draught, Lucinda had come back out and replaced the
vial. Lord Cantley had been watching her, but then, he always watched her.

She should have suspected that he was up to something when she finally emerged from his wife's bedchamber to find him extending a hot cup of tea toward
her. Gratefully she'd drunk the tea, preparing herself for
the long walk back to the village. But when she awoke in
the morning, she did not recall the long walk back to her
cottage.

Lucinda did not recall anything past drinking the tea,
all the while the earl staring at her, smiling as if he knew
something amusing that she did not. The first thing she'd
noticed when she awoke in her cottage was the soreness
of her breasts and then, when she moved, down below . . .
the soreness there. She had suspected in that instant
something had been done to her and suspected also by
whom it had been done. There had been traces of blood
on her thighs.

After two months of missing her monthly menses, Lucinda knew that she was with child. The earl had drugged
her, defiled her, and then gone on with his life as if he'd
done nothing despicable. She'd confronted him. No
mouse, Lucinda would not allow him to commit a crime
against her and pretend ignorance about what he'd done.

At first, Lord Cantley had denied having touched her.
But like all men who enjoy committing crimes, in the end
he had to boast to her. He had to tell her what he'd done to
her while she lay helpless. Then the foul man had tried to
make her feel as if the whole matter were her fault. If she
hadn't tempted him, if she hadn't teased him, he wouldn't
have had to have her, and by any means. Lucinda had told

him about the child in a rage of anger, not that he wouldn't have noticed in time.

Her temper was something she'd struggled with all of her life. The red hair, the only thing her father had ever given her. Lucinda had made threats against the earl. She'd told him she would have his child, a male child, and that someday her son would lay claim to all that the earl possessed. It had been a mistake.

A week later Lord Cantley's men had come for her. Lucinda, gifted in sometimes knowing things before they happened, had already gathered a few of her belongings and had taken refuge in the forest. She later learned that Cantley had placed a price upon her head. For theft, he'd said. But Lucinda knew the man had begun to worry about his wife learning of his infidelity and about the babe, who one day might threaten the throne of England if he carried his father's mark.

Sebastian stirred and brought Lucinda back from the past. How content he looked, how warm, how well, how safe. She couldn't bear the thought of uprooting him, of sleeping in the streets and having to do anything necessary to see that he was fed. Tears, those strange drops of human joy and sorrow, were seldom her companion, but they visited her now.

She blinked them back and walked to the bed where Martha usually slept. Although she doubted that sleep would come for her, Lucinda lay down upon the soft mattress. She should be packing, and as quickly as she could. She should flee into the night, go somewhere Jackson Wulf could never find her. But again, she was torn.

Why did Jackson Wulf have to come back from the dead? Sporting those innocent dimples, baring that tawny muscled skin, standing naked before her as if he had nothing to be embarrassed about, no human physical flaw that he must hide from her? *Because he has no physical flaws,* she answered her own question. But he did have weaknesses. The bottle. His own inflated sense of worth. His curse.

Do you plan to share my bed tonight? It was probably the first time a woman had said no to him. And he had to remind Lucinda about the kiss they had once shared. He'd said her lips were sweet. Lucinda unconsciously traced the shape of her mouth. That one, she imagined, would say anything to get a woman into his bed. There was a weakness, as well. That rather large piece of meat dangling between his legs.

If she had to, Lucinda supposed she could offer herself to him in exchange for his not killing her, for his allowing her to stay with her child. But surely his curse meant more to him than a tumble with a willing woman. There would have to be more between them. There would have to be . . . love.

Abruptly she sat. Why hadn't it occurred to her before now? Well, for one thing, Lucinda hadn't thought she'd find herself in this predicament with Jackson Wulf. It was so simple. All she had to do was make the man fall in love with her. Become her slave. Fall deep under her spell. But she would have to hurry, for his brothers could return soon and put a fast end to her plans.

Lucinda rose and left the room. She stood outside the bedchamber where she'd earlier slept, and listened. A smile curved her lips when she heard his drunken snoring. Softly she opened the door and went inside. He lay sprawled upon the bed. She took a moment to study him. Good Lord, what perfection. What total maleness. What a shame he was a drunkard and a soon-to-be murderer.

Creeping to her sewing basket, Lucinda removed a

pair of small scissors. She went to the bed and leaned over him. A quick snip and she had what she wanted. A lock of his pretty blond hair. She would begin the ritual tonight. By morning, Jackson Wulf would already be half in love with her.

Chapter Five

The witch had not left. Jackson sensed her presence in the house, smelled her tantalizing woman's scent. He lay abed, his eyes closed, his head pounding from the liquor he'd consumed the previous night, and he felt oddly relieved that she had not gone as he'd instructed her to do. Why he did not know. Perhaps because if she'd left the child behind, Jackson would not know how to make good the promises he had made her. Perhaps because if she stayed, he would have longer to consider whether he could kill her or not.

Perhaps only because she intrigued him. He didn't affect her the way he affected other women. If he did, he would not have awoken alone this morning. The fact that she could resist him also intrigued him—that along with the reason she had clipped off a piece of his hair late last night. What was she up to?

A soft rap sounded upon his door. Thinking the summons was from Hawkins bearing breakfast, Jackson bade the steward to enter. The door opened. It was not the solemn-faced Hawkins who entered but a redheaded vixen wearing a pale yellow gown. The gown hugged her curves and displayed the figure she had in so short a time regained. Her hair hung loose around her shoulders, reminding him of red silk shot through with gold thread.

His interest was immediately piqued . . . or something along the lines of interest. He was also a little angry that she had not done as he told her to do the night before.

"You are either very brave or very stupid," he said. "I expected to wake and find you gone this morning."

"And a bright good morn to you, too, my lord," she said, sarcasm dripping from her voice. "I have brought you breakfast. We must talk."

"We talked last night," he reminded her. "I thought I made myself clear to you."

She set the tray on the table close to the bed before seating herself next to him. She seemed not to even consider the impropriety of being in his room, much less placing herself in such a compromising situation. She might not be highborn, but her earthy beauty nearly stole his breath. With the sun peeking through the curtains, shimmering upon her fiery hair, she looked like a fairy sprite and not a flesh-and-blood woman. Certainly not a witch.

"I've been thinking," she said, handing him a cup of strong-smelling tea.

Jackson eyed the tea warily, then reached across her and set it back upon the tray. "Obviously thinking I am slow-witted," he said. "The tea doesn't smell quite right."

She glanced toward the cup in question. "I wish I had your nose, or that I had had it at one time. Hawkins has a rather impressive herb garden. I mixed you up something special this morning . . . to help with the headache."

His head was pounding, to be sure, but he couldn't see how she would know that. But then, she was a witch. Perhaps she could read his mind, as well. "Maybe a permanent solution?" he asked.

She sighed dramatically. "I don't plan to kill you, but I think that I might be able to help you. As for the headache, I assume a man who drinks too much in the eve will suffer for it in the morn." Lucinda lifted the cup again and handed it to him. "If I am to help you, you must trust me."

Rather than take the cup from her, he stared into her eyes. They were clear and as green as spring grass. He saw no dark motives lurking there. His gaze drifted downward to the Cupid's bow of her mouth. Her lips were full and inviting, and sweet, if he recalled correctly. Lower still his eyes drifted, settling upon the firm rise of her breasts. They looked plump and delectable, but not swollen with milk as one might expect of a mother nursing a babe.

"Why were you sleeping in here last night instead of in the same room with your son? Wouldn't it be simpler to feed him during the night?"

"My face is a good deal higher than where you are staring," she said.

His gaze lifted abruptly. Her cheeks were flushed a becoming shade of pink. He wouldn't expect a witch would blush. Certainly not a woman who'd borne a babe out of wedlock.

"I can no longer feed him," she said. "It greatly aided my decision to pass myself off as your wife, and Sebastian off as your son. Hawkins has secured a wet nurse for me. I fear it was the starved state I was in when I bore Sebastian. My milk dried up a scarce month into his life."

"Pity for the babe," Jackson said, thinking it rather than meaning to comment aloud. He wouldn't mind suckling at her breasts.

"Will you accept the tea?" She brought them back around to the subject at hand. "Will you dare to trust me?"

Jackson shoved his hair back from his face, recalling that she'd stolen a lock of it last night. "There are a good many things I'd dare to do with you, but trusting you with my life is not one of them. Why are you still here, Lucinda?"

The spell Lucinda cast did not seem to be working. The tea was the test. If he was suddenly so smitten with her that his mind was befuddled, he would have been too blinded by his attraction toward her to suspect she'd put something in his tea. It was in fact a harmless mixture meant to soothe the ill effects of too much drink, but still, he maintained the sense to remain distrustful of her.

"I am still here because I have nowhere else to go," she answered. Lucinda blinked back tears and straightened her spine. "The babe would not fare well on the streets of London, and I cannot bear to leave him behind as of yet. I offer you a trade. Safe harbor for both of us, and in exchange, I will help you break the curse that haunts you and your brothers."

He drew his knees up, and the thin sheet covering his lower half slipped lower. She could tell he had at some point shucked the trousers he'd worn the previous night and now was naked beneath the covers. Odd, but that was very distracting to her.

Lucinda had seen many men in various states of undress due to her healing abilities. She'd never been affected by the sight of male flesh before . . . but then, she'd never seen such an impressive display of it before now.

"Do you really think you can break the curse?" he asked.

"I can try," she answered. "Perhaps that is what led you

to me, and not the notion you've taken that killing me will break it."

"You said you wanted safe harbor. Why do you not go to the child's father for help?"

She feared now that she'd said too much to Jackson the day he'd busted into the cottage and helped her deliver Sebastian. He wouldn't let her stay if he knew a man hunted her and her child. Another man bent on killing them both. Those of a loftier position in life were known to stick together. She would lie if she had to. Not for herself, but for her son.

"The child's father does not want us. He took his pleasure of me, but pleasure was all he wanted. He accused me of being a thief and put a price on my head to throw suspicion off of himself as being the child's father."

Jackson shifted and the sheet draped around his hips slid lower. "Why would he go to such lengths? All he need do is deny being the babe's father. Men do it all the time."

She had trouble keeping her gaze off of the smooth skin of his flanks. The sheet still covered him, but barely. She hadn't noticed before the thin line of dark hair that started below his navel and made a path downward. It intrigued her now for some reason.

"The birthmark upon Sebastian's thigh," she answered, regaining her wits. "If the child were born with it, as Sebastian was, it marks him as belonging of his seed. Everyone in the village would know, and I suppose the father thought I would use it to drain him of coin throughout the years. The man has a wife, children of his own. He did not need another mouth to feed, much less two."

"Did you love him?"

Her gaze lifted abruptly to his. In the light of day, his eyes were dark, almost black. A startling contrast to his blond hair. Only at night did they glow blue. His question surprised her. Why would that matter to him? Should she lie and therefore make him believe better of her? The conception of her child was through no doing of her own, but she very much doubted that Jackson Wulf would believe that. He believed only the worst of her, so why not allow him to do so?

"No," she answered. "I did not love him. But I do love my son. I would see him have a better life than what I alone can give him. If you had children of your own, you would understand."

"It does not take having children of my own to understand," he said quietly. "I saw the love for the babe come upon you the first time that you held him. In that moment, you looked like an angel."

She glanced away from his eyes. "You and I both know that I am no angel. But then neither are you. Will you accept the trade I offer?"

"My face is up here."

A blush burned her cheeks. She'd been staring at the sheet again or, rather, what was beneath the sheet. Her gaze lifted to his face.

"And all you want in exchange is to stay here with your son? Food and lodging until the curse is broken?"

It was not all she wanted, but Lucinda knew it was all that she could ask for. She would stay with her son until he became a man if such an option were open to her. But she knew it was not possible. Regardless of Jackson's curse and the mystery and rumors surrounding his family, he and Lucinda were worlds apart.

"Yes, that is all I ask," she answered.

He stared at her long enough to make her fear all that she had asked for was still too much to give. "Agreed," he finally said, and she almost sagged with relief.

"Why did you take my hair last night?"

The sudden change of subject startled Lucinda. She'd thought he'd been passed out with drink when she'd done her deed. What explanation could she give him but the truth? It seemed silly now, her plan to make him love her. Such spells seldom lasted long. And if not for the prospect of staying with her son, Lucinda cared little to be the object of Jackson's affections. Especially if his affections had been summoned by magic rather than given freely. She hadn't been thinking clearly last night when the idea had first occurred to her. She'd been frightened and desperate.

"I wanted to cast a spell over you," she admitted, glancing down at her hands, which nervously plucked at the borrowed daffodil gown. A gown far grander than anything she had ever owned or ever would. "A love spell," she went on to explain, feeling her face flush again.

He cocked a dark brow. "To what end?" he asked curiously. "If you want to share my bed, all you need do is say so."

Lucinda's gaze lifted to his. "Is that what you believe love is? A physical exchange between two people? A lusty romp beneath the sheets? I don't imagine I'd have to cast a spell to get you into bed with me. I imagine my being a woman is all the incentive you need."

He placed a hand against his heart. "You wound me with your sharp tongue. You are no innocent. I am no gentleman. It would only be natural for us to end up in my bed, making love."

His conceit greatly annoyed her . . . his conceit and the fact that she couldn't keep from staring at his bare skin. It looked so smooth, so warm, so enticing. She had never been enticed before. Perhaps he was the one who'd cast a spell over her.

"What a nice word you have for it," she snapped, regaining her composure. Lucinda stood, suddenly realizing that she was already in his bed. "I have no interest in you other than the bargain I ask you to make with me. Certainly you can find your pleasure elsewhere. I have already learned the result of such folly."

"I will be careful," he offered.

Her face flamed again. She'd hardly blushed a day in her life and now she couldn't seem to stop. Blushes were for innocent maids and ladies. Not for her.

"A claim all men probably make to get what they want," she scoffed. "Sharing your bed is not part of our bargain."

He abruptly changed the subject again. "How do you plan to break the curse?"

There was the tricky part. Undoing another's curse would be difficult. "There are several things that I can try," Lucinda provided. "You said there was a riddle. I must study it, study you. It is not something that I can do overnight. Not an easy task, I will warn you now. You will have to cooperate fully with me. Are you up for that?"

"According to my brothers, I can rise to any occasion," he said drily.

Lucinda held her hand out to him. "Then we will shake as men do to seal our bargain."

Her hand slid into his when he reached for her. It was not a hand, she noted, that knew hard work. His skin was smooth and warm, his fingers long and sculpted, like the hands of an artist or a musician. It was a hand that would feel good against a woman's flesh. Rather than shake her hand, he pulled her down onto the bed with him.

"You're not a man, Lucinda," he said, his face only inches from hers. "I won't treat you like one. My home, my protection, my trust—you ask for a lot. I will have something in return from you."

There were no dark thoughts of rape to throw Lucinda

into a panic, no remembered humiliations done to her, but
her heart sped and sudden fear gripped her all the same.
In the past, her body had been hers. She'd never been
tempted to share it with another, for she understood that
such an act of intimacy would call for sharing much more
of herself than just her body.

She had no heart to open to others, all save Sebastian.
Her heart was guarded, scarred by cruel words and cru-
eler deeds. To give, to love, she would have to learn to be
soft. She could not be soft and survive in such a cruel
world.

"Whatever you want from me you will have to take,"
she said, meeting his stare with a hard one of her own.
"You may use my body, but you will never touch my
soul."

He reached for her face and she automatically
flinched. But he did not strike her, simply cupped her chin
and turned her face up to his.

"I will not take anything from you," he said. "I only
ask for a kiss. One given willingly, without a knife aimed
at my back. Is that so much to ask for all that you have
asked of me?"

Staring into his dark eyes, his sensually shaped mouth
close enough for her to feel the warmth of his breath, Lucinda had trouble reasoning. A kiss was a little-enough
thing. For a home for her son, a future for him, it was
nothing to ask at all. Slowly, she leaned toward Jackson.

Chapter Six

Jackson made her come to him. He did not meet her halfway, although the distance between them was hardly a hair's breadth. She touched her mouth to his. Her blood immediately began to tingle, to warm in her veins. His lips were soft and yet firm and molded to hers as if their mouths had been fashioned to fit together. When he made no further move to participate in the kiss, she realized he wanted her to do the kissing.

Lucinda had never kissed a man of her own free will. Her past was littered with unpleasant incidents of men trying to grab her, trying to force their slimy, foul-breathed mouths upon hers and crush her lips. Jackson's mouth was neither slimy nor foul-breathed, and the contact between them was as light as a whisper. His passiveness fueled her bravery, and her curiosity.

Had that kiss three months past in a crumbling cottage, her body bruised and weak and bleeding, her life and the life of her child in danger, really been as good as she thought? It seemed impossible under the circumstances. Desire certainly must have been a misunderstood emotion, for no woman in her right mind would desire a man after suffering the pain of childbirth. She'd told herself that countless times over the past few months when she thought about that kiss. Now, she could make certain.

She pressed harder against his lips and they parted beneath hers. Their breaths mingled, then their tongues touched. She tried to recall what he had done with his tongue in her mouth that day in the cottage. Caressed, yes, that was what he'd done, so she did the same. A peek from beneath her lashes caught him staring at her. She broke contact.

"How is it that a mother, a woman wise in the ways between men and women, kisses like she has never kissed a man before?"

The damnable blush rose in her cheeks again. He thought her experienced. He probably thought her a whore. Most men did without any evidence to fuel their suspicions. She would be all he thought she was, at least at this moment in time. Lucinda slid her hand behind his neck, conscious of the silky brush of his hair against the back of her hand. She pulled him closer, closed her eyes, and did her best to convince him that she was exactly what he thought her to be.

When her tongue thrust boldly into his mouth and she moved her head in rhythm with the mating of their mouths, she peeked from her lashes again. His eyes were closed, his long spiked lashes dark against his high cheekbones. It was a dance, she realized. The movement of lips against lips, like the ebb and flow of an ocean. Coming together, then breaking apart, together, then apart, while their tongues did a dance of their own.

How her hand came to be pressed against his bare chest she did not know. But he felt just as she had thought he would. Warm, smooth, either hairless or what hair he had was so fine and light she could neither see nor feel it.

His heart pounded beneath her palm, hard, strong, fast. His hand cupped the back of her head, just as hers held his. He twisted his fingers in her hair, a firm hold but not hurtful. Then he became a participant in the kiss.

He came to life and he brought her to life, as well. Life in a sensual realm where she had never walked before. The heat of their bodies touching blended with the cool morning air to create a steamy mist around them. His mouth drew responses from her whether she wanted to give them or not. Soft moans, deep sighs, little sounds in her throat that slipped past her defenses. His hands slid from her hair, down her neck to her shoulders, spreading the heat even through the fabric of her gown.

She craved his touch and never knew it until this moment. But as strong as any potion she had ever created was her pull to him. The way he drew her out of herself, to stand by and watch a stranger take her place. A woman who only felt, only desired, only longed, and couldn't shield herself from emotion. A woman who couldn't guard her heart against him.

Lower his hands moved, down her arms to her hands, where he locked his fingers with hers, the palms of their hands burning against one another. Palm against palm, he turned her so that he could easily press her down onto the bed beside him; then he was over her, using the skill of his mouth, his teeth, his tongue, to flood her with sensation and destroy all ability to grasp reason. He made her breathless, he made her burn, and the feel of his body pressing into hers made her realize he also planned to make her his.

It was much more difficult than it should have been, but Lucinda grasped wildly for the threads of her sanity. She pushed against his chest, the long, solid length of him pressed against her, only the flimsy sheet and her thin summer gown a barrier between their bodies. "You tricked me," she accused. "You're trying to seduce me!"

Staring down at her with his dark eyes, eyes awash with desire, he said, "If I were trying very hard, you would already be naked beneath me."

"Get off of me!" she demanded. 'I will not yield to your lust."

"Won't you?" he asked softly.

"This is not part of our bargain," Lucinda said through clenched teeth.

"How badly do you want to stay with your son?"

Lucinda went limp beneath him. So, this was how it would be? She should have suspected as much. It was the way of life. The strong taking from the weak. The higher class using the commoner for whatever purpose suited them at the moment. She should have known he couldn't be trusted. He was a man . . . worse, he was a wolf.

"You know that I would do anything for Sebastian," she said. "Take what you will."

He stared down for a moment at her; then he sighed and rolled off of her. "I've never had to take what a woman is all too willing to give. I won't start now. I imagine you will come to me in time."

His arrogance fired her temper. "Without threat or force, I will never surrender to you," she assured him, but she wasn't all that certain. A moment ago, he'd had her squirming beneath him . . . and she hadn't been squirming to get away. "How manly that must make you feel."

He shoved his hair away from his handsome face. "I've never considered my masculinity an issue," he remarked. "My common sense is another matter entirely. I am a man led by my emotions. Lust and addiction thus far proving to be my strongest."

He rose from the bed, startling her that he didn't take

the sheet with him. Bare-assed, he walked to the liquor cabinet and poured himself a drink. With his back to her, Lucinda's gaze traveled him from head to heel. The spit in her mouth dried up.

Thankfully, Sebastian set up a wail in the next room, shaking her from the spell Jackson's nakedness had cast over her. Lucinda scrambled up from the bed and was out the door without a glance or a word of parting cast behind her. She shut the door with force to announce her departure.

Jackson raised the glass to his lips, noting the slight tremble of his hand. Not a reaction to needing a drink . . . a reaction to Lucinda, a witch with no last name. He stared into the amber liquid's comforting depths for a moment, then, with more effort than he would like to admit, set the glass back on the table untouched.

It was only a kiss, he told himself. What in heaven's name had him shaking like a man left out in the cold too long? It was not only a kiss, he admitted. He'd kissed countless women, bedded countless women. He'd never felt like she had just made him feel. As if she'd reached inside of him and touched all he thought was dead there. She had for a moment brought him back to life.

He shook his head and walked to the wardrobe. He kept several changes of clothes at the town house to save himself the bother of packing when he took a wild hair to visit London. The estate held little appeal for him since he'd returned from abroad a changed man. Gabriel, his older brother, thought him lazy when it came to the care and raising of the fine horses they bred for sale. The truth was, the horses sensed the wolf beneath his skin and acted skittish around him. It had taken him a great deal of time to train the horse he'd left in Whit Hurch to accept his strange scent.

Jackson had feared Gabriel would know. Having fallen victim to a curse, and not even getting the girl in the bargain, had been an embarrassment to Jackson. Lady Anne Baldwin, sweet gentle creature, was the first thing he'd ever truly wanted in his life that had been denied him. And it was with her rejection that the rest of his circumstance came to the forefront. He was shunned by society. No proper match for a lady. Highborn and wealthy, he was no proper match for a common girl, either.

Jackson moved to the bed and sat. He stared across the room at the glass sitting a short distance from him. The sun sparkled through the amber-colored liquid. It called to him. But not as strongly as the soft sound of Lucinda's singing in the next room. Ignoring the liquor, Jackson slipped into a pair of clean trousers, pulled a white linen shirt over his head, and padded barefoot into the next room.

A plump woman with plumper breasts widened her eyes upon seeing him at the door. He put a finger to his lips to silence her. The wet nurse scurried past him and down the hall toward the stairs leading to the bottom landing. Lucinda had her back to him. She sat in a rocker, the edge of a small blanket peeking out over one side. Jackson stood and listened to her for a moment. She had a lovely voice. It was low and husky and penetrated a man's soul. Softly, he walked up behind her, staring over her shoulder.

The babe had grown. Sebastian, she called him. The child's cheeks were plump and pink. A tiny fist was entangled in his mother's long hair and he stared adoring up at her while she sang to him. The babe's gaze wandered up, and upon seeing Jackson he smiled. Jackson couldn't help but smile back.

Lucinda glanced behind her.

"He's a fine boy," Jackson said.

Her eyes were so soft he thought he would drown in

them before she seemed to recall who it was she was looking at. She glanced away from him.

"Sebastian is a good baby. Hardly raises a fuss at all unless he's hungry or needs changing."

"Does he have his father's look?" Jackson was curious.

She was silent for a moment. "Aye. Unfortunately he does. But I'll not hold it against him."

"Then I won't, either," Jackson decided. "He smiled at me just a moment ago."

Lucinda made a clucking noise. "Has to belch, I imagine. He's too young to smile." As she said so, Jackson watched her prop the babe upon her shoulder and pat him gently upon the back. Her efforts were rewarded a moment later when the child belched loudly and, to Jackson's horror, a white stream of milk came pouring from the babe's mouth onto his mother's shoulder.

"Good Lord!" Lucinda exclaimed, good-naturedly. She rose and handed the child into Jackson's arms. "This isn't my gown. I should have thought to throw a rag over my shoulder before burping him."

Jackson held the child awkwardly beneath his arms. Sebastian's tiny legs kicked while Lucinda hurried to a washbasin, dabbed a cloth inside, and began dabbing at the stain upon her shoulder. She glanced in his direction and frowned.

"You're not holding him right. Cradle him in your arms."

Through a series of awkward starts and stops, Jackson managed to do as she instructed. Sebastian stared up at him with the biggest, bluest eyes he'd ever seen. A thatch of dark hair covered the baby's head. Sebastian grinned at him. He grinned back again.

"I swear, I do think he's smiling at you for a fact," Lucinda commented, still dabbing at the shoulder of her gown. "He likes you. Why I can't imagine."

"Maybe because he knows without me he wouldn't be here on God's green earth."

He'd only been teasing, but at Lucinda's silence Jackson glanced across the room at her. She stood stark still, her face suddenly ashen.

"You are right," she whispered. "There is no way on earth I can ever repay you for that. For giving me my son's life."

To be held in such noble esteem was both an unwanted feeling and an unfamiliar one to Jackson. He suspected he hadn't done a noble deed in his life. Considering what he'd wanted to do to the child's mother only a short time ago in his bed, he accepted that he was unworthy of her sudden reverence toward him. He shrugged.

"I'm sure we can think of some way to repay me." He gave her a wicked smile.

The color returned to her face with force. "Lout," he heard her mutter, and he was much more at ease with insults. She glanced at the stain on her gown and he thought she might cry. "I've ruined it," she choked. "I've ruined the lady's gown. I had no right to wear it, but Hawkins was certain that she wouldn't mind and I had nothing else except the rags I brought with me."

His heart twisted. He took so much for granted. Even wallowing in his self-pity over the hand fate had dealt him, he supposed it could be worse. "Then we shall have to remedy that. I will not have you wear rags. Or borrowed clothes. Hawkins, I imagine, knows ways to remove a stain even the finest laundress in London hasn't heard of. He'll see to it. Don't cry."

Her back straightened. "I am not crying," she announced. "I do not cry. Tears are for the weak." She came to him and took the babe from his arms. As she bent toward him, he closed his eyes for a moment and inhaled the sweet fragrance of her hair. Honeysuckle.

"In fact I will see to your wardrobe immediately," he said. "I myself know nothing of women's fashions, but I know someone who does."

Lucinda glanced up at him. Was he serious? He would clothe her? She cocked a saucy brow. "I imagine you do." And she imagined any gowns he would provide her with would be a whore's offcasts.

He almost smiled. "She's the love of my life," he teased her. "We'll visit her right away. Change your gown and give that one to Hawkins to see to. I'll meet you downstairs."

Chapter Seven

Beggars could not be choosers, Lucinda had decided. She and Jackson sat in a fine carriage drawn by the loveliest matched set of horses Lucinda had ever seen. It felt odd to be traveling in such grand style, wearing yet another borrowed gown from Rosalind Wulf's wardrobe, seated across from a man who Lucinda supposed was the most handsome man in all of London . . . perhaps the most handsome man alive.

"The horses," she commented. "I noticed they shied as you approached the carriage. They sense there is something not quite right about you?"

"A bloody inconvenience considering horses is what we do," he said bitterly. "We raise them," he explained. "We are unrivaled in England as breeders of fine horses."

Lucinda was surprised. "I thought you were inherently wealthy. Born into it."

"We are," he admitted. "But a man must have something to do. Or at least my brothers consider the horses an honorable way to keep the family fortune healthy."

"I like the thought of it," Lucinda decided. "Of Sebastian working with the horses. It will be good for him."

Jackson smiled sadly. "I once enjoyed it myself. Until . . ."

"I can do something about that," Lucinda offered. "An oil to coat your skin and disguise the scent of wolf the horses react to. We can try it if you'd like."

He suddenly moved from his seat and perched beside her. "Do you smell it? I've often wondered if I put off a strange scent to other people, like I do to the horses."

She was taken off guard when he suddenly bent close to her and tugged his high starched collar aside. "Smell me," he instructed.

Lucinda had been asked to do some strange things in her life, but never before had a man asked her to smell him. "I'm sure that you don't," she assured him. "I-I would have noticed."

"You may have been distracted," he suggested, a hint of a smile tugging at his disturbingly sensual mouth. "Smell me now while you are focused on that alone."

She wanted to roll her eyes. Instead, she leaned toward him and pressed her face against his throat. She breathed in his scent. It was in no way offensive. To the contrary, he smelled of soap and water, and maybe a hint of sandalwood.

"You smell very nice," she said.

"So do you." His head was turned toward her hair. "Honeysuckle?"

Lucinda straightened abruptly. She put distance between them. "Yes. I dry the flowers, crush them, and add them to my soaps."

"Very nice," he commented, his voice low and husky. "You smell good enough to eat."

Lucinda wasn't certain how to take the compliment. She glanced out the window at the teeming London streets and said nothing at all. She thought she heard him chuckle softly a moment later.

She expected Jackson Wulf's experience with women, and fashion, would lead them to perhaps a brothel hidden away on the outskirts of the city. She felt her mouth drop open when the coach pulled up before the grandest house she'd ever seen. It was more like a castle. The footman got the door for them. Jackson bounded out, then held his hand for Lucinda.

He did so without thought, she realized. He might claim to be no gentleman, but the schooling was there, whether he wished to acknowledge it or not. She took his hand and alighted. Quickly he steered her away from the coach and from the horses that were already beginning to stomp nervously. Jackson led her up a long path to the front door.

"Who lives in such a place?" Lucinda whispered, fearing her eyes were bulging and her mouth was gaping like the commoner she was. "The king himself?"

"A friend," Jackson answered. "And no, not the king."

He said the word "friend" with a warmth to his voice that caused an odd reaction inside of her. She didn't like it, she realized. The familiarity with which he spoke of this woman. Was she a lover? Oh God, worse, was she the woman he had given his heart to?

She and Jackson reached the massive front doors and they swung open. A man, one almost as stuffy looking as Hawkins, greeted them.

"Her grace is expecting you," he said formally. "This way please."

"Why is she expecting us?" Lucinda whispered as they followed the man inside.

"I sent around a note before we left," Jackson explained. "It isn't proper to drop in unannounced."

Seeing him in this suddenly very proper light was intriguing. He was dressed immaculately. Even in one of Rosalind Wulf's fine orchid gowns, Lucinda felt she paled in comparison to Jackson Wulf.

They were led into a large parlor where an old woman sat upon an overstuffed velvet bench. Her gray hair was thinning and she was nearly bald on top of her head. There was a twinkle in her eyes when she looked at Jackson, however, that allowed Lucinda to glimpse the girl who still lived in an old woman's body.

She held out her age-spotted hands. "Jackson, my boy. I so prayed the rumors concerning your death were false. It broke my heart, and it has been too long since I've seen your handsome face."

He went to the woman, took her hands, and dropped to one knee. "Duchess, you grow more beautiful each time I see you."

She giggled like a young girl before her wrinkled face turned serious. "Dear boy, what has happened to you? Where have you been?"

Lucinda watched Jackson closely. What explanation would he give the woman? He seemed to measure his words carefully.

"I have been on a personal mission," he answered. "In a small village. There was a fire. All thought I had perished. I was injured and it took some time for me to make my way home."

The woman's intelligent eyes moved toward Lucinda. "And what of the rumors that you had married? That there is even a child?"

Now came the test of Jackson's word. Lucinda lifted a brow when he glanced toward her. To deny Sebastian was his son would be to already break their agreement. He tugged at his collar. "There is a child," he admitted. "A son. But I did not marry his mother."

The woman pursed her lips. "And why not, Jackson?"

Again, his gaze strayed toward Lucinda. "She is common, your grace."

When the lady glanced at her, Lucinda straightened her spine. Common she might be, but she had her pride. It was about the only thing she had left.

"Does *she* have a name?" the lady asked, her lips curling slightly at the corners, almost as if giving Lucinda a nod of approval for her defensive stance.

"Lucinda," she answered softly.

"And is it agreeable to you, Lucinda, that this man bedded you, carelessly planted his seed inside of you, and has no conscience to make his sins right in God's eyes?"

Lucinda didn't know how to respond. She supposed the only way she could. "Doing all is a habit, I'm thinking, with the upper classes, my lady."

To her surprise, the woman threw back her balding head and laughed. "How right you are, my dear, and you must address me as 'your grace.' I am the Dowager Duchess of Brayberry. Common is not only a state of birth."

What an odd woman, Lucinda thought. To champion a horse, then cut its legs out from beneath it during the race. But the woman commanded respect. Anyone who could make Jackson Wulf squirm beneath her accusations had earned it in Lucinda's mind. "Yes, your grace," she said.

"You will marry the girl, Jackson," the duchess suddenly blurted.

It was difficult to say which one of them looked the more shocked. Lucinda supposed her face drained of color. Jackson's eyes widened.

"Not even you, dear lady, can demand such of me," he said, no longer resembling a blushing boy being scolded by his mother.

The woman cocked her head to one side and regarded him. "Not in a legal sense, but I did promise your mother

I would look after you. Steer you in the right direction when I am able. You are a man without responsibilities, Jackson. It's time you answered for your wild ways. Lucinda might in fact be common, but you could do worse, and I imagine you have," she added drily.

"Lucinda is a witch."

Now it was the lady's turn to blanch. Her steely gaze snapped toward Lucinda. "Is the lad merely insulting you or is he speaking literally, dear?" the woman asked her.

Lucinda's chin came up another notch. "I am a witch," she answered. "Just like my mother and hers was, and hers before that."

The duchess simply stared at her. Lucinda was prepared to be ordered from the grand house, any thoughts of marriage between her and Jackson promptly dismissed by the woman. "How interesting," she finally responded. "Still, as I said, he could do worse. You are quite lovely."

Although she felt a blush rising, Lucinda fought it down. The lady had taken the game too far, and surely she wasn't serious, merely nettling Jackson Wulf. "I'm thinking I could do better, as well," she said in what she hoped was a haughty tone. "That he stands by his word to care for my child, to see that he's raised properly and not misused is all that matters to me."

"Is it, indeed?" the woman asked.

"Now that the issue is settled, may we move on to the reason I brought Lucinda today?" Jackson interrupted, and Lucinda thought he looked relieved to dismiss the subject of marriage, and conscience, and duty to his mother. "Lucinda is in need of a new wardrobe and I thought you might help her in that regard, your grace," he said. "I know nothing—"

"Not so fast, my boy," the duchess interrupted him. She turned back to Lucinda. "So, you are telling me that you do not mind if this man wishes to treat you, the mother of his child by his own admission, as he would a whore?"

"Of course I mind," Lucinda snapped without thinking. "But," she quickly added. "We have an agreement between us."

The woman lifted a brow and looked at Jackson.

"Yes, an agreement," he stated.

"What is this agreement?" the woman wanted to know.

Lucinda was thinking it was hardly the woman's business. Jackson echoed her thoughts.

"That is between Lucinda and myself."

"Does it have to do with the curse?"

Jackson's eyes widened for a moment again before he recovered. "As I said, your grace, and with no disrespect, the issue is a private one."

"You think she can break the curse," the woman suddenly speculated. "Is that the bargain between you? She will break your curse, and in return, you will show responsibility to a child you should be responsible for regardless?"

The silence grew awkward. Jackson had stood by his word to claim Sebastian, even to a woman with obviously close ties to his family. Lucinda was under no such obligation. "The child is not his," she said. "I want Sebastian to have a better life than I can give him. Jackson has agreed to do this for me and I have in turn agreed to help him with his . . . problem."

"Then he told you about his family curse?" the duchess asked. "The truth to it? Not the rumor?"

Jackson suddenly came forward to stare down at the woman. "Duchess, what are you asking?"

The woman met his stare. "I know the truth, Jackson. I was your mother's closest friend and confidante. I know what drove your father to suicide and your mother to madness, and then death."

"Then you should know why I cannot marry," he responded stiffly, but Lucinda saw that he was visibly shaken by the woman's admission.

She waved him off. "Armond is married."

"And on his way to ruin," Jackson bit out. "I would spare him that."

The woman reached out a hand to him. "Jackson, Armond and Rosalind are happy. I'm not sure what happened between them. They attended a social ball I gave, then I became ill and they departed for the country estate. Armond sent around a note promising me a long audience upon their return. Whatever might have stood between them, no longer does, I'm thinking. I'm praying."

Jackson finally reached out and took the hand she held extended to him. He bent on one knee. "But for how long? And what of their children? Their sons? You accuse me of being irresponsible, and rightfully so, but I will break the curse upon my family. I will do it for Armond and Gabriel, if not for myself."

Lucinda felt as if she had intruded upon a private moment. The woman squeezed his hand. "It is an honorable quest, Jackson. But your actions are not honorable toward this woman you will allow to live beneath your roof. This woman whose child you will take as your own. Give her your name. Your mother would wish it."

He bent his blond head and closed his eyes for a moment. Without looking up, he said, "My mother abandoned us. I do not live my life to please the dead."

"Or the living," the duchess added with sarcasm. The woman's eyes softened upon him. "She loved you, Jackson. She loved all of you. She was weak. You must have more strength, and you do. I can see you do."

Caught up in the exchange, Lucinda felt tears gather in her eyes. To see Jackson Wulf bent before the woman, his pain evident, affected her more than she wished. It was as if they had both forgotten she stood in the room. She would remind them.

"I have no wish to marry Jackson," she said to them. "The bargain is all I care about."

Jackson stared into the woman's eyes for a moment longer before he released her hand and rose. He turned stiffly toward Lucinda. "The duchess is right. We will marry, but we will hold to our bargain. After you have broken the curse, you will leave."

Lucinda's knees nearly buckled. "Marry?" she whispered.

"It was by your doing that most of London believes we are already married," he reminded her. "Besides, it will be better for Sebastian. Do you want people to call him a bastard behind his back? Do you want him to live with that shame?"

Lucinda had lived with the shame all of her life. Could she marry Jackson Wulf? For Sebastian, she supposed she could, as long as Jackson understood a marriage between them changed nothing. "In name only," she specified.

He shrugged. "If that is your wish."

"Then it's settled," the duchess breathed, looking smug with herself.

"Obtaining a special license will not be easy," Jackson said to her.

"Line the archbishop's pockets well and it will be easier than you think, my boy," the woman countered.

Lucinda's stomach rolled. She tried to assure herself a marriage between them changed nothing. In fact, it was good. Good for Sebastian. That was all that mattered, wasn't it?

"Now, what were you trying to say about a new wardrobe for Lucinda?" her grace asked Jackson.

"She's in need of new clothing," he answered distractedly. "I knew a seamstress wouldn't come to the house, certainly not alone. I thought you could help."

"Of course." The woman studied Jackson for a moment. "Why don't you take yourself off and let Lucinda and me see to this? You look like you could use a good strong drink, my boy."

Panic nearly overwhelmed Lucinda. She didn't want to be left alone with a virtual stranger. But then, Jackson was nearly a stranger to her, as well. Would he leave her?

He nodded. "You're right, I could use a drink."

"I'll send Lucinda home in my coach once we've finished," the woman said. "Off with you now."

Did Lucinda dare send Jackson a message that she didn't care to be left alone in strange surroundings and in a place where she was clearly out of her element? He was staring at her, she realized, waiting for permission to leave. She didn't want him to think she needed him, not for a moment. Sebastian needed him, but Lucinda did not. And where would a drink lead him? Into the arms of a willing woman? That shouldn't bother her either. She'd told him to find his pleasure elsewhere. Then why did it bother her?

"I'll be fine," she lied.

His sensual lips quirked. "What more could a man ask for? A wife who gladly sends him off into debauchery."

"I'm sure you could find your way easily enough without my help," she countered. "Your past is proof of that."

They stared at each other for a moment longer. He finally turned and walked away.

"Oh my," her grace remarked. "Such wonderful sparks between the two of you. I think you'll be good for Jackson, my dear."

Lucinda took a deep breath. "I'm not so sure he will be good for me."

The woman patted the seat beside her. "Come and sit, my dear."

Lucinda did as she bade. They sat in silence for a moment, then the woman turned to her.

"Are you really a witch?"

Lucinda sighed. "Yes."

"Can you give me something for my hair?" The duchess bent her head so that Lucinda saw the baldness beneath the thin strands scraped back from her head. "I don't think anyone has noticed, but I'm going quite bald."

Her lips twitched. Lucinda almost smiled. Sadly, she couldn't remember smiling much in her life. When her mother had been alive, she could coax a smile or an occasional giggle from her, but for the most part, Lucinda was a very serious person.

"I believe that I can mix you a potion to put on your hair that will help," she said.

"That would be wonderful, my dear," the duchess said. "Now stand up; let me have another look at you."

Lucinda wasn't used to doing another's bidding. She'd been alone in the world since she was sixteen, four years now since her mother had died. Nevertheless, she rose from the bench as the woman had instructed.

The duchess twirled her finger. "Turn around."

Again, Lucinda obeyed.

"You thankfully have a lot to work with, Lucinda. Your hair is beautiful, but of course red is never 'in' among the ton. Still, you have a nice figure, and your skin is perfection. So many times those with your coloring are plagued by freckles, but you are blessed with pure white skin. I know a seamstress on Bond Street who will know just which colors will enhance your beauty, and which to stay away from. I'll send a note to her immediately and ask her to visit us here for a fitting."

"Today?" Lucinda blinked. "She'll come today?"

"If I ask her to," the duchess answered with a chuckle. "I've paid her very well for her services over the years. She knows which side her bread is buttered on."

"That would be wonderful," Lucinda responded.

"I'm thinking you should have a special gown for the wedding."

Lucinda's stomach churned again. "There's no need," she argued. "It's to be a short marriage. There needn't be any sentiment tied to the affair."

The duchess simply stared at her. Stared at her a good long while. Long enough to make Lucinda fidget with the folds of her gown.

"But you would like it to be more, yes?"

"No," she automatically answered. "Why would I?"

The lady shrugged. "Why wouldn't you? The man has agreed to see to the welfare of your son. Will it be so easy for you to be parted from the child?"

The thought nearly brought tears to Lucinda's eyes. "No," she answered. "It will kill me to leave him. I love him so."

"Then why not try to make the marriage one in truth?" the duchess asked. "Can't you cast a spell over young Jackson?"

Lucinda glanced at her rough hands. "I tried that," she admitted. "It doesn't seem to be working."

"I hope you're better with hair," the woman worried. She waved a hand to dismiss the worry. "You'll simply have to win him the old-fashioned way then. With beauty and charm and grace."

"What makes you believe that I would even want Jackson Wulf for a true husband? He's arrogant, not to mention cursed. He's—"

"I know," the duchess cut her off. "He's quite the ladies' man, and a drunkard some say. But if you get him out of the brothels and off the bottle, he might make a good husband. And he's not hard to look at; that is for certain. All the Wulf boys are as handsome as sin. If you say he is not pleasing to the eye, then you are either a liar or blind."

"I am not blind. He is very handsome," Lucinda admitted. "But his good looks are not as important to me as his good deeds. Besides, we are both different, from the rest of society and from each other. I have not been raised as he has been raised. I do not know about manners and such for a lady."

"Not a worry," the duchess chortled. "I will take you under my wing, Lucinda. In short order, you will be every bit as refined as the young ladies born with a silver spoon in their mouths. I'll make you a wife Jackson can be proud of."

The lady's assurances stung somewhat. What did Lucinda care if Jackson Wulf found her pleasing? If he did grow to care for her, why couldn't he care for her just as she was? She shook her head. What was she thinking? The bargain had been made. Her son's future was set, and her future as well.

"And he is rich," the duchess added thoughtfully. She suddenly smiled. "We shall spend lots of his money while he's off drinking and, pardon me for saying so, but knowing Jackson, whoring as well."

The thought shouldn't bother Lucinda in the least. She'd given him her permission, after all. She chewed her lower lip and tried to ignore the stab of unwanted jealousy that rose inside of her. A moment later, she took a deep breath, turned to the woman, and smiled.

"Yes, let's do spend his money."

Chapter Eight

Lucinda's head was spinning by the time the coach delivered her back to the town house. She'd had everything ordered from underwear to outerwear, from fine nightgowns to fine ball gowns. Good Lord, she surely had spent the whole of the Wulf fortune. The duchess kept assuring her that such things were necessary and that Jackson could well afford to outfit her in style.

Now she felt a bit sick to her stomach. If her stay with Jackson was to be a temporary one, where on earth would she wear all the finery being made for her? She could sell the gowns if need be, Lucinda decided. She was surprised that as she reached the front door Hawkins didn't have it open before she reached the front steps. The man had an uncanny ability to know what she needed before she even thought to ask for it. She let herself in.

Halfway down the entry hall, she heard male voices coming from the front parlor. The front parlor was her favorite room in the whole house. She loved the rich furniture, the blazing hearth, and the striking portrait of the Wulf family that hung over the fireplace. It was a welcoming room. She paused at the entrance of the parlor to be greeted by a heartwarming sight. Jackson was holding Sebastian upon his knee while the usually stuffy Hawkins made faces at the child, obviously in hopes of wrenching a smile from him. Baby Sebastian's expression was nothing but serious.

"I don't believe he smiled at you, Lord Jackson." Hawkins finally gave up the game. "He's quite fond of me and he has never regarded me with anything but the somber little face he's pulling now."

Lucinda tried to hide her smile when she stepped into the room. "I believe it is time for Sebastian's nap," she said.

"Lady Lucinda, I did not hear you drive up in the carriage." Hawkins looked as if he expected fifty lashes for his oversight.

"I let myself in," she stated the obvious.

"I shall see how Cook is coming with sup," Hawkins said formally, hurrying from the parlor.

Lucinda walked over and took Sebastian from Jackson. The babe's little eyes lit up upon seeing her. She hugged him to her and kissed him.

"How did the fitting go?"

Her spirits immediately sank. "I fear you have no fortune left to squander," she admitted, feeling the damnable blush blossom in her cheeks. "The duchess convinced me I needed much more than I would have otherwise owned in a lifetime."

Jackson merely shrugged. "I'm sure if she thought you needed it, then you did. The Wulf fortune can afford a great many wardrobes."

Lucinda felt only slightly less guilty.

They stood in awkward silence for a moment. What did a woman say to a man who had earlier been forced into marriage with her? Lucinda's little world in Whit

Hurch was different. She'd had problems there to be certain, but this world was completely foreign to her.

"The marriage changes nothing," she finally blurted. "But for Sebastian's sake, I thank you for agreeing to wed me. You were right, I would not want him called a bastard behind his back."

"Well, there are worse things than being a bastard," he said quietly. "We both know that. As long as we both also understand the original bargain still holds."

"Yes," she agreed.

Another long pause followed.

"Ah, when—"

"As soon as I can secure a license and you have something of your own to wear. The where and how I will decide later."

She nodded. They were back to thick silence. Sebastian was already asleep on her shoulder. She had a perfect excuse to leave.

"The potion you told me about today," Jackson suddenly said. "I'm anxious to try it. I miss being among the horses."

Lucinda was relieved he had changed the subject.

"It's nothing more than some fat, herbs that I imagine I'll find in Hawkins' garden, melted together and made into either a soap or an oil to be applied directly to the skin. I'll see to it as soon as I put Sebastian down for his nap."

Jackson walked over and took Sebastian from her arms. "I'll take him up. Ask Cook for anything you need in the kitchen."

Cook had not been pleased to have a woman nosing about his kitchen. And it was a grand kitchen indeed. Lucinda had five bars of soap cooling and a jar of oil made from animal fat and various herbs known to mask a scent. As always when she was working, she became totally engrossed in the task. She'd eaten her dinner right there in the kitchen, regardless of Hawkins's disapproving scowl. Now she took the jar of oil and went in search of Jackson.

She found him upstairs in his room. The door was open. He sat upon the bed, looking over what appeared to be an old piece of parchment. Lucinda rapped softly against the door frame. He glanced up at her.

"I have the oil," she said.

"Come in." He placed the parchment on the bed and rose, meeting her when she stepped into the room. "I'm to rub it on me?"

"All over you," she instructed.

He brought the jar to his nose and sniffed. "It doesn't have a scent."

"No," she agreed. "And it won't make you have one, either. It's also very good for the skin. For dryness," she specified. "Although your skin doesn't look dry, or what I've seen of it doesn't."

"Will you go out to the stables with me after I've applied it so we can see if it works?"

"If you wish," she answered. "While you undress and apply the potion, I'll see that Sebastian is tucked in for the night." She turned on her heel and went to the room next door, where her son and the wet nurse slept.

Once Lucinda and Jackson had struck their bargain, she'd asked for the bedchamber on the other side of the nursery to be prepared for her. It must have seemed odd to Hawkins, but the man's expression never gave a hint that he found a young married couple sleeping in separate bedchambers anything out of the ordinary. And perhaps among the wealthy it was not.

In the small cottages of her village, it wasn't unusual for husband, wife, and children to share the same bed, so little space was to be had, especially for large families.

Sebastian was already sleeping. Martha sat in a chair by the hearth, her head bent to a sampler. The woman smiled at her, but they didn't speak lest they wake the child. Lucinda walked to the large cradle and stared at her sleeping son. Just looking at her babe brought her joy. He was an angel. An angel with the mark of the devil. But he would be safe now from harm . . . or would he?

If she couldn't break the curse, Jackson might harm the babe while the beast ruled him. She hadn't yet made it past the relief of knowing Sebastian would be well cared for to consider that her son might be in danger from the very man who had promised to look after him. They had not discussed that issue. They certainly would. With only a nod of parting to Martha, Lucinda hurried from the room.

She burst into the room next door unmindful that Jackson would be in the process of doing what she had told him to do and was therefore only half-dressed.

"I'm glad you're here," he said. "I can't reach my back." He held the jar toward her. "Would you mind?"

She did mind. Touching him made her feel odd. For some reason, when she touched him she forgot to breathe. Still, how could she refuse without admitting that he had an effect upon her that she would rather not admit?

"I need to talk to you about Sebastian," she said without answering.

He walked to her, placed the jar in her hand, and said, "Talk while you rub."

When he turned his broad bare back to her, what else could she do but comply? She stuck her fingers into the jar and dipped out a handful of thick oil. The moment her hand touched his warm flesh, her knees went weak. She loved the color of his skin. There was a slight red scrape where she had once thought to stab him. She rubbed extra oil into the scratch to help it heal.

"What did you wish to speak to me about regarding Sebastian?"

It took her a moment, lost in sensation, to clear her head. The subject she wished to discuss with him was very serious business, so she tried to blot out the feel of his skin beneath her hands.

"When you are at the mercy of the beast, how do I know that you will not harm Sebastian?"

The muscles in his back stiffened. "I thought you were going to break the curse," he reminded her. "Then you will have no reason to worry."

"But what if I cannot?" she insisted. "Or cannot before the curse comes upon you again?"

Suddenly he turned to face her. His dark eyes stared down into hers. "Whatever you think of me, know that I would never put Sebastian in danger. I know when it is coming. It happens when the moon is full. I take myself off and spend those days alone in the woods."

Since Lucinda's hands were still covered in oil, it seemed only logical to press them against his chest and continue rubbing the mixture into his skin. "Always it is tied to the moon?"

He shook his head. "Once, when I was very angry, it came upon me and there was no moon to set it into motion. But I do not anger easily. And I know when it is beginning and can act with human thought until it takes me completely."

Curious, she glanced up at him. "And after it does, are your thoughts your own?"

His disturbing mouth formed a frown. "No. That is the worst of it. Not knowing what I might do when the wolf takes me. Who I might harm. That's why I never allow myself to be around those I care for when I know the change is coming."

Her hand had moved up his chest and she now rubbed the oil into his neck. "How long do we have?"

"Not long. Three weeks or around that."

His voice had become very low, very husky. He stared into her eyes and she saw a flash of blue enter his. Night had fallen, she realized. He had night eyes.

"If you don't finish, and quickly, I won't be able to stand here and remain passive much longer. Your hands are driving me insane."

Lucinda snatched her hands away. "I didn't mean to; that is, I—"

"I am well aware that you have no desire to seduce me, Lucinda," he interrupted her blabbering. "It takes little to excite me these days. It's not your fault."

She had an odd notion that he'd just insulted her. Lucinda's face started to burn and she turned away from him. "Will you hurry and dress? I'm tired and wish to retire shortly."

"I have offended you."

She heard him shuffling around and assumed he had resumed dressing. "Offended me in what way?" she played ignorant.

"The remark about being easily excited. I haven't been with a woman in a good long while, and am therefore more excitable than usual. I didn't mean it as an insult to you. You're very desirable, Lucinda."

Her face grew hotter and she was glad he couldn't see her silly blushes. "I thought you took yourself off today to visit some of your old friends," she commented. Finding him at home playing with Sebastian when she returned had come as a shock to her, but still, she'd been gone a good long while. She had no idea how long he'd been home.

"The thought occurred to me," he admitted. "But then I realized drink usually went along with female companionship for me, and I decided to come home instead. I'm thinking I shouldn't drink so much. Would set a poor example for young Sebastian, would it not?"

Her anger and embarrassment seemed to slip from her like sand through her fingers. She turned to look at him. "Yes, it would. You've made a wise decision." That he would do that, for her son, a child not his own, took her totally by surprise.

"Shall we go?" he asked.

Still flustered, she could only nod. He moved forward, took her arm, and steered her out of his room.

Jackson loved the smell of the stables. It was an honest smell. Horses, hay, leather, and even manure. All combined, the scent brought him a strange feeling. One of coming home. Henry, one of the grooms, was pitching hay to the horses lined up in the stalls.

"Lord Jackson," Henry said upon seeing him. "I heard you were back. Not used to seeing you much around here."

"I'll do that." Jackson nodded toward the pitchfork in Henry's hands. "You can go on home now."

Henry looked surprised but moved toward him. Jackson had yet to move from the entrance of the stable farther inside. He didn't know how the horses would react upon his approaching them and wanted no witnesses to the event. None save Lucinda.

The groom handed Jackson the pitchfork, tipped his hat to Lucinda, and hurried on his way. Jackson stepped inside the stables. He propped the pitchfork against a wall. The horses stood, heads bent over their stall gates in preparation to be fed. They regarded him curiously, but so far none seemed uneasy with his presence. Bolstered by their reaction, Jackson moved closer to the first stall.

He slowly reached out his hand to a tall black stallion.

The animal sniffed at him, then pressed his muzzle into the palm of Jackson's hand. He rubbed his hand over the horse's muzzle, then up, to scratch behind his ears. Jackson moved to the next stall and petted the stall's occupant, and the next, making his way down the long roll of stalls.

"Do you see, Lucinda?" he asked excitedly, glancing toward her. She leaned against the stable entrance doors watching him.

"Yes, I see," she said, and he thought her smile was lovely. Soft and womanly.

Jackson turned back to a delicate gray mare and pressed his face against her satiny coat. The mare whickered softly, a welcome to his attentions. For a moment as he stood there, his face buried in the mare's long mane, his eyes misted over. He'd forgotten what it felt like to be accepted among God's creatures. Sometimes he forgot what it was like to be only a man.

Women helped him remember, Jackson admitted. It was because they welcomed him into their arms that he went sometimes all too willingly. He needed to feel like a man and nothing but a man, if he realized he held an unfair advantage with the ladies. He'd used it, too, which made him somewhat of a hypocrite. Jackson didn't mind using the curse to his advantage, but wishing it was gone from him once it no longer served his purposes.

In the past, plying himself with liquor and crawling between a woman's legs had dulled the pain of his seemingly useless life. He had longed for a way to connect in a society that had turned their backs on him. He had longed for a touch, a kiss, a way to feel only human.

One woman did not seem affected by his ability to easily lure women to him. Jackson pulled back from the mare and glanced toward Lucinda. She did not hunger for his kisses, his touch. She knew what he was. And perhaps it was because she did know that he desired her attention more than the others before her. Could even one woman accept him as he was? Curse and all?

Stepping away from the stall, Jackson walked to where he'd laid the pitchfork, grabbed it up, and began feeding the horses.

Lucinda watched Jackson work. His muscles moved beneath his shirt and she found she enjoyed watching him. At the moment he might look like a man, but he still moved like an animal. Graceful even while doing something as mundane as pitching hay. There were a good many horses and a good amount of hay to pitch. She saw a trickle of sweat make a path down his temple.

About halfway down the row of stalls, he paused and removed his shirt. He seemed engrossed in his work and Lucinda doubted that he even recalled she stood watching him. She swallowed hard at the sight of so much masculine flesh. His muscles rippled while he worked, and a thin sheen of sweat coated his honey-colored skin.

What was it about a man working that made a woman feel as if she labored alongside him as well? The body, the movements, the concentration. He'd made it to the last stall and had just pitched a large load of hay inside when the horses began to stomp in their stalls, making uneasy nickering noises to one another. Jackson glanced toward Lucinda as if in question.

"You're sweating," she called to him. "It allows your scent to resurface."

He backed away from the stall, moving slowly down the rows of horses. As the horses continued to stomp and snort in their stalls, he propped the pitchfork against a wall, reached down, and grabbed up his shirt, walking slowly toward Lucinda. For a moment, when his eyes met hers, she felt uneasy as well.

When he stood before her, she also caught his scent. It

affected her as surely as it affected the animals, but not in the same way. Suddenly her skin grew warm, her heart sped a measure, her nipples hardened, and below, between her legs, she grew moist and achy. She had no idea what he saw as he stared down into her eyes, but she strongly suspected that he knew what effect he had on her.

She suddenly understood. "You use it to your advantage."

He placed a hand on either side of her head, trapping her against the wall. The lanterns lit along the walls of the stable suddenly dimmed, as if he commanded the more intimate lighting.

What little light remained danced in the long strands of his hair and glowed golden against his sweat-moistened skin. She fought the urge to touch his chest, to run her hands along his smooth, warm contours. What was he doing to her? She didn't like it, or maybe she did.

"There is an animal in all of us, Lucinda," he said softly. "I call to yours is all."

He did. He called to something inside of her that had never drawn breath until he awoke the slumbering beast inside of her. Temptation. Desire. Sin. He commanded them all. Her powers, her gifts, as her mother had called them, seemed sorely lacking in comparison.

"You have an unfair advantage among mortal men," she accused.

"I have a couple." He bent to brush her lips with his.

Her body melted into the wall behind her. Her knees felt weak, but she tried to reclaim control over her emotions. "Your dark appeal is wasted on me," she assured him, although her voice sounded breathless, husky, and not at all assuring.

"Why do you fight me?" He gently nuzzled her ear. "It's not as if you are saving yourself."

Whatever spell he cast was outwitted by his worst enemy and his greatest tool for seduction—his mouth. She pushed him away. "I may not be a lady, but neither am I a whore," she bit out. "You'd do well to remember the next time when casting your spell over a woman to keep your mouth closed."

Lucinda had to get away from him, and quickly. She shoved past him and out of the stables. The summer night was cool and damp and helped revive her senses. She heard Jackson pull the stable doors shut behind her and soon he joined her on the path to the house.

"I do thank you for the gift you have given me to-night," he said. "I can run among the horses, again, if I must make certain not to sweat while doing it."

Nor should he sweat around her, Lucinda decided. She had no more than hatched the thought when a vision flashed inside her mind. A vision of Jackson looming over her, his body slick with sweat, his dark eyes alive with fire. Lucinda shook her head to dislodge the vision. She sometimes caught glimpses of things before they happened. Was this one of them, or had her imagination simply turned traitor against her?

"When we reach the house, I'd like for you to join me in my bedchamber."

She drew up short. Her hands clenched at her sides. "Do you never give up? Is it so inconceivable to you that a woman would not desire you?"

He turned back toward her. The night sky was alive with stars behind him. They danced in his eyes. "You said you needed to see the riddle. I had been reading it earlier. I wanted to give it to you."

She was glad the cover of darkness hid the embarrassed blush she felt stinging her cheeks. "Oh," she said softly. "Of course I need to see the riddle."

They resumed the path. She thought he would say more, perhaps tease her about which one of them could not get the act of lovemaking out of her mind. The silence stretched as they walked.

"See, already I have taken your advice into consideration."

She glanced toward him, but the darkness stole his expression from her.

"The one about keeping my mouth closed," he answered, although she had not asked.

Chapter Nine

After Lucinda surprised Jackson with the fact that she could read, and even Latin, for her mother, despite being a witch, had been a learned woman, Jackson had surrendered the riddle to her for study. It was actually a poem. Lucinda had studied it long into the night, and this morning she felt groggy-headed and short-tempered due to a lack of sleep. She was just about to get out bed, check on Sebastian, and see about getting breakfast when a soft rap was followed by a tall man carrying a baby bursting into her room.

"What is your opinion of the poem?"

She wanted to yell at Jackson. His manners were awful, and if she thought so, she couldn't imagine what high society thought of him.

"Do you mind?" she asked, pulling her covers up around her neck. "I'm not yet dressed for the day."

He moved toward the bed and seated himself. His dark eyes travelled over her. "You have nothing I haven't seen before," he said. "In fact, I've just about seen everything you do have, now that I recall."

Her face burned. "I'll thank you not to recall," she muttered darkly. "That wasn't the same at all."

"No need to be modest around me, Lucinda. We are to be wed."

"In name only," she reminded him, but had trouble staying cross when Sebastian looked so content cradled in Jackson's lap. She reached for the baby. "Come here, sweetheart."

"Since you asked." Jackson slid across the bed toward her, bringing Sebastian along with him.

"Not you." She scowled. "The invitation is for my son only."

Jackson handed her Sebastian and frowned. "You're so cold, Lucinda. What will it take to melt the ice around your heart?"

"It is not my heart that you are interested in," she countered. "Do not pretend otherwise."

"No," he agreed. "Giving my heart was never in my best interest."

What woman had managed to capture this man's heart? Lucinda was curious and, if she was honest, maybe a little jealous, as well. "Why did you not marry her? Did she not return your love?"

He didn't answer for a moment, and she thought he wouldn't, when he finally admitted, "She did not even know of it." Jackson rose from the bed. "I will bring your breakfast while you dress. I'd like to discuss your impression of the poem. The riddle hidden within."

The subject was closed. His equally closed expression told her so. "All right," she agreed. "I am famished."

He left the room, and cuddling for a moment longer with Sebastian, Lucinda gathered her thoughts on the poem.

" 'Damn the witch who cursed me,' " she repeated the first line of the poem. And with that line Jackson had damned Lucinda, as well. Ivan Wulf, who had composed the poem and been the first recipient of the curse, had not blamed himself for his tragedy but a woman. A witch. It was a fault of men, to blame others for their own bad deeds. Lucinda knew that better than anyone.

She laid Sebastian in the middle of the bed, then rose and dressed for the day. She'd barely gotten a brush through her long hair when Jackson returned. He did not carry the tray himself, but Hawkins followed him inside the room.

"I thought Hawkins could take Sebastian back to his nurse to have his own breakfast," Jackson explained.

Lucinda rolled her eyes. "Martha is just in the next room," she reminded them both.

"Hawkins insisted." Jackson shot her a meaningful look that said not to argue the matter further.

"Very well, then," she said. Lucinda reached down upon the bed and scooped Sebastian up. His little eyelids were heavy and she imagined he'd soon be back to sleep. Once Hawkins settled her breakfast tray on the stand next to her bed, she handed him the babe. A slight smile touched his mouth as he stared down at the child; then, posture rigid, he quit the room. Jackson walked over and closed the door behind him.

"So, what did you make of the poem?" Jackson asked.

Lucinda seated herself on the edge of the bed and uncovered her breakfast plates. The smell wafted up and made her stomach rumble. She never forgot while being served a fine meal in this house how she had once worried where her next one would come from. She took a bite of fluffy eggs and savored them before answering.

"The woman who cursed your forefather must have had very strong magic to do so. To cast a spell that has lived all these years. She also must have been very angry."

"I had nothing to do with that," Jackson said, coming

to sit beside her on the bed. "And yet I suffer for whatever sins he committed against her."

"He would not wed her," Lucinda explained. "Because of his position," she further explained.

"I know he refers to her as 'this witch I loved but could not wed.' He also says 'betrayed by love, my own false tongue.' He lied to her."

The old parchment rested on the stand where her tray sat. Lucinda reached across the small table and plucked it up. "Yes. He probably led her to believe a lie, that he would one day marry her despite their differences. Thus the lines 'Alas, no woman understands duty, / be it to family, name, or war,'" she read. Glancing up at Jackson, she said, "He obviously chose another when it came time for him to wed. A woman who would be in keeping with his higher position and please his family."

"Again, not my fault," Jackson grumbled. "What do you think about the riddle? 'Seek you and find your worst enemy; / stand brave and do not flee. / Love is the curse that binds you, / but 'tis also the key to set you free'?"

The riddle perplexed Lucinda. She wasn't certain she wanted Jackson to know that. If he thought she could not break the curse, he had no reason to allow her to stay. It would take some time . . . she would make certain of that, for the thought of leaving Sebastian behind was still too raw a wound to patch. But she didn't have long before another full moon would transform Jackson.

"It could mean a number of things," she hedged. "The poem says nothing about killing your worst enemy, and even later your ancestor admits to battles fought and won, and still defeat he leaves in his stead. I would think the answer lies in discovering your worst enemy but perhaps defeating them in some way other than in normal battle or death."

Jackson looked thoughtful. "And what plans do you

have for trying to break the curse yourself? The poem also says than Ivan Wulf had found no way to break it, 'no potion, chant, or deed,' which to me means he might have gone this same path with another . . ."

"Witch," she provided. "Perhaps he did. But then, the woman he sought out didn't have as much a stake in the breaking of the curse, I'll warrant."

Their eyes met.

"You don't seem like a witch," Jackson said. "I've seen no proof that you have powers any greater than my own."

"My powers are not to be used to impress anyone," she said. "I am a white witch, and am therefore bound to only practice good magic. If I could turn you into a toad, believe me, I would, but then, I'm thinking someone already has."

Her temper was as fiery as the color of her hair. Jackson was no fool, regardless of what his brothers thought of him. He'd easily believed Lucinda to be a witch when he'd come across her in the cottage. But since he'd returned to London to find her posing as his wife, she seemed an ordinary woman. Staring at her flawless skin, her sunfire hair, her shapely figure, he retracted the thought. She was not ordinary, but was she truly a witch?

She'd fashioned the oil for him last night, but any herbalist might have just as easily known about the mixture.

"You take my name, ask for me to raise your son. I want proof that you are all that you say you are."

"I have something in mind," she said. "In two nights' time, there will be a red moon. A red moon is very powerful. Since the moon curses you, I will appeal to it to also set you free. It is a ritual that must be performed at midnight, and must not be witnessed by anyone."

Jackson was still skeptical. "But I will not know if it has worked until the full moon is upon us again, correct?"

Her brow furrowed. "Are there certain characteristics of the wolf that you feel inside of you, even when the moon does not command you?"

All of his life, even before the curse took him, Jackson had been aware of his differences from others. It was something he and his brothers all shared. An unnatural sense of hearing for Armond; for Gabriel, well, surely no mortal man could work from sunup until sundown and still come in looking like he'd lounged around doing nothing all day. All of them could see well in the dark.

Women. For Jackson it was the women. They came around him as if he put off a scent that attracted them, and he knew by Lucinda's reaction to him last night what he had long suspected was in fact true. They could not resist him . . . except for Lucinda, and Lady Anne Baldwin, who'd stolen his heart and never even known it.

"Yes," he answered. "I suppose I would know even before the full moon. I would feel different."

"Then we will see," she said, "in two nights' time."

Chapter Ten

The night was foggy but warm. Mist rose from the ground in Lucinda's magic circle. She'd placed the candles in the four directions. Each one bore the color of the element it represented. To the North, she lit the black candle, to the South, the white, the East the red, and the West the gray candle. The circle she had thrown stood firm against outside elements. All negative energy had been chased from the circle.

She glanced up at the sky, but the moon chose to hide from her. She would sing to the clouds, seduce them into parting. To beseech the moon to release its hold upon Jackson, she needed to see it.

Lucinda said the ancient words her mother had taught her, spoken in a tongue only those of another world, another time, still understood. Softly she began to sing. As always when communicating with an element of the earth, she closed her eyes and lifted her face to the sky.

The mist boiled and rolled around her, but the clouds overhead did not do her bidding. She sang with greater passion, swayed in time to the soulful moans of the wind.

Lucinda turned to the East, the North, the South, and the West, concentrating harder. In her mind's eye, she saw the clouds overhead part, allowing her direct contact with the moon. But when she opened her eyes and looked heavenward, she found that she had not seduced the clouds and they still stood firm against her.

Her skills at seduction were weak, she admitted. Desire, both feeling it and purposely inspiring it in another, was new to Lucinda. She closed her eyes again, but this time she sought a vision of Jackson Wulf's face. Slowly, she lifted her arms above her head, reaching toward the sky as if reaching for a lover. Freeing her mind from inhibitions, she swayed and sang, danced and dipped within the magic circle, all the time keeping Jackson's image inside her head.

With her barriers lowered, her thoughts free to go where she usually would not allow, Lucinda acknowledged her own desires. She thought of the way his mouth moved against hers, the way his flesh felt beneath her fingertips. She thought of his scent and the way her own body reacted to it. And suddenly she no longer danced for the moon but only for him.

Jackson watched Lucinda from his window. Her voice, raised in song, had called to him, roused him from sleep, and brought him to the window to stare down upon her midnight ritual. He recalled that she'd said the ritual was to be private, unseen by others' eyes, but he could not look away from her. The mist swirled around her, and her body swayed to a melody he could not hear, but he understood all the same.

The sensuous sway of her hips mesmerized him. It was a dance as old as time. A dance meant to seduce a man, and whatever spell she might be trying to cast was working on him. His heart beat hard and fast inside of his chest. His heavy breathing fogged the windows, and more than once he'd wiped the steam away so he could see her. Desire, red-hot and knife sharp, rose inside of him. He slipped into a fog of want, of need, of hunger. Rational thought had no place here. Not when she called to the deepest, darkest recesses of his soul.

Her slender pale arms, which she held up toward him in the darkness, lowered to the clasps on either side of her gown. Like a shimmering veil, the garment floated to the ground. Now she stood naked in the mist. A goddess.

She was the embodiment of womanhood. Her skin glowed in the mist. The flickering flames of the candles surrounding her danced across the rises and valleys of her perfect form. Her breasts rose firmly away from her rib cage; her nipples, small and rose colored and hard, beckoned to him. He was hard, too. Painfully hard.

Her waist was small, flaring gracefully into hips probably wider than they once were but still round and smooth and welcoming. Her legs were long and shapely, her ankles thin, and her feet small and delicate.

She seemed born of the night, a stark contrast to it but at home in the darkness. In that moment Jackson wanted her as he had never wanted another woman. He pressed his hands against the cool glass, wanting to put them on her skin instead. Did she know she danced for him? Seduced him? Did she know that she called to the beast in him, the beast that lived in every man? The last vestiges of control snapped.

All he could think about was having her. Dominating her. Possessing her. His nostrils flared, as if he could catch her scent through the glass. Then he turned from the window, naked from sleep, hard with need, and beyond calling humanity back. He wanted her. He would have her.

◆ ◆ ◆

Her body was damp with perspiration, her hair wild around her shoulders, and her heart thundering to the pagan rhythm in her head when Lucinda felt a presence invade her sanctuary. She whirled to a stop, opened her eyes, and saw him standing just outside her magic circle. She wondered if her mind had conjured him. Was he made of mist instead of flesh and bone? *Flesh,* she answered, her gaze roaming his naked body, naturally coming to rest on the hardened member protruding from between his legs.

It was a sight to make a maiden faint or a whore smile. Lucinda was neither maiden nor whore. The sight of his nakedness did not embarrass her. She marveled at his perfection, even that which made him a man. Her gaze roamed him without shame, lifting to his face, where her eyes locked with his. His glowed blue in the mist. They spoke of ancient rituals between man and woman, of promises of pleasure beyond her wildest imaginings.

"Come to me," he commanded.

Lucinda wanted to obey. She wanted to go to him so badly that her body vibrated with a need stronger than anything she had ever known. She took a step toward him, one her feet made without permission from her mind. This was not part of their bargain. He took too much from her already. He took her very life, her joy, her son.

"Go away," she said softly.

He did not go away.

"Lucinda."

Her name upon his lips was like a touch, gentle, hypnotizing, and yet so very commanding. She swallowed hard and shook her head. "I do not want you," she said with more force.

"You lie." He nearly growled the accusation, but again, his voice was soft, compelling. "I smell your desire on the mist. Let us end this game between us. Come to me."

Her knees grew weaker, but she resisted. "No."

His eyes glowed brighter for a moment. "Then I will come to you." He took a step, then came up against the protective barrier of her magic circle. He placed his hands against it, as if it were glass. "Let me in," he instructed softly.

Feeling safer because he could not enter the circle without her permission, Lucinda walked to the barrier. "You cannot enter without my invitation, and I will not extend it to you."

One hand slid lower against the barrier, as if he could touch her breast. Lucinda was curious as to what it might feel like to have his hands on her. She stepped closer and when she pressed against the barrier felt the warmth of his touch. Her skin tingled and she sucked in a soft breath.

"Lucinda." His voice was low and husky. "Let me in."

She dared not. Lucinda knew what would happen if she did. The lowering of her inhibitions made her vulnerable to him. She would give herself to him, become a slave to his passion, and to hers, as well. He would use her, as all men used women, without thought or care to what the morrow would bring or who must suffer for the sins of the night.

Having regained a measure of her common sense, Lucinda started to back away. He pressed up against the barrier and temptation pulled her back under the spell. She wondered what it would feel like to experience all of his heat, the whole naked length of him pressed against her.

She might have resisted if the barrier were not in place. If she did not know for certain that he could not breech it. The barrier more than protected her; it gave her control. Lucinda pressed her body against his. His heat quickly spread to her and set her on fire. A soft moan escaped her throat.

There was nothing in the world like it, she suddenly understood. The slide of flesh against flesh. The heady elixir of passion shared and not stolen. The melding of mind, spirit, and flesh with another. For the first time, she understood the call to mate. She understood sexual attraction and why few could resist. It was enough for her at the moment, simply feeling, simply understanding, but it was not enough for him. The sharp sound of his fists hitting the barrier startled her from the spell.

Lucinda stepped away from the barrier quickly. Jackson stared at her, eyes glowing, a look of pure torture upon his face. Between his parted lips she caught a glimpse of fangs. Her hand snaked to her throat in an unconscious gesture. She backed away until she stood next to her discarded gown. Never taking her eyes from him, she bent and snatched it up, holding it before her like a shield.

Glancing up, she noted that the clouds still covered the moon. What was happening? How had she called his beast to the surface without the full moon to set the curse in motion? She must send it back, must call the man forward to take the beast's place.

"I call to you, Jackson Wulf," she said. "I call to the beast that dwells within you. Let me see only the man, and crawl back inside of him until the night is yours to command. I banish you from this place, beast. You are not welcome here."

His fists pounded against the barrier again and Lucinda jumped. She must have confidence in her powers. To waver would lower her defenses, would possibly allow him inside the circle. The man could be reasoned with. The beast could not. She stood her ground. Fear weakened the body, the soul, the mind. Fear alone could defeat her if she gave in to it.

Gradually, the glow dimmed in Jackson's eyes. His

fangs retracted. Lucinda did not dare breathe a sigh of relief until he turned and walked away from her. Once he had gone, her knees gave way and she crumbled to the ground. This was no ordinary curse that haunted Jackson Wulf. Obviously, the moon alone did not always set it into motion. He'd said it had once come upon him before without aid of a full moon.

She needed to learn the circumstances that had provoked the beast before. And to cover her own weaknesses this night she would cast a spell of forgetfulness upon Jackson. Tomorrow she must pretend that none of this had happened.

Lucinda found Jackson in the dining room the next morning. She stopped just outside the door to gather her wits. He seemed focused upon his plate, but she could see that he had not eaten, nor did he look inclined to do so. She drew in a shaky breath and entered.

"Good morn, my lord," she said with false cheerfulness.

He glanced up but said nothing. When she walked to the chair beside him, he stood and pulled it out for her, but again, he seemed distracted, as if he simply performed his gentlemanly duty out of habit. Lucinda sat. Hawkins bustled in. The steward lifted silver covers from the platters so that Lucinda could pick and choose. Once she filled her plate and Hawkins bustled out again, she glanced at Jackson from beneath her lashes.

"You are quiet this morning," she said.

"I had the strangest dream last night," he finally responded. His gaze met hers. "But I think maybe it was not a dream."

That he remembered took her off guard. Sometimes a will was too strong to practice magic effectively against the individual. Jackson was obviously such a person. The fact didn't bode well for her or for him if the beast inside

of him had a will to match the man. "Do you feel any different today?" she asked to change the subject. Lucinda
knew the ritual had not worked, but still, she had to ask.

"No," he confirmed. "Nothing has changed." His dark
gaze steadied upon her. "I was there, wasn't I? I came to
you but could not reach you."

Lucinda fought down the blush she felt rising in her
cheeks. If he remembered all, he would also remember
her curiosity, and where it had led. A woman who didn't
want to find herself in his bed didn't give a man like Jackson Wulf such information. "The ritual cannot be repeated." She again avoided his question. "The red moon
was only for one night until the next one. We will have to
try something else."

"I frightened you."

She thought to glance away from him, but he reached
out and gently took her chin, forcing her to look at him. "I
have never frightened a woman before, at least to my
knowledge. I could not control myself. What is happening
to me?"

At least she could answer this question. "The wolf
tried to surface last night," she answered, stirring eggs she
now had little appetite for, either. "You told me that had
happened once before. Were you with a woman then,
also?"

He shook his head. "No. I had left a tavern and saw a
man beating a poor orphan in the streets for trying to pick
his pocket. Something about seeing someone so big and
strong beating someone so small and helpless brought
forth a rage I had never felt before. I confronted the man.
He hit me, as well, and told me to mind my own business.
Then I felt the wolf rising up, hungry for the man's blood.
Whatever he saw when he looked at me frightened him,
him and the child. They both ran away into the night."

"Then it is not the moon alone that rules the beast inside of you," she said. "Rage and . . ."

"Lust," he provided what she did not say. "Although I have never before felt lust as strongly as I did last night. Were you dancing for me?"

To glance away, to blush, would tell him more than she wanted him to know. "No," Lucinda lied. "Your breakfast grows cold," she said to turn his burning gaze off of her and onto something else.

He lifted his fork. His hand shook so badly that he quickly set the utensil down. Lucinda turned a questioning look upon him.

"The liquor," he explained. "Or rather, the lack thereof."

His weakness and his obvious distaste of it softened her heart toward him. Such a physically strong man to have so many weaknesses. "I can make you a potion," she offered. "To ease—"

"No," he interrupted. "This is something that I must fight on my own. I won't trade one addiction for another."

Before Lucinda thought, she reached forward and placed her hand over his. "I know you can do this," she assured him.

His eyes softened. He brought her hand to his lips, kissing her fingers softly. The result was an immediate burst of warmth that spread from her fingers down her arm.

"Last night," he said, staring into her eyes. "Did I dream you came to me? Did I dream you pressed against me? Did I dream you wanted me?"

Denial would be best, but Lucinda had a feeling he would see the lie in her eyes. "I was only curious," she admitted. "If I would feel different with another man."

His jaw tensed. Lucinda realized it wasn't the right thing to say. She had meant if she would feel repulsed as she suspected she would feel if Lord Cantley ever touched her again. Perhaps she had wondered deep down if the contact of Jackson's flesh against hers would stir any memory of what had happened to her the night Lord Cantley defiled her. There were things she did not care to share with Jackson. Her humiliation at the hands of another man was one of them.

"And was it?" he asked stiffly. "Any different?"

"I do not know," she answered, but of course she did know. She hadn't felt repulsed by the feel of Jackson's body against her. Far from it. "And I do not wish to discuss it further."

He opened his mouth as if he'd argue, but Hawkins suddenly hurried into the dining room. "A note, Lord Jackson," the servant said formally. Hawkins extended a highly polished silver platter on which a dainty note rested.

Jackson took the note and opened the wax-sealed envelope. "It's from the duchess," he told Lucinda. "I recognize her seal."

Lucinda's heart sped a measure. Had a portion of her wardrobe been completed? She longed to wear something that didn't belong to Rosalind Wulf. Not that the lady didn't have impeccable taste, but Lucinda always worried about ruining one of the nice gowns she borrowed from Rosalind's wardrobe.

"Her Grace and the seamstress will arrive here shortly. The necessities have been completed and the seamstress wishes to do any last-minute alterations."

Lucinda was both thrilled and horrified. "Here?" she whispered. "They're coming here?"

Jackson glanced around. "The place isn't that shabby. Not as grand by half as—"

"It's not that," she interrupted. Embarrassed by

Hawkins's presence, she glanced meaningfully at the servant. Jackson dismissed the man and she continued, "I have no idea how to entertain a lady. Where will I receive them? Should I serve—?"

"Her Grace knows you haven't been schooled in such matters," Jackson assured her. "She won't expect you to have everything just so."

Lucinda discovered something she'd never known about herself in that moment. She wanted to have everything "just so," as Jackson had put it. She didn't want to be an embarrassment, to either Jackson or herself. "I should serve tea," she decided.

"Hawkins will serve tea," Jackson said.

"And I need to serve some of those little iced cakes. Do we have any?"

He almost smiled. "If we don't, I'll send Hawkins quickly to Gunter's to fetch some."

Breakfast forgotten, Lucinda stood and began to pace. "Should I dress my hair?" She'd never done so in her life but thought she might struggle to at least put it up off her neck.

"I love your hair down," Jackson said softly. "The way the sun catches your lovely curls and shoots gold through them. You are very beautiful, Lucinda."

When he looked at her that way, Lucinda could almost believe him. She didn't consider herself beautiful. She was too tall and too shapely and as common as mud. If men had paid her heed in the past, it was because she was a lone woman and one rumored to be easy with her charms, as all witches were.

"Flattery will get you nowhere," she clipped.

"I'm beginning to see that," he countered. "You admit-, ted to being curious. I'm curious, too. Why not resolve the issue?"

"Curiosity killed the cat."

"Satisfaction brought her back." He rose and walked toward her.

Lucinda stifled the urge to flee. When he stopped before her, she had to lean her head back to look up at him. "Satisfying your curiosity is not part of our bargain," she reminded him. "I like to think of our arrangement as more of a business venture."

"Nothing wrong with mixing business and pleasure," he said, running a finger along her collarbone and making her shiver. "Why do you bring the beast out in me?"

He was perfectly serious, she realized. "I assumed all women brought it out in you," she answered.

"No," he said. "Not like that. Not like last night. Have you cast a spell over me?"

Lucinda thought back to the first night he had arrived at the town house. Could the spell she'd cast be working? But no, she'd cast a spell to make him fall in love with her. Any attractive young woman could probably inspire lust in him. But then again, maybe all he associated with love was lust. Maybe he did not know the difference.

"You seem immune to my spells," was her answer.

"As you are to mine," he countered, and then perhaps just to prove he didn't believe his claim for a moment, he ran his finger along her collarbone again.

Try as she might, Lucinda couldn't suppress another shiver.

Chapter Eleven

Lucinda spent the remainder of the morning preparing for the duchess's visit. After taking tea in the main parlor, Her Grace and the seamstress joined Lucinda upstairs in her bedchamber. The dowager held Sebastian on her lap, cooing and clucking to the child and making a general fuss over him.

"I think just another nip here at the waist," the seamstress said while Lucinda stood before a cheval glass admiring the woman's handiwork. Lucinda wore a satin gown of ivory, one she knew the duchess had chosen for her wedding day. The gown was lovely and delicate.

"By all means," the duchess agreed. "Lucinda should show off her hourglass figure. With that hair, that skin, and that figure, she's going to be the toast of London, as far as the gentlemen are concerned leastwise," she added with a chuckle.

"I doubt that I will be included among London society," Lucinda said, uncomfortable because the seamstress was present. The woman went about her tucking and measuring as if she wasn't listening to the conversation. "If what I've heard is correct, Jackson isn't even accepted."

"Perhaps," her grace agreed, tickling Sebastian beneath his double chin and receiving nothing but a piercing look for her efforts. "But no one dictates to me who attends my own social functions, and I am still powerful enough among the ton that no one dares snub my invitations, either. You will have a chance to show off these lovely gowns, I promise you."

The thought rather sickened Lucinda. If Lord Cantley was an example of the upper crust, she wanted nothing to do with them. She decided not to worry over the matter. She doubted she'd be in London long enough to attend any parties and doubted that Jackson would want to be seen in public with her even if she was.

"There, I think we've finished for now," the seamstress said, helping Lucinda from the gown. "The rest of your wardrobe should be finished next week."

"Thank you," Lucinda said to the woman. Her once empty wardrobe now stood with the doors open, holding a variety of nice day gowns and evening attire, the drawers full of lacy undergarments, stockings, and nightgowns. It was overwhelming to think she owned so many clothes. Lucinda's mother had taught her to sew, but the coarse fabrics and simple frocks she'd made for herself were shabby compared to her current finery.

Slipping a lace robe over her new undergarments, Lucinda moved toward the duchess to take Sebastian from her. Lucinda knew that Hawkins lingered somewhere near the top landing, waiting to escort the ladies back down and out.

"You will come visit me soon, won't you?" her grace fussed. "We must begin your lessons before I show you off to society."

"Of course," Lucinda lied. What use did she have for

fancy manners? Still, she would humor the lady for the time being. "Oh!" Balancing Sebastian upon her hip, Lucinda suddenly rushed to her dressing table and retrieved a jar. She returned to the duchess and pressed the jar into her hand. "For your hair," she whispered. "Apply it nightly and sleep with a wrap around your head."

"You remembered." The older woman leaned forward and kissed her lightly upon the cheek. "You are a dear girl."

Lucinda was stunned by the show of affection. She simply stood and stared as the duchess and the seamstress bustled out of the room.

"Hawkins, help an old woman down the stairs," she heard the duchess call.

Slowly Lucinda lifted a hand to her cheek where the old woman had kissed her. No one had ever treated her so kindly. Even those whom she once helped in her village usually only nodded a brief thank-you, their eyes never really meeting hers. They had been afraid of her, she realized. Even Lord Cantley perhaps had been afraid to pursue her as a man would normally pursue a woman.

Had he thought Lucinda would curse him? Make his manly parts shrivel between his legs and fall off? If only she could. Lucinda's magic could do no harm. Her gifts could only be used for good deeds, or they would be taken from her.

"I like that outfit you're wearing very much."

Startled, Lucinda glanced toward the door to see Jackson lounging there, his back pressed against her door frame. He shrugged away from the door and entered. "I wanted to see what you've spent the family fortune on," he explained. His gaze ran the length of her. "I approve."

Her cheeks were burning. The delicate underthings showed more than they hid. "You have no call to enter my bedchamber at will," Lucinda reminded him. "The clothes might legally belong to you, but what is in them does not."

He lifted a brow. "We are to be married. You do understand English law regarding the subject of marriage? Everything you own will belong to me."

"I own nothing," she was quick to point out.

"Except what is in those fetching undergarments." He walked to her, and his hand lightly brushed against her breast in the process of taking Sebastian from her arms. She jumped as if he'd scorched her. Lucinda took a step back from him, immediately clutching her wrapper tighter around her.

"We have a bargain, remember?"

"I can hardly forget when you remind me every time I come within touching distance." He held the babe up in front of him and grinned at the child, who made a squealing noise of delight. "Wish your mother would squeal for me like that," he said to the child.

Frowning, Lucinda moved forward and took the child from him. "You're getting him much too excited. It's his nap time. Look in my wardrobe all you want. I'll take Sebastian in to Martha."

Lucinda wanted away from Jackson. She kept remembering the feel of his flesh against hers. The disturbing way her body reacted to him whenever he was close. He thought she had cast a spell over him. She very much believed he had cast one over her. She entered the nursery and handed Sebastian to Martha. Lucinda lingered for a moment, intending to give Jackson an opportunity to look over her wardrobe and, she hoped, be gone by the time she returned.

Martha seated herself in a rocker, unbuttoned her frock, and brought Sebastian to her plump breasts. The poor woman had lost her own babe, and Lucinda wasn't certain there was a husband. She hadn't wanted to pry.

As she watched Sebastian nurse, she felt a pang of envy. How she would love to nurse her own babe. Lucinda moved to Sebastian's cradle and straightened the covers, even though Martha had already done so. Her thoughts turned to Jackson. In her room next door, his fingers running over the fabrics of her new gowns. Then a vision flashed in her mind. Jackson at her breasts, which caused a very different reaction from longing to bond with her son. Her nipples hardened immediately.

Heat crept up her neck into her face. Why would she have such thoughts? And why was she suddenly curious to know what it might feel like to have Jackson's mouth against her skin? Lucinda should have never dabbled in things better left alone last night. There had already been an initial spark between them when they met. Why add fuel to the fire?

She glanced toward Martha. The wet nurse now had Sebastian propped upon her shoulder, patting his back even though his eyes were closed in sleep. Hoping she'd given Jackson enough time to survey her new wardrobe and leave, Lucinda tiptoed out of the nursery. When she entered her room, Jackson was sitting on her bed, staring at the open doors of her wardrobe.

"I thought you would have looked your fill and left by now," she said. Lucinda walked to the wardrobe. The sight of all the rich materials and the beautiful gowns still took her breath away. She turned toward Jackson. "Well, do you approve?"

His gaze drifted down her body. "As I've already said, I very much approve."

Jackson was trying to unnerve her with his hot glances and suggestive remarks. Lucinda needed to set him straight again. She flounced to the bed and stood before him, hands on hips.

"My face is up here."

"I know where your face is," he said, never glancing up at her. "And it's a lovely face, but at the moment it takes a poor second to the sight of your nipples straining against your chemise."

Lucinda hadn't quite gotten the vision of him suckling at her breasts from her mind before she'd left the nursery. She should have taken more time to bring her emotions under control. Self-conscious, she started to pull her wrapper closed. He stopped her.

"Don't," he said. "Just this once, don't."

He held her hands pinned at her sides. She thought he simply meant to stare, but he leaned forward and traced the shape of her nipple through her chemise with his tongue. She swallowed the gasp she felt rising in her throat. He had no right. She could struggle. But she didn't. Perhaps her vision had been one that simply told her this would happen. Perhaps she wanted it to happen.

She felt ignorant at times about intimate matters between men and women. She dealt often with the results of such folly, but she had never felt passion herself. Not until she met Jackson. It was as heady as any mulled potion and as hard to resist. She closed her eyes and allowed herself the small sin of pleasure.

As if sensing victory, Jackson released her hands and pulled her closer. His hot, moist mouth closed over her nipple through the thin fabric of her chemise. He drew her gently into his mouth and sucked. Lucinda couldn't control the soft moan that escaped her lips. Her hands strayed to his hair, fingers entwining in the silky locks that brushed his broad shoulders.

Her chemise had a velvet ribbon that gathered it at the neck. Jackson loosened it with his teeth. His hands slid up her waist, her rib cage, and a moment later he tugged the chemise down, exposing her breasts. Lucinda refused to open her eyes. Behind the darkness of her eyelids, she could pretend she didn't know what he was doing.

His hands closed around her breasts, and just as she had imagined, they felt good against her skin. He took her nipple into his mouth again, the silky brush of his hair against her skin nearly as erotic as the deep pull of his mouth upon her nipple. Her hands twisted tighter into his hair. Her knees shook.

"Do you know how perfect you are?" he asked, his face nuzzled against her breasts. "How beautiful."

Jackson made her feel perfect. He made her feel beautiful. He pushed the chemise down farther, causing her thin wrapper to fall off of her shoulders and hang from her elbows. His tongue traced the lower shape of her breast, then drew a hot line down her stomach. The question of where he might be going with that sinful tongue of his caused her to open her eyes. The first thing Lucinda focused upon was the open doorway. It was as effective as a cold bucket of water thrown in her face.

"The door," she gasped. Lucinda shoved him away, nearly tripping on her long robe while trying to back away from him.

"I'll close it," he said.

Jackson rose and moved to the door while Lucinda struggled to put everything back into place. She yanked her wrapper tight around her and joined him, stopping him before he could pull the door closed.

"Put yourself on the other side of it," she said, her voice shaky. "I—we shouldn't have."

He reached out and ran a finger down the front of her robe. "Why shouldn't we have? I was very much enjoying myself, and I don't think you were minding too much, either." He leaned forward and brushed her ear with his lips.

Her legs shook so badly she feared he'd notice. Lucinda liked being in control of her life, in control of her emotions. Lord Cantley had taken away her control, her right to say no to him. Jackson might not be the type to take what a woman wasn't willing to give, but he wasn't above seducing her in order to achieve the same goal. She knew what had just happened between them wasn't entirely his fault. Still, she needed to remind him and herself that it wasn't part of their bargain.

"It is my body," she said. "What happens or does not happen between us is my decision to make."

He pulled back from her, staring down into her eyes. "I never said it wasn't."

"Yet you have purposely tried to seduce me on more than one occasion," she accused.

"I never said I wouldn't."

His calm in the face of her churning emotions angered Lucinda. He was in control. She was not. Lucinda wheeled away from him. "Please leave."

"Why is it so hard for you, Lucinda? To give? To be soft? You are soft. Your skin, your hair, everything but your heart."

With her back turned to him, she scoffed at his remark. "Again, you pretend an interest in my heart when we both know that is not what you are after at all."

His hands on her shoulders made her jump. "And if I was, would you give it to me, or would you be as stingy with that as you are with the rest of you?"

Lucinda's heart was guarded. It had always been guarded. Only Sebastian could lay a rightful claim to it, and in the end even he would break her heart, through no doing of his own. She drew a shaky breath. "Please leave as I've asked you to do. We have a bargain and nothing more. That is all we will ever have."

He removed his hands from her shoulders. "Pack a bag. We wed tomorrow. We'll leave at first light."

She turned to see him now standing at the door. "The license," she reminded him.

"I have it. And you will have your precious bargain. I hope it keeps you warm at night."

The door closed.

Chapter Twelve

The quaint country parish was two hours' ride from London. The vicar had agreed to marry Jackson and Lucinda once Jackson had provided the necessary license. The man had sent his wife in search of proper witnesses. Lucinda sat in a small room staring out an open window at a field of wildflowers. The day was beautiful, sunny and warm. She'd removed the ivory gown from her valise, hoping the wrinkles would disappear with the help of the humid heat.

It was silly, but she wanted to look particularly fetching. She had no veil, but the beautiful flowers called to her and so she climbed from the window and walked into the field. She picked enough to make herself a small bouquet, then extra to make a wreath to wear around her head. By the time she climbed back into the window, the vicar's wife had entered the room and stood wringing her hands.

"Thought you'd had a change of heart and escaped through the window," the woman said. "Didn't want to have to tell the handsome gentleman."

If running away was an option, Lucinda supposed she

might have done exactly that. She had to remind herself that this was no marriage in truth. It was only a bargain.

"I found a couple in the village who have agreed to stand in witness of your marriage," the woman said. "It is time to ready yourself."

"Was it difficult?" Lucinda asked, sitting in a rickety rocker in order to fashion her head wreath. "To find someone willing to stand for us?"

The woman wrung her hands some more. "It's that he's a Wulf," the woman whispered. "His family has a dark stain upon their name. But to look at them you'd think they were angels," she added, rather wistfully.

It shouldn't have surprised Lucinda that Jackson and his dimples had already seduced the woman. With a sigh, Lucinda turned her attention to the wreath she fashioned. She had been taught to weave when she was a child and it took her only a short time to make the headdress.

"I will prepare now," she announced, hoping the woman would leave.

"I'm here to help you." The vicar's wife glanced toward the gown Lucinda had spread out upon a small cot in the room. "It is a lovely gown you'll be wearing. I'm thinking you need help getting into it."

An argument formed on Lucinda's tongue, for she was uncomfortable with others helping her dress and undress. She'd told Hawkins so when she'd first arrived at the London town house and he'd fretted over securing her a ladies' maid. But Lucinda admitted the gown would only wrinkle more without an extra pair of hands to help her with the buttons up the back.

"All right," she agreed. "I suppose the sooner I prepare, the sooner the wedding will be over."

A mischievous spark entered the woman's eyes. "Anxious for the wedding night, are you?" She giggled. "Can't say as I blame you there, child."

There would be no wedding night, at least not in the traditional sense. Lucinda very much hoped that her handsome bridegroom remembered that.

Jackson found he had little in common with the country vicar. Their stilted conversation had fallen flat, and the couple who stood in the corner eyed Jackson as if they expected him to fly into an insane rage at any moment, find an ax, and have their heads on a platter for his wedding feast. He should be used to being treated like a leper, but he admitted it still bothered him. It more than bothered him. It made him cross.

He glanced toward the door of the crude church, and his sour mood immediately diminished. Lucinda stood poised in the doorway. She was a vision. The lovely satin gown was simple but hugged her woman's curves to perfection. The wreath of wildflowers she wore around her head made her look like a fairy sprite. Her long hair hung loose around her shoulders, and she carried a small bouquet. He felt like a cad in that moment. He should have thought to pick the flowers and present them to her.

Never taking his eyes from her, he walked to where she stood, took her hand, and led her to the front of the church. The vicar was a no-nonsense man and the ceremony proceeded. Vows were spoken, Jackson's voice sounding nearly as hollow as Lucinda's in the small church. He'd at least thought about a ring, and Lucinda blushed when he slipped the thin gold band upon her finger. He was a little unnerved that it fit her perfectly. As if it belonged on her finger.

Once their names were signed to the proper documents, he reached in his pocket and paid the witness couple, who only thawed toward him when they realized he might be responsible for their next cow. Noting the roof was in shabby repair, along with the rest of the parish church, he also made a generous donation to the vicar and his wife.

"Is there an inn close by where we might spend the night and get a bit of supper?" Jackson asked the vicar.

"The Crow's Foot is not an hour from here," the man answered. "Though a rough crowd is known to frequent the lower tavern."

Tavern? Jackson's mouth nearly watered.

"Perhaps we should press on for home," Lucinda said quietly.

He glanced at her, sparing her a strained smile. "You sound like a wife already."

The Crow's Foot did indeed host a tavern full of rough-looking patrons. Jackson wondered if having a scar was some sort of password to gain entrance. Lucinda still wore her ivory gown, and in the dark, smoky tavern she appeared as out of place as he would at a hog-calling contest. She hadn't spoken another word since his snide comment at the church, and with difficulty he tried to pretend that the very smell of stale ale and sour wine didn't excite him every bit as much as she did.

"Will ye be wanting a tankard, 'andsome?"

A serving wench with her booty falling from the front of her stained blouse paused at their table. He tried not to notice that the edges of her large, dark nipples could be seen just dancing above her blouse, being as he'd only been married for one hour.

"Sup," he answered. He glanced at Lucinda. "To drink?"

"Milk," she answered softly.

The serving wench scowled but nodded. "We've a fine venison stew and hard bread for sup tonight. Cook might be missing a few fingers, but he makes a good stew."

As long as the fingers are not in the stew, Jackson thought. "That will be fine," he said.

"And for ye to drink, my lord?"

Jackson wanted to say "ale" so badly he had to bite his lip to keep it from spewing forth. "I'll have milk, as well," he finally answered.

He hated milk, but the slight touch of Lucinda's hand beneath the table was almost worth passing on the ale. Almost.

Jackson glanced around, noticing they were the object of most men in the tavern's attention. Or rather, Lucinda was.

"Wish you weren't so fetching," he grumbled.

"I told you we shouldn't have come," she whispered.

He turned to her. "Can't you cast a spell on yourself to make all who look at you find you disgusting?"

She rolled her eyes. "If I could go around casting spells to serve whatever purpose I required at the moment, I wouldn't have lived the kind of life I've lived."

Lucinda said little about her past. Jackson was curious. "Was it horrible?"

Her lashes drifted downward. "Not always," was all she said.

A moment later she glanced back up at him. "And what of your life?"

A father who had turned into a wolf one night at supper and had later killed himself? A mother who had followed him to the grave? A younger brother who had gone missing? Two older brothers who stood staunch against assault after assault and never shed a tear? Yes, Jackson was different from them all. The black sheep. The jokester. The drunkard. The womanizer. Jackson had cried when his parents died. Alone, in his room, he had wept for them and for the bleak future that stretched ahead.

But he had learned to find solace in other things. Foolish thing perhaps, but they had saved his sanity in truth.

"My life has been better, I suspect, than yours," was his answer.

" 'Ere's your sup." The serving wench set a tray upon the scratched table. "And your milk," she added with a snort. She glanced around. "Best you eat quickly and be gone from here."

"We were planning to secure a room upstairs for the night," Jackson said. "It is our wedding day."

The woman frowned. "You'll not be wanting to stay." Leaning closer, she lowered her voice. "I 'ear talk at the tables. Some are planning to spend your wedding night with the young bride 'ere. The further they get into their cups, the braver they will get. Take my advice, eat and go out the same way you came in."

The woman sashayed off. Lucinda, he noted, looked worried. "Think I can't protect you?"

"I think it would be foolish for you to even try, given the odds," she mumbled, dipping a bite of stew into her luscious mouth. "I say we take the woman's advice, eat up, and get out. We can sleep in the coach on the way home."

As much as both women were probably right, Jackson didn't like to be chased away. He wasn't a coward. Although, to his knowledge, he wasn't really a fighter, either. Should he sacrifice his manly pride for the sake of Lucinda's safety? Glancing around the room at the men eyeing his bride lewdly, he decided that he could and that he should. He had the responsibility of a wife now . . . for however long she continued to be his wife.

"Very well," he finally agreed. "We'll sup and be on our way."

Chapter Thirteen

Lucinda was pleased that Jackson showed common sense regarding the matter of leaving the inn. She felt eyes moving over her, undressing her. A man with a face like Jackson's and hands that had never known hardship did not inspire confidence in his protecting skills. His skills at seduction were another matter. Resisting those skills in a room upstairs held as little appeal to her as the trouble she felt brewing in the small tavern room.

She finished her stew and bread before Jackson but managed to hold her tongue in urging him to hurry. Like the beasts in the woods that sensed fear and reacted by attacking the weaker prey, she didn't want the men present to know she was terrified. Nor did she want Jackson to know that she lacked confidence in his ability to protect her.

Finally, he shoved his food away, left coin on the table, and helped her rise. A chorus of male sounds of appreciation followed them through the tavern and out the door. Jackson scowled at the men on his way out but thankfully did not challenge anyone.

The night air was doubly sweet after the smells of male sweat and stale ale in the tavern. Lucinda breathed deeply, now able to relax as they moved around the back end of the tavern toward the carriage house.

They nearly made the relative safety of the carriage house, where both coachman and footman slept with the coach, when five shadows broke from the night and blocked their path. Lucinda sucked in her breath. Jackson grabbed her arm and pulled her behind him.

"We want the woman," one voice broke the sudden silence.

"I want her, too," Jackson drawled. "The problem is, the choice is the lady's, and I think she prefers me, her husband, over the five of you."

"We aim to change her mind," another man said, and snickers followed from the others.

"Over my dead body," Jackson said, his voice now low, deadly.

A knife appeared from the dark, catching the glint of the half-moon overhead. "That can be arranged," the knife wielder assured Jackson.

"Leave us alone." Lucinda darted around Jackson, facing the shadows. "I'm a witch and I'll curse you all if you do either of us harm."

Jackson pulled her behind him again.

"Don't know about the others," the knife wielder said. "But I'll take my chances with the witch. Figure what she has under that gown is worth being cursed to have some of."

Lucinda's stomach lurched. Jackson lunged.

His swift action took her by surprise and obviously the shadow men as well. He kicked the knife from the leader's hand, following through with a jab to the head that sent the man stumbling backward. A growl sounded in the dark, but Lucinda didn't know if it came from Jackson or one of the shadows. Like a pack of animals, the shadows pounced upon Jackson. She nearly screamed when they wrestled him to the ground. The men came flying up and off of him before she could express her terror. Somehow, Jackson had gained his feet again.

If she found his strength unnatural, the shadow men were slower in their thinking. They stormed Jackson again. Again he drove them back with his feet and his fists. In the darkness, one shadow in a group of six stood out clearly. She saw the blue glow in Jackson's eyes. Driven now by bloodlust, his attackers seemed not to notice their victim was no mortal man.

Jackson fought with grace and finesse and Lucinda wondered how she could have ever doubted his abilities to protect her. It was, perhaps, the rest of mankind that needed protecting . . . from him. Distracted by the fight, she hadn't noticed that one shadow had slipped away from the others. She smelled him before he clamped a dirty hand over her mouth.

"We'll have our fun while everyone else is busy," he whispered harshly in her ear.

Lucinda recognized the man's voice as belonging to the leader. She was at first too stunned to struggle, but when he tried to pull her away from the others instinct penetrated shock. She tried to kick out at him, her efforts hampered by her long gown. He had an arm around her, just below her breasts, nearly cutting off her breath. She saw Lord Cantley in her mind's eye and allowed all the rage simmering inside of her to surface. She could not fight back while he'd done his dark deeds to her, but she could fight now.

"No," she said. "Not ever again!"

She clawed at the man's arm with her nails. She kicked back and managed a blow to his shin, which was less effective because of her delicate slipper. Still, the man loosened his hold on her, issuing a foul oath in her ear. Lucinda nearly got away before he reached out, grabbed her shoulder, and tore her gown in his attempt to pull her back to him.

A low growl sounded behind her. The man's hand fell away from her shoulder. She couldn't see what stood behind her, but she saw the whites of the eyes of the man who had attacked her when his gaze widened.

"Holy mother," he whispered, stumbling back. "What is he?"

Slowly, Lucinda turned to face what had driven fear into the leader's eyes and voice. Jackson stood before her, his strange eyes glowing in the dark, his fangs flashing in the moonlight. She knew his intent. Knew it by the twisted expression on his face. He meant to kill the leader. He meant to rip the man's throat out with his teeth. Although Lucinda felt no great compassion to see a man spared who had planned to defile her, she did feel compassion for Jackson. The beast ruled his head now, but the man would face the consequences of the beast's deeds.

She stepped toward him. "No, Jackson," she said softly. "Let him go." He growled at her in response, but she stood her ground. "You are a man," she continued, "not a beast without the ability to reason. Come back to me."

Behind her, she heard her attacker's footfalls as he ran to escape them. Jackson's head snapped in that direction. He started to pursue, but again Lucinda placed herself between Jackson and the fleeing man.

"I need you here with me, now," she commanded. Bravely she stepped forward and ran a hand down the side of his cheek. Softly she began to sing. A lullaby that she often sang to Sebastian in order to quiet him. Jackson was clearly torn, his glowing gaze fixating upon her, then straying past her where he no doubt still saw and heard the fleeing man in the darkness.

Lucinda continued to sing, to draw his gaze until the light began to fade from his eyes. His teeth retracted by degrees. His body reacted violently—sudden shudders wracking his tall frame as if a battle between man and beast took place inside of him. He went to his knees, and Lucinda went with him. There in the moonlight, she wrapped her arms around him and held him until the shudders subsided.

She didn't realize that she was shaking, too, until he rose, gathered her close to his body heat, and carried her back toward the inn. She wanted to protest entering the place again, but her teeth were suddenly chattering so that she couldn't speak. Two men stumbled out, allowing Jackson to easily slip inside the lower tavern while holding Lucinda in his arms.

A deathly hush fell over the revelers as they saw Jackson and Lucinda standing there. Jackson, like a true lord, simply ignored them, throwing instructions over his shoulder as he climbed a set of stairs leading to the upstairs rooms and, no doubt, expecting his orders to be followed. He walked into an open room, a lamp left burning on a table as scratched and scarred as the one downstairs, a welcome sight. He carried Lucinda to a lumpy bed and gently laid her upon it.

Rising, he removed his fine coat, which did not look nearly as fine as it had earlier. He gently placed the coat over her, and she snuggled into the heat his body had left behind.

The serving wench from earlier appeared with a pitcher and basin, cloths for washing draped over her arm. "Told you there was trouble brewing," she muttered. "The two of you are lucky you're not lying back of the tavern with your throats slit."

"Set the basin here." Jackson indicated the table. "Bring up a glass of warm brandy."

The woman started to huff up, but Jackson interrupted. "Please," he added. "You'll be paid well for the trouble."

The woman nodded and hurried off to do his bidding.

Lucinda watched Jackson pour water into the basin, dip a cloth, and wring it out. He returned to her, gently wiping her face and neck.

"You need that more than I," she managed through her chattering teeth. "Your lip is bloodied."

"It's nothing," he said. "I was so enraged at the thought of one of them touching you, I hardly felt what blows they did manage to inflict upon me."

"I owe you an apology," she said.

He lifted a brow.

"I didn't think . . . that is . . . I didn't place much confidence in you. I was wrong."

"Confidence is hardly an emotion I inspire in most," he said. "I should have never brought you here. We should have made for home as you suggested at the parish church."

The serving woman and a man, from the looks of him perhaps the proprietor of the inn, entered. The woman set a glass of gold liquor on the table, then went to a small hearth and knelt before it, her intent obviously to start a fire.

"I am most distressed to hear that you were set upon by some of my rougher patrons from the tavern," the man said. "Please accept my sincere apologies."

"No real harm done," Jackson clipped. "The lady, my wife, however, has been unnerved by the incident. A good night's rest will see us off in the morning."

Jackson walked to the bed, removed his coin pouch from the pocket of his jacket, and handed the man a good sum. "I trust this is sufficient to see that we are not further disturbed tonight."

The man's eyes lit with obvious pleasure. "I'll put my

best man at the bottom of the stairs to see that no one comes up," he said. "Although," he added, his brow furrowed, "it will be difficult if someone else wishes a room for the night."

Jackson poured more coins out and handed them to the man. "You have no rooms available. That should pay for the whole floor. Also, send someone trustworthy out to my coach and have our luggage brought up and set by the door."

The man inclined his head. "As you wish, my lord."

Both the owner of the inn and the serving woman left the room. Jackson lifted the glass of brandy. He swirled the brandy in the glass and sniffed it. Lucinda quietly waited for him to down the contents. She couldn't blame him for a lapse in discipline considering what they had both been through. He walked to the bed and sat beside her.

"It's not the quality I would have wished, but drink it anyway. It will take the edge off." He extended the glass toward her.

"For me?" She was surprised.

"You didn't think it was for me, did you?" he teased. "I don't drink."

She might have refused, for Lucinda had never touched spirits, but how could she? Besides, she feared if she refused it would give him reason to drink the brandy himself. It wouldn't do to have it sitting around, tempting him. She struggled up on her elbows, pushing back his coat to take the offered glass. She brought the glass to her lips and sipped. The liquor burned a path down her throat and caused her to choke.

"It's good, isn't it?" Jackson continued to tease.

"It's horrible," she managed to gasp.

"But it will warm you up," he assured her. "Drink it all."

Lucinda steeled herself and drank the whole glass

down. She spent several minutes coughing afterward, but he was right; a nice fire now burned in her belly. Jackson took the empty glass, rose, and walked back to the table where the pitcher and basin sat. He eyed the glass for a moment, and she halfway expected him to tip it up for even a drop, but he set it aside. He moved to the door, opened it, and stepped outside, entering a second later with her valise and his.

"Did you bring a nightgown?"

She shook her head. "No. I thought we'd be driving straight back to London after the ceremony."

He moved back to the table with the basin and pitcher, then pulled his shirt over his head. Lucinda gasped, not because of the amount of firm, muscled flesh suddenly on display for her eyes but because he had several scrapes and bruises already forming on his upper torso. She threw his coat aside and rose, going to him.

She took the cloth he'd dipped into the basin from him and wrung it out. "Let me help you."

"You should stay in bed," he argued. "This is nothing. A couple of scrapes and a few bruises."

Lucinda ignored his protest. She went for the blood on his lip first. Dabbing gently, her gaze focused upon his mouth, she was once again intrigued by how perfectly formed his lips were. The flash in her mind of his extended teeth earlier she tried to ignore. He brought the matter up.

"It's happening with more frequency," he said quietly. "What does it mean? Will the beast take over completely soon? Will the man be lost?"

Lucinda had a theory about the matter. "I can only assume your emotions are simply more engaged," she answered. Her gaze lifted to him and the worry reflected in his dark eyes. "The man is still the stronger of the two. You proved that tonight."

"But stronger for how much longer?"

The question was directed more to himself than to Lucinda, so she said nothing. The room suddenly felt too warm as she brushed the damp cloth over his skin. Her head felt light. The liquor, she realized. It wasn't an altogether unpleasant feeling, she admitted. She found her inhibitions slipping from her, and once she forgot to use the cloth to wipe his skin and instead ran her hand down the slopes and contours of his chest.

"Are you trying to seduce me, Lucinda?" he asked softly.

Her gaze darted up to his face. "No," she blurted, perhaps too defensively. "I'm . . . I'm drunk," she suddenly realized, swaying slightly until he steadied her. His warm hands burned into her shoulders, one completely bare, she realized, her attacker having ripped the material clean away.

"Let's get you undressed and into bed," Jackson said.

She stepped away, still swaying a little. "You'd like that, wouldn't you?" she slurred. "Dull my senses with drink and have your way with me while I'm defenseless against you? You're like all men."

Jackson reached out and steadied her again. "I'm not like all men, and you know it," he said. "I have bedded many a drunken woman, Lucinda, but always they made their wishes for intimacy known to me before we—"

"What a thing to say to your wife on her wedding night," she interrupted. "No wonder your lady love would not wed you."

"It is not a wedding night, in truth, Lucinda," Jackson reminded her. "Not unless you would like for it to be."

"You know that I do not." She tried to walk but stumbled. He steadied her again. "You may have seduced many a maid with that silver tongue of yours, but you will not defeat me with it."

He sighed, as if she tried his patience. Suddenly he bent and scoped her up in his arms, carrying her toward the bed. "You have no idea what I can do with my tongue," he said, then deposited her upon the bed.

Chapter Fourteen

His new bride looked particularly alluring with her red curls a mess, her green eyes flashing fire, and the shoulder of her gown missing. How Jackson would like to kiss her into silence . . . into submission, but after his behavior toward her the night of her midnight ritual, he'd promised himself he would exercise control where Lucinda was concerned. He especially meant to stand by that pledge tonight, while the beast still hovered so close to the surface.

Lucinda had said his emotions were more engaged. Were they? And if so, why? She'd made it clear to him that she did not desire him . . . yet at times, when he looked into her eyes, he thought he saw more than a cold bargain between them. He thought he felt more, too. More than just a need to end his family curse. More than just the desire to straighten himself out and become something other than what he had been in the past. Was it Lucinda who made him want to be a better man? Perhaps the spell she admitted to casting over him that first night he arrived home to find her in his bed was working.

Perhaps he'd simply gone without female companionship for too long. His choice, he realized. Again, out of character for him.

"You promised me," she said, but the fire had left her eyes and her lids looked heavy. "You promised you would not take advantage. You said the marriage would be in name only."

"No," he corrected her. "You said all of those things. I merely said I would abide by your wishes, whatever your wishes might be at the time. I never promised that I wouldn't try to change your mind."

"My mind is not my own tonight," she said. "You understand that well enough, don't you?"

He brushed a stray lock from her forehead. "Close your eyes and sleep, Lucinda. You are safe with me. At least for tonight."

She didn't want to trust him. He saw that she fought the effects of fatigue, shock, and the brandy, but in the end she surrendered to sleep. She looked uncomfortable in the torn gown. He imagined she wore a corset, as most women did, and would sleep much sounder without the contraption. Jackson nudged her over gently until she slept on her stomach. He slowly undid the fastenings at the back of her gown.

Her skin called to him. So pale and smooth and soft, every accidental brush of his fingers against her back sent shock waves of desire though him. He tried to blot out the sensations, tried to focus on the task at hand and look at it only as a chore that must be done for her comfort.

That he was highly uncomfortable was not the issue. He could earn her trust. He could be trustworthy if he concentrated hard enough. Her corset was laced up the back, and, experienced in matters of undressing women, Jackson had the laces loosened in a short amount of time. He turned her onto her back again, then set about removing the torn gown.

The silk of her undergarments whispered against his hands. He imagined her skin would feel even smoother than silk and fought not to touch her any more than was necessary. The beast was still too close to the surface to make the battle easy for him.

He was sweating by the time he'd removed the gown and her petticoat. He slid her dainty slippers from her feet and eyed the thin silk of her stockings. His hands nearly shook as he ran them up her slim legs, beneath her knee-length satin drawers, to the places upon her thighs where they fit snugly enough to keep them up. He tried to ignore the feel of her warm, smooth thighs. He failed.

Once the task was done, his nerves raw and scream-ing, he rose and draped her discarded clothing over a chair back. He restocked wood onto the fire and then stood before it for a moment, staring across the room at Lucinda.

Pieces of the night drifted through his mind. The fight, his rage that any man would dare lay a hand on Lucinda. Any man, obviously, but himself. He recalled something that had penetrated his rage then. As the other men had faded into the night and Lucinda had struggled with the leader, she had said, "No. Not ever again!" *Not ever again what?* he wondered.

She stirred, shifting to her side. She drew her knees up closer to her body. His gaze fastened upon her breasts, which nearly spilled from her low-cut chemise. They were perfect to him, filling his hands but not overly large. He recalled the feel of her small rose-colored nipples in his mouth, her hands twisted in his hair.

Jackson moved to the bed and stared down at her. He had two choices. Crawl into bed with her and try to get some sleep before morning . . . or throw on a shirt, go back downstairs, and get rip-roaring drunk.

• • •

Lucinda awoke with her head pounding and the feel of hot, firm flesh pressed against her. She opened her eyes and froze. She was half-sprawled across Jackson. All she saw was his naked chest, her head being lodged beneath his chin. She immediately tried to jerk away. Her head bumped his chin. She heard his teeth click together. He swore.

Scrambling up, she glared down at him. "What did you do to me?"

Rubbing his chin, he said, "You're the one who almost knocked my teeth out."

"I don't mean just now," she huffed. "Last night. What did you do to me?"

Her heart was already hammering. The sight of Jackson Wulf, leaning back against white sheets half-naked, was enough to send it speeding on. Rather than answer, he lowered his gaze to her chest. She glanced down, realizing that she was only half-dressed herself. And half falling out of the front of her chemise. She clutched the material together, wondering where the silk ribbon that kept it tight had gone.

"You undressed me!" she accused.

"You looked uncomfortable," he responded.

"You had no right!"

"I am your husband."

Her speeding heart lurched, then nearly stopped. Did he insinuate that he'd had the right to do more than undress her? And that he'd taken those rights while she lay unconscious from drink? She didn't feel much different than she had when they had married, other than the headache. That was to say she didn't ache in places she had ached when Lord Cantley had defiled her. But did that mean anything?

"Did you . . ." She paused to take a deep breath. "Did you . . ."

"Have my wicked way with you?" He suddenly leaned

up and toward her. "Did I kiss every inch of your soft skin? Did I use my hands on you, my tongue, any- and everything to bring you pleasure?"

She swallowed loudly, their eyes locked, his mouth only inches from hers.

"Did I wedge my way past your defenses and come inside you? Did I fill you, complete you, take you to dizzying heights you have never been before?"

Again, she had to swallow the lump in her throat.

"Did I make you scream my name when release finally found you, and, in turn, call yours when the pleasure became so intense I could no longer resist surrender?"

She couldn't look away from him. It was as if he'd cast another spell upon her. Her face should be flaming, but all she felt was the heat between her legs. "Did you?" she whispered.

He leaned back against the pillows. "No. But I wanted to," he added. "I spent the whole night wanting to."

They sat on the bed, still staring at each other, for an uncomfortably long time. Finally, Lucinda said, "I want to go home. I miss Sebastian."

Jackson glanced away from her and the spell was broken. "Then by all means, let us leave this dreadful inn and return to London."

She started to rise, but he wrapped his hand around her bare arm. The air nearly cracked with static at his touch. "I have stood by my end of the bargain. Now it is time for you to stand by yours. I want this beast who now rules me even when the moon is not full gone. I want it banished from my brothers' lives, as well. If you have deceived me by making promises you cannot keep, you will not hold me to my own. Is that understood?"

Slowly, she nodded. This was the darker side he hid from the rest of the world. This was not a man to be taken lightly. This was not the jokester or the drunkard or the ladies' man. This man was dangerous. This man held the future of her child in his hands.

"I understand," she said.

As the coach passed through the parish village, Lucinda noted that villagers glanced fearfully at the coach and scurried into their cottages, slamming doors against them. She glanced across the coach at Jackson. He had also been gazing outside. He flashed her a smile.

"Welcome to the world of the damned."

"It is not a world that I am unfamiliar with," she assured him. "Who is to say they are hiding from you, or from me?"

"The wolf and the witch. We make a pair, don't we?"

At least Jackson had hope. When she broke the curse for him, he would no longer be a wolf. Lucinda would always be a witch. She had been born into it, with no say in the matter and no way of changing who she was. She realized all too well had Jackson not been cursed, fate would have never led him to her door and he would have never given her a second glance.

Instead, she was now his wife. For the time being, leastwise. Since he'd glanced back outside, she assumed he did not expect an answer from her. The coach slowed, and obviously curious as to why, Jackson leaned his head out the window. Lucinda did the same.

A man stood in the road, waving his hands in the air. By his dress he was a common peasant, but his face was blanched white and his eyes looked like those of a madman.

"Please, I beg your help!" he called.

The coach lumbered to a halt in front of the man. Jackson had swung out of the coach before the footman could get the door.

"What is your problem, man?" Jackson called to him.

"My wife," the man croaked. His wild gaze strayed past Jackson to the coach and to Lucinda, who still had her head hanging out of the window. "Please, whether you be a witch or not, use whatever magic you have to save her. She has labored for two days with the babe, and still it will not come. I fear I am losing them both."

Lucinda was out of the coach in a flash. "Where is she?"

"This way."

The man turned and hurried across the road. Lucinda meant to follow, but when she passed Jackson he reached out and took her arm. "You are my wife now," he reminded her. "Not a common country witch."

His words surprised her. Surprised and angered her. "Oh, I see," she said. "It is all right to be a witch for your cause, but not for anyone else's." She jerked her arm from his grasp. "I may be your wife now, but it doesn't change what I am. No more than being my husband changes what you are." She flounced past him and followed the man.

Jackson fell into step beside her a moment later. He didn't argue further, but she could tell by his tight expression he was not happy with her decision.

The cottage they came upon was small, but then, Lucinda realized it was not smaller than most; it just seemed so because she now lived in a grand house. She stepped inside the darkened cottage and immediately caught the scent of death. She walked to a small room, not comforted to see a frail young woman lying very still in the bed. Had the woman been thrashing about and moaning it would have been a better sign.

"You must save my Miranda," the man choked. "It's not much I've given her since we wed, but she's always had my heart. I cannot live without her."

Lucinda smiled softly at the man. "I'll do what I can," she promised. "Build a fire. It's chilly in here."

It was not so chilly, but Lucinda wanted to give the man something to do, something to keep him occupied while she examined the woman. Lucinda swept into the room and walked to the small bed that the couple shared. She placed a hand against the young woman's forehead. She was cold and clammy. Not a good sign. The young woman opened her eyes.

"Are you the angel come to take me and my babe to heaven?"

"No," Lucinda assured her. "I'm here to help you and your babe stay in this world."

"I wasn't asking you," the woman surprised her by saying. "I was asking him."

Lucinda glanced over her shoulder to see Jackson standing behind her.

"I'm no angel," Jackson said to the woman. "But I am your guardian. Your husband sent me to watch over you."

"Gerard?" she whispered. "Where is he? I would say good-bye to him."

Lucinda touched the woman's swollen stomach. She waited; then, relieved, she felt the child move beneath her hand.

"I'll hear no talk of good-byes." Jackson moved around Lucinda, took the woman's hand, and seated himself on the edge of the straw mattress. "Your man has no place here. He wouldn't be a help to you, although he told me to tell you he loves you."

The woman's pale face brightened. "He's a good man, my Gerard. I had hoped to give him a fine son to help him in the fields."

"And so you will." Jackson's gaze found Lucinda's.

She had lifted the sheet and felt where she needed to feel. Her fingers were gentle, but the child was not even on its way. The woman's passage was very narrow, the bulge of her stomach large. The child could not come into the world. Not in normal fashion. Lucinda tried to relay that sad message to Jackson with her eyes.

He glanced back down at the woman, smiled, and Lucinda saw him squeeze her hand gently. "What name have you chosen for your child?"

"We were thinking Gerard after his father if it is a boy. Of course we must call him Gerry so as not to get the two confused."

"Of course," Jackson agreed. "And what if the child is a girl?"

"Elizabeth," she answered, her voice fading. "After my mother."

"That's a beautiful name," Jackson said. When he glanced again at Lucinda, she motioned him to her.

"You must rest, Miranda," he said softly, tucking her hand at her side. "Rest so you may find your strength again."

The young woman closed her eyes. Jackson rose and joined Lucinda at the bottom of the bed. "Is there nothing you can do for her?" he whispered. "No magic, even?"

"Only the magic of the knife."

His eyes widened. "The knife?"

Lucinda glanced at the sleeping woman, took Jackson's arm, and led him from the room. The woman's young husband stood staring down into the small fire he had built. When he saw them, he hurried forward.

"Can you save them?" he asked Lucinda.

"Perhaps," she answered. "I must cut your wife to remove the babe. The child will not come on its own and then both of them will be lost."

"Cut her?" The man looked horrified. "You are a witch, just as it is rumored. And you." He turned his maddened gaze upon Jackson. "No one even knows what you are."

Jackson stepped forward and grabbed the man by the

throat. "I know what I am. I am not a man who would let my wife and child die because of superstition. If I had to sell my soul to the devil himself, I would do so to save someone I loved."

The man swallowed hard. Jackson released him. "Now, do we go, or do we stay and make this a happy day for you instead of a sad one?"

Rubbing his neck, the man glanced at Lucinda. "Do what you must."

The ice around her heart had chipped when Jackson had made his passionate declaration to the man. She doubted that she could have swayed the farmer without Jackson's help.

"I'll need some things," she roused herself to say to the man. "A large knife. Sharp. Lots of rags. A good strong thread and a large needle. And liquor," she added.

"I have all," the man responded. "As for the liquor, not much in the bottle. I have it hidden away so Miranda doesn't fuss when I take a small nip now and again."

"Just be sure a small nip now and again doesn't turn into a big nip more often than not," Jackson said drily.

"I need to wash my hands," Lucinda said. "Have you a good strong soap?"

The man motioned Lucinda toward a pitcher and bowl on a table in the corner. "Miranda makes a soap that will peel the skin right off your hands."

"Then let's start to work," Lucinda said, moving toward the basin.

Chapter Fifteen

Lucinda's hand shook when she held the blade against the woman's stomach. Due to the raging fire in the next room, the cottage had heated up and Lucinda felt sweat gathering upon her brow. She had everything she needed. Except perhaps the courage to go through with her plans.

"You have done this before, right?"

Pausing to draw a sleeve across her brow, she glanced toward the edge of the bed where Jackson sat next to Miranda. "Once," she assured him. "On a cow."

Jackson looked at the sleeping woman. Lucinda had used half the liquor to cleanse her hands and the knife and had Jackson force the other half down the woman's throat. Lucinda knew he had wanted to take a drink himself, but again he had refrained. His willpower amazed her.

"Did the calf live?"

"Yes," she answered, poising the knife again. "But the cow did not."

Jackson swore softly. "You know if you kill this woman, regardless that she would have died anyway, they will crucify us."

"It is a chance I must take," she said. "If it is not one you are willing to take, best to return to the coach and run at the first sign of trouble."

"I won't run," he said. "And I won't leave you here to face possible crucifixion without me. Whatever happens, we are in this together."

It was odd to hear him say so and to feel as if she wasn't totally alone in the world. Lucinda had been since her mother died. In a small country village, one did not befriend the local witch without becoming the object of persecution right along with her. Lucinda had never had a friend. Not even in childhood.

"Time to hold her," Lucinda said. "She may be resting now, but in a moment, she will come fully awake. Her strength may surprise you, so don't spare yours. You must keep her still."

Although she hadn't wanted to, Lucinda had used rags to tie the woman's legs to the short posts of the bed. Lucinda couldn't have her kicking out and thrashing about in the lower half, either. She'd draped the woman in a way to afford her some dignity since Jackson was present, but he barely would glance past the woman's face anyway. The husband Lucinda had sent on an errand to find an array of wild-growing herbs she would need later. She didn't want the man in the house, listening to his wife's screams.

"I will begin." Lucinda steadied the knife in her hand and pressed it against the woman's skin, below the bulge of the child. Blood immediately welled up.

There was a soft hiss from the woman's lips; then she came alive. Jackson held her shoulders. When Lucinda cut deeper, the woman screamed. Miranda kept screaming, but due to Jackson's strength, he managed to keep her still enough for Lucinda to work. She had to cut deep to reach the womb. She often had to grab cloths and soak up the blood in the process.

The woman thankfully passed out from the pain, but Jackson still held her down lest she recover, all the while speaking soft words to her. The words helped to calm Lucinda, as well. Just the sound of his deep voice. Soothing, almost hypnotic.

Finally, she had cut deep enough and wide enough to slide her hands inside the woman and find the babe. Pulling as gently as she could, she managed to bring the child out. She didn't like the babe's bluish tinge. Her hands were slippery with blood and she needed Jackson. The woman was still passed out, or at least Lucinda hoped that was the reason she wasn't screaming or fighting.

"I need you to see to the babe," Lucinda said to Jackson. She quickly tied and cut the cord; grabbing up a large rag, she handed both babe and rag to Jackson.

"Hold the child up by the feet, like you did with Sebastian," she instructed. "Then take the cloth and rub the babe. Do not be gentle."

"It's so still," he said softly. "Is it dead?"

"Not dead," she answered. "Just not yet among the living. I must quickly sew the woman closed while she's unconscious . . . she is only unconscious?"

Jackson bent close to the woman's face. "Yes. She is still breathing, but shallow."

"We must do the best we can, Jackson," Lucinda said. "Sometimes God, or the fates, or whoever decides such matters takes a soul regardless of those who fight to keep it in this world. I had to learn that at an early age."

The babe suddenly made a small squeaking noise. Lucinda glanced up from her stitching. Jackson smiled at her. He continued to rub the babe until the small squeaks turned to screams of outrage. Lucinda smiled back at him.

Upon hearing the screams, Miranda stirred. "Is that my babe?" she whispered weakly. "Is he alive?"

Jackson wrapped the child in a clean rag. "The babe is

pink and beautiful, and he is a she." Jackson held the child close so Miranda could see her daughter. "Elizabeth is so beautiful you will have to guard her carefully," he said. "From foul men like me who will one day think to steal her from you."

Only love could blight the pain the young woman must be feeling, because despite her being sliced open and carefully stitched back together, her face filled with color and she smiled brightly down at the child.

"Miranda?"

The young husband suddenly stood in the bedroom doorway. He held a sack of herbs, which fell from his hand to the floor.

"Gerard," she whispered, turning a blinding smile upon her husband. "Come see your daughter."

The man went to his knees. He covered his face in his hands and wept. Jackson nestled the babe in her mother's arms, then went to help Gerard rise.

"Be strong," Jackson said. "You've a daughter to raise, and she'll look to you for strength and guidance." Suddenly he looked very far away and very sad. "Be there for her always."

Gerard nodded, wiped his eyes, and rushed to his wife's side. "My God, Miranda," the man choked. "Just look at her. She's a beauty to be sure."

Lucinda finished cleaning up the young woman while she and her husband cooed and clucked over the babe. She glanced toward Jackson, who stood leaning against the door frame, watching the family. She thought he still looked sad, and a bit melancholy.

"Gerard," Lucinda said. "You must set a kettle over the fire so I can show you how to prepare strengthening draughts for your wife. And she must stay in this bed and rest. No working around the cottage or toting heavy buckets of water and such, not until she is healed."

"I can fetch her mum to come help out," he said. "She lives not a day's walk from here."

"Good." Lucinda piled the bloody rags in a bucket. "Burn these." She nodded toward the bucket. "In a few days' time, only when you feel the wound has closed, carefully remove my stitches. Now, start the kettle. Did you find the herbs I asked for?"

The husband nodded. "Aye, took some time, but I found them."

"I will show you how to squeeze one of the plants and mix a salve for Miranda to coat the wound with. It will help it heal, though from this day on she will bear the scar."

The young man kissed his wife and new daughter on the head and rose to do Lucinda's bidding. He paused before Jackson.

"Whatever you are, devil or saint, from this day on, I will call you friend. And the fine lady, as well."

Jackson slapped a hand on the man's shoulder. "It has just occurred to me that I have no friends. I accept your friendship and give mine in turn."

Lucinda's eyes grew annoyingly moist over the exchange. "Jackson, go and help him. Lay out the herbs for me so I can get them boiling and we can go on our way. I want to go home."

She missed Sebastian to the point of madness, especially after seeing the woman holding her own babe close to her, staring in wonder at what she had created.

Jackson ushered the young husband from the room with him. Finished with her work below, Lucinda moved up and sat on the edge of the bed for her first good look at the babe. Jackson was right. She looked like a little princess, regardless of her shabby surroundings.

"I thank you, milady, for what you have done for me this day," Miranda said softly. She took Lucinda's hand

and squeezed. "I will tell Elizabeth stories one day about the fine lady and gentleman who helped her into the world."

To cover her emotions, Lucinda turned to business. "It will hurt to rise, but tomorrow you must. Do not overtax your strength, but the sooner you move around, the sooner you can abide the pain of doing so. Allow your husband and your mother to bring the child to you for a while. Nurse her, love her, but allow everyone else to care for her until you get your strength back. You have lost a lot of blood."

"I was going to die, wasn't I? Me and Elizabeth?"

Lucinda saw no point in answering. She reached out and ran a hand over the babe's blond head. "Jackson is right. You'll have to guard this one."

Miranda glanced up at her. "I thought he was an angel, your Jackson." She glanced toward the door as if to make certain they would not be overheard. "I didn't mind so much, the dying, if he was here to take me with him," she confided.

"Not all angels are handsome," Lucinda said drily. "Devils can be handsome, too. Rest. I must go and instruct your husband on all that needs to be done for you."

The young woman took Lucinda's hand and squeezed again. "Like my husband, I will call you friend. You are always welcome here in my humble home."

Lucinda allowed herself to soften. Never had she been offered so fine a gift for her services. She squeezed the young woman's hand in return. Lucinda rose to see to the business of preparing the strengthening draught and instructing Gerard about which herbs should be used for what.

She felt emotionally drained, and a little surprised by Jackson. She'd just seen a side to him he had kept hidden from her. She'd just seen a glimpse of his heart, and for the first time she wondered if it truly wasn't worth winning.

Jackson tried to nudge Lucinda awake. He had held her the entire way home while she slept, although she would have no doubt fought the arrangement had she not been exhausted. He saw her now in a new light. He saw the world in a new light. Watching the young couple, so much in love, blessed with a daughter, he realized for the first time how much he resented his awkward life. He would give all he had, the Wulf wealth, just to be a common farmer with a wife who loved him and sons who were not cursed.

And Lucinda might indeed be a witch, from a common background, but she had the gift of healing in her and today Jackson had been shown what a gift it was. She had saved two lives. She'd performed a miracle. And she'd done it with a strength and dignity he doubted most men could muster. He gently nudged her again.

"Wake up, Lucinda. We are home."

She snuggled closer to him. He wasn't vain enough to believe she wanted to be near him. She wanted his heat. Just as she wanted a future for her child. Lucinda was a woman who knew what she wanted and how best to get it. Soft feelings, he imagined, did not figure into her equations. And yet he knew she had them. She'd shown them to him on a few occasions. Today was one of them.

"Sebastian will think you have abandoned him. Wake up so you can assure him you have not."

She stirred at the mention of her son. She also tensed the moment she roused herself enough to realize she was pressed against Jackson. She quickly scrambled back.

"I must have fallen asleep," she murmured. Raking a hand through her long hair, she glanced toward the open door of the coach and the footman who stood outside waiting. Her ability to remain unaffected by Jackson wore upon his ego. Instead of alighting first and helping her out, he made her squeeze past him, smiling at her when she was forced to brush up against him. Her plump, ripe lips thinned and she narrowed her gaze upon him. He continued to smile at her until she made the door and the footman helped her out.

Jackson followed lazily behind her, watching the sway of her hips. It was some ridiculous hour of night, but Hawkins, ever at his post, had the door open for them before they reached it.

"I have supper trays up in your rooms and both of you a nice hot bath," he announced.

Jackson wondered how the man had managed to keep the baths hot, but the thought of relaxing his cramped muscles in a steaming bath appealed to him. He followed Lucinda up the stairs, surprised she didn't take them two at a time to see Sebastian. She wanted to, Jackson could tell. He found himself a little anxious to see the babe as well.

She'd already reached the nursery and gone inside by the time Jackson made the first landing. He paused at the open doorway and leaned against the door frame. Her back was to him as she stared down into the cradle, but as he watched her every muscle in her body seemed to relax. He half-expected to see her melt until she was nothing more than a puddle on the floor. How was she ever going to leave her child behind?

As if Lucinda sensed him staring at her, she turned. She did not motion him inside, and he realized she took his presence as an intrusion. He shrugged away from the frame and moved to his room.

Just as Hawkins promised, a tray had been left of cold ham, bread, and cheese. No wine, Jackson noted. A bath sat steaming in the middle of the room, and he stripped down and climbed in, sighing with contentment as the warmth of the hot water seeped into his stiff muscles.

While he soaked, a thought occurred to him concerning Lucinda and Sebastian. If she stood by her bargain and broke the family curse for Jackson and his brothers, he could still provide for both her and Sebastian. He could find them a nice place of their own, see that Sebastian had proper schooling and everything that wealth could buy him but that his bloodline could not.

Who was Sebastian's father? Lucinda said a man who wanted pleasure from her and nothing more. Bastard. He had touched her. He had made love to her. He had received all she would deny Jackson. Her own husband. As he took a brave step forward with his thoughts, it occurred to him that if Lucinda broke the curse, he need not make her an offer of money and a place to live so that she could stay with her son . . . he could offer her the continuance of the arrangement they had now. She could remain his wife, raise her child.

But then Jackson thought of the couple in the small cottage earlier. The love between them. Could he be content with Lucinda's coldness when another woman might give him her warmth, her heart, children of his own seed? He was shocked that he entertained such thoughts at all. Once he did not care to be tied to a woman or children, but then he'd had little choice in the matter.

If Lucinda broke the curse for his family, perhaps things would change for them. They might once again be accepted into society, have normal society lives. Armond's wife, Rosalind, was of noble blood. She would fit in with society. But Lucinda? She was not common; in fact, she was perhaps too uncommon. Jackson could not see her moving easily among a society with so many rules, nor, if he were honest, could he see himself doing so. Not now. Maybe at one time, before he knew of the curse and the heartache it brought to his family.

The water had grown cooler than he liked, and Jackson climbed out, toweled himself dry, and slipped into a pair of clean trousers. He moved to the tray left for him, thinking he would rather he and Lucinda shared the meal. He had a wife now, a child to care for, and yet he still felt as alone as he always did in this house.

Jackson left the food untouched, walking instead to the door and out into the hallway. Quietly he slipped into the nursery next door. The wet nurse snored softly in her bed. He walked to the cradle and looked down. In the soft glow from the night fire Sebastian looked pink and content. The babe opened his eyes and stared up at Jackson before grinning his toothless grin. Jackson reached down and gently lifted Sebastian into his arms.

"You can't sleep, either?" he asked softly. He ran a hand over the babe's soft, fine hair, holding him close. Sebastian smelled of his mother. The subtle honeysuckle scent of her soaps. Jackson closed his eyes and inhaled deeply. Odd, that that scent alone could bring something very close to longing swimming to the surface of his emotions.

"You'd best go to sleep, little man." He kissed Sebastian on the head, laid him back into the cradle, and gathered his covers over him. "You're a Wulf now. Try to bring more honor to the name than I have."

He turned to see Lucinda standing at the open doorway. She wore her silk finery, her long hair still damp from her bath. The subtle scent of honeysuckle teased him, and he wondered how long she had been standing there, watching him. The firelight brought a soft glow to her eyes. He thought for a moment, before she turned and quickly sought the safety of her own room, that he had seen longing in her gaze, too. A longing that matched his own.

Was she lonely, as he was lonely? Had she gazed at the young couple in the village, joyful over the life of their child, and felt as if something hollow and cold rested inside of her?

Why did she deny him even the pleasure they might find for a short time in each other's arms? She said she would never surrender to him. Never give herself willingly. What did she have left to protect? Her heart? Perhaps she had lied to him about Sebastian's father. Perhaps she had loved him and he had broken her heart.

Jackson left the nursery and went back to his lonely room. He returned to his tray, lifting a thin slab of cheese to his mouth; then he hesitated. Something had just occurred to him.

Lucinda had said seeking out his worst enemy and defeating them in the traditional sense might not be the key to breaking the curse. If not through battle, if not through killing, how else might he defeat her? With her heart? With her surrender to him? The thought intrigued him.

Seduction Jackson could do, and do well. So far, he'd only been toying with her. He would not use force in any way; he'd made himself that promise after the night he nearly lost all control with her during her midnight ritual. But he'd never had to use force before with a woman. He'd never had to do much of anything but come within sniffing distance of one to get her attention . . . and usually anything else he wanted. Lucinda would be a challenge. She wasn't like other women. She wasn't like anyone he knew.

And he need not feel guilt about his intentions. Lucinda was no proper virgin miss. He wouldn't be taking anything she hadn't willingly given before. She wouldn't be harmed . . . no, he would make certain that her surrender resulted only in her pleasure. He could never kill her.

He knew that now. Not even if it truly meant breaking the curse for his family.

But surrender, seduction in truth, would not harm her. And if it truly broke the curse for him, and for his brothers, it would still be in a way by her doing. Her giving. Her surrender. Jackson considered the matter further as he nibbled on the food Hawkins had left for him. Something very akin to guilt, to conscience, plagued him. It had never plagued him before where women were concerned.

They gave. He took. But Lucinda wasn't like those women. All she wanted from him was the cold bargain they had first made. But she had not fulfilled her end, and he was beginning to wonder if she could. Perhaps it was time he took matters into his own hands. Having made his decision, he attacked the tray of food with more gusto. He would need his strength.

Chapter Sixteen

Two days later, the rest of Lucinda's clothing arrived. It was overwhelming to have so much when once she had owned so little. The duchess had also spent the past two days trying to school Lucinda in matters she had no interest in. Lucinda saw no point in learning all that the woman seemed determined to teach her, and teach her quickly.

"Please, Your Grace, if I see one more fork today I will scream."

The duchess sighed and steered her from the dining room table into the parlor. "I want you to be ready, Lucinda."

"Ready for what?" Lucinda tried to curb her snappish tone. "What is the point of all of this? It's not as if I will be invited—"

"Oh, but you have been," the duchess interrupted. The woman smiled smugly at her.

Lucinda's stomach dropped. "What?"

"'Beg your pardon' is the correct form to use," the duchess corrected her. "And yes, an acquaintance of mine, a countess, no less, is hosting a ball in two weeks' time. I happened to mention that I hate attending such affairs alone and that I wished to bring a young man and his new wife along with me. Of course she couldn't refuse. It would be rude."

"I cannot go," Lucinda whispered. "I am not ready. I will never be ready." She walked to where the woman had seated herself. "Did you happen to mention who it was you planned to bring with you to this woman's affair?"

The lady frowned. "Well, no, but then she didn't ask, either. A person really should ask," she continued. "And of course you can go. In fact, you must, the way I see it. For Jackson if not for yourself. He needs to rub elbows with his peers now and again. You do plan to give the Wulf brothers normal lives, don't you?"

Lucinda had been thinking on that, and thinking rather frantically. She'd thought of something that might work . . . although Jackson wasn't going to like it. Not at all.

"Yes," she answered. "That is the bargain. It is also the bargain that I will leave Jackson once I've broken the curse. I would think the less we were seen together the better for him . . . for later."

"Sit down, Lucinda dear," the dowager instructed. "You wear me out with all your pacing back and forth. I wish I had your youth."

Lucinda took a seat across from her. The tea service sat ready and waiting, and Lucinda took it upon herself to pour.

"Now, as I was saying, Lucinda, you must attend. If you become all that Jackson desires in a wife, if you manage to win over the ton, with my help of course, then why on earth will you ever have to leave?"

The thought of leaving tore Lucinda up inside. Not the thought of leaving Jackson but the thought of leaving Sebastian. At least seeing them together that night in the nursery, seeing how gentle Jackson was with her son, how he spoke softly to Sebastian, held him close, even kissed him on the head, had warmed her heart.

For the first time, she realized if she did break Jackson's curse, Sebastian would do well having him as his father. She'd almost been tempted to join them beside the cradle. To wrap her arms around both of them, but she had refrained . . . as she always refrained from showing too much emotion.

"I don't want to leave," she admitted. "It tears me apart to think of living my life without my child. Not knowing what he is doing. Not seeing how he has grown. Worrying that he is wondering about me, and where I've gone, and why I've left him." Tears gathered in her eyes and she had to blink them back. "But a bargain is a bargain."

"The way I see it, bargains are meant to be broken," the duchess countered. "Besides, bargains have no place in matters of the heart. Do you believe that Jackson has any feelings for you at all?"

Jackson had feelings for her all right, just not any that had to do with the heart. He was up to something. Since they had returned from their wedding, he'd been nothing but charming to her. Often she caught him staring at her. On those occasions, when their eyes met, she felt suddenly scattered. As if she couldn't think or speak or do anything except stare helplessly back at him.

"Not the proper feelings I suppose a husband should have for a wife," she finally got around to answering. "How is your hair doing?" she decided to change the subject.

The duchess fiddled with her teacup and kept her gaze averted. "Well, to be honest, I can't abide the smell of the potion you gave me to put on it. It stinks so that it makes my eyes burn and my nose run. I have decided I would rather be bald than subject myself to it again."

Lucinda hid her smile behind her teacup. Of course, the potion would not work; nothing worked for baldness, no matter how many times men, and women, too, asked her if such a potion existed. She'd decided at one point to make something so foul smelling those who asked for the potion would resign themselves to being bald rather than subject themselves to the unpleasantness of using the potion.

"Well, that decision is yours to make," she said.

"I don't think it's so noticeable anyway," the woman fussed. She turned to Lucinda. "Now, about the affair, you will come, won't you? And I want you to come here beforehand so that I can help you prepare. You'll need my maid to dress your hair. You really should have one of your own."

Ladies' maid was a position Lucinda could see herself in more than lady of the manor. She saw no need for such things. She'd never had them in the past. Why accustom herself to luxuries that she would soon be forced to give up?

"I suppose if Jackson isn't against going, we will attend," Lucinda gave in. "But I fear befriending outcasts so publicly will make you an outcast yourself, Your Grace."

The woman reached over and patted her hand. "I'm too old to be an outcast, dear girl. You have made me very happy. I do so love to champion the lesser horse."

Lucinda simply lifted a brow, then took a drink of her tea. The lady was just as rude most of the time as she accused Jackson of being. Perhaps that was why they got on well together. But Lucinda couldn't get angry with the duchess. She found that she adored the older woman. Lucinda counted her as a friend, and friends were never something Lucinda had had in the past.

"I must see you every day up until the event, Lucinda," the duchess said. "We have too little time to prepare as it is for you to attend your first social function as Lady Lucinda Wulf."

The name startled Lucinda. From simply Lucinda all her life to Lady Lucinda Wulf? How had she become trapped suddenly in this world so foreign to her? By her own doing, she admitted. She should have taken Sebastian and run the first night Jackson returned to the town house, very much alive, and very naked, as she recalled. But where would she be now if she had? She shuddered to think. She shuddered just as much to think about being presented to a society that had never been anything but distrustful and cruel to her.

Suddenly needing to see Sebastian desperately, Lucinda finished her tea and bid the duchess good day. Once Lucinda reached the town house, she took Sebastian into her room for his playtime. Glancing out the window, she saw Jackson below, out toward the stables. He was in an enclosure working a horse on a long rope. Jackson looked at peace with himself. He'd obviously used the soap she'd given to him. The horse seemed accepting of him and his scent or, rather, his lack of scent.

She had trouble looking away from him. He was a startlingly handsome man, even from a distance. Lucinda forced herself to leave the window. She laid Sebastian upon the bed and stretched out beside him, staring down at his perfect features. She supposed his father was a handsome man, although she had never noticed. He was of a station far above her, and a married man at that. Yet here she was now, a titled young woman. She glanced around at her rich surroundings, at the wardrobe that stood open, ripe with fancy gowns and sensible day gowns.

Sometimes her circumstances overwhelmed her. *Ofttimes,* she mentally corrected. When she pictured herself back in the life she had always known, an empty feeling came over her. She would be alone. Not even her son to brighten her dreary days. He cooed up at her and she smiled.

"What will I do without you?" she whispered down at him. She kissed his soft cheek, snuggled him to her, and lay back to look at the ceiling. "A bargain is a bargain," she said, maybe to remind herself. She had thought more and more upon Jackson's curse and what else she might do to try to break it.

Something barbaric had come to mind. She wasn't certain that she could perform such an exorcism. Still, it had been used throughout the ages to drive demons from a human host. She would speak to Jackson about it over dinner.

Glancing down at Sebastian, Lucinda saw that he had fallen asleep snuggled against her. She closed her eyes and tried to rest, tried to mentally prepare herself if Jackson did agree to have the beast purged from him. She would need perhaps more strength to do it than she possessed.

Lucinda entered the dining room for dinner that evening and drew up short. Only one candelabra with two candles alight flickered upon the long table. Usually the lamps were lit and Hawkins and a servant from the kitchen stirred about. The room was empty. But no, there in the shadows, she made out the shape of a man. He stepped forward and the candlelight danced in his hair. He held a glass of wine. Lucinda wondered if she stopped the frown from forming on her face before it took shape.

Jackson stepped forward and extended the glass to her. She took it automatically. He pulled out a chair for her to be seated. Some inner voice whispered for her not to take the seat. It told her to run . . . while she still could.

She sat. "Where . . . where is Hawkins?" she managed. Jackson looked good enough to eat. He wore black, a tight-fitting waistcoat and equally tight-fitting trousers, black boots, and a white shirt open at the neck.

"I will be serving you tonight," he informed her. "I thought Hawkins could use a night to himself. I dismissed him earlier."

Lucinda didn't like the sound of that.

"You look uncomfortable." He pulled a chair very close to hers and seated himself. "Do I make you uncomfortable, Lucinda?"

"No." She did not fear him. But she did fear his ability to make her lose her head. Since they'd first struck their bargain, Lucinda felt as if he'd merely been toying with her. Like a cat played with a mouse before gobbling it up. She had a feeling he was tired of playing. "What has Cook prepared for us?" she asked, hoping to sound casual.

He leaned closer. "We will have dessert first."

She turned her head toward him in surprise, only to find his mouth nearly touching hers. "Dessert?"

He reached forward and brought a bowl of ripe strawberries toward them, then a small bowl of cream. He took a plump berry, dipped it in the cream, and held it to her lips. Staring into his eyes, she simply opened her mouth and allowed him to dip the end of the fruit into it. Rather than bite, she instinctively sucked the cream off the tip. The blue glow in his eyes suddenly flared.

Jackson took the same piece of fruit, also dipped it in the cream, but this time brought it to his own lips. His tongue flirted with the creamy tip for a moment before he stuck it into his mouth and, like she had done, sucked the cream off. Her nipples immediately tightened.

"Have you ever noticed how fruit resembles men and women?" he asked softly.

Lucinda could only shake her head no.

He held the strawberry up. "The shape," he answered.

"Symbolic of both male and female." Dipping the tip of the fruit again, he continued, "See how it resembles a woman's nipple?"

She saw that it did and when he sucked the cream from the tip a second time felt as if he were doing the same thing to her. Squirming in her seat, Lucinda refused to answer. Her lack of response didn't deter him. Jackson chose a larger berry, round and plump, dipped it, and brought it to her lips again. Her mouth automatically opened and again she took the tip of the fruit to steal the delicious cream.

"For a man," he said, "it is the shape of the head of his cock."

She bit down, she supposed due to the shock of him saying something so vulgar to her. Jackson flinched slightly, but when she felt the sweet juice fill her mouth he leaned closer, took the fruit away, and placed his lips to hers. She didn't have time to swallow before he parted her lips and shared the fruit with her. It was the most sensual thing she had ever experienced.

He lingered at her lips, sucking, nibbling, and teasing until she grew breathless. "Jackson," she tried to warn him, but he hushed her by taking full possession of her mouth. He had kissed her before, but this kiss was different. Commanding, demanding, a man no longer content to play at seduction. Lucinda with her limited experience with men was no match.

She felt as if the bottom had suddenly fallen away from her feet and she was falling down a deep dark well of sin. But she did not mind the drop. He pulled her to her feet and stood with her, never surrendering her lips. The dining table pressed against the backs of her legs and forced her to sit. Her gown was full enough at the skirt to allow Jackson to wedge himself between her legs. She knew the position was highly provocative and highly improper.

How odd that she could fathom anything but the feel of his mouth moving over hers, his hands at her throat, unbuttoning the high-necked gown she wore. He did not hurry, unbuttoning one button, his fingers brushing against the skin he uncovered before moving to the next. Her breasts swelled, her nipples growing painfully hard with anticipation. Innocent as she was, she knew what he planned before he did it.

He broke the contact of their mouths when he had unbuttoned her gown to the waist. He stared into her eyes, mesmerizing her before his gaze slowly moved down to her breasts. A gentle tug at the ribbon loosened the shift; then his fingers slowly slid the fabric down past her aching breasts. He knelt between her legs, took one finger, dipped it in the bowl of cream, and laved it upon her pebbled nipple.

Lucinda held her breath until his tongue circled her nipple, swirling the cream before he took her into his mouth to suck. Only then did her breath leave her in a relieved sigh. Her fingers twisted in his silky hair and she pulled him closer against her. She couldn't think past sensation, and Jackson's reputation, she supposed, was well deserved. He teased one nipple, then the other, until she squirmed against him, breathing ragged, the throbbing between her legs so intense she had no idea how to quiet the need that roared inside of her.

Somewhere the voice of reason tried to call to her, but his scent smothered it. He put it off now, like sweet venom meant to paralyze his prey. And she did feel somehow outside of herself. And yet more alive than she'd ever felt before. His hands were suddenly upon her legs, pushing her gown up, sliding along the silk that caressed her thighs, winding like a serpent to the tapes at her waist. She should say something, protest, but voice and inclination to struggle were suppressed by his power over her. His scent filled her, excited her, made her a prisoner of her desire, and of his.

His hand slid into the top of her drawers. She gasped at the contact of his fingers against her skin. His mouth inched up her neck and he rose to stand, capturing her mouth again. Slowly, his hand inched farther down. The hot thrust of his tongue in her mouth made it difficult not only to protest his forwardness but also to really want to. She knew she was losing control, and Lucinda feared that above all else.

Once, her control had been taken from her. Her mind had haunted her with that. Had perhaps provided worse horrors than Lord Cantley might have actually done to her. It was the thought of being helpless, the thought of being unable to command her mind and her actions, that nearly undid Jackson's spell. Nearly, until he touched her . . . there.

His touch was soft, gentle, unlike how she had imagined Lord Cantley had handled her. But then, everything about Jackson Wulf was soft, his skin, his hair, his eyes. He pressed against her and she had to withdraw the thought. Not everything.

"No," she managed to whisper against his lips. "I'm not ready."

He kissed her softly, but he did not remove his hand and step away from her. "I'm not going to make love to you with my body," he said. "I only want to give you pleasure."

And so saying, he found the hidden bud within her and stroked her into awareness. Her nails dug into his shoulders. She opened her mouth wider to him and he ravaged her, if below he was nothing but tender . . . and persistent. She opened to him wider there as well, spreading her legs, pressing against his fingers to increase the pressure.

He seemed to know her thoughts, her desires, what she needed, even if she did not.

The pressure inside of her rose. Hunger clawed at her, made her tremble and twitch, building, always building. Jackson trailed a path of kisses to her ear. While his fingers pleasured her, his other hand cupped her breast, his thumb brushing sensuously over her nipple.

"You must let go, Lucinda," he whispered. "Surrender yourself."

His husky words alone nearly pushed her over the edge of insanity, but she fought against the tide of pleasure rising inside of her. She felt as if she was losing total control. Panic penetrated pleasure. "No!" The cry left her lips and she shoved at him. "Don't!"

He pulled back to look at her. His expression was startled, as if he thought he might have hurt her without realizing it. Lucinda clawed at his hand shoved down into her drawers. She pushed him with all her strength and he stumbled back a step. With a sob, she shoved her gown back over her legs and tugged the gaping edges of her bodice together

"Did I hurt you?" he asked.

Emotion clogged her throat. Tears welled in her eyes. "I cannot," was all that managed to come out.

His brow furrowed. "You cannot what, Lucinda? Take pleasure from my touch? I think you can," he argued. "I think you were. I think you were only a stroke away from—"

"I cannot lose control!"

He took a step toward her. "That's what it is, Lucinda. That's what two people do when they share their bodies with one another. They trade control for emotion. They feel instead of think. They trust, if only for that moment in time; they trust totally in one another. You know that, don't you?"

She knew nothing about lovemaking, nothing except what he'd taught her or, rather, tried to teach her. If she told him the truth, if he knew that by being in danger herself she had perhaps put him in danger as well, he might turn her out tonight. She couldn't leave Sebastian. Not yet. If she didn't break Jackson's curse, she couldn't leave Sebastian at all, she realized. Not with a man she didn't know for certain she could trust.

"Our arrangement did not include you pleasuring me," she reminded him. "Or me pleasuring you."

"So far, it hasn't included you holding to your part of the bargain, either," he said, and his voice was tight now. Angry. He walked to the table, pounded a fist on it, and made her jump. "Dammit, Lucinda. I cannot kill you. I cannot . . . seduce you. I'm becoming frustrated with my own options of possibly breaking the curse, and you are doing nothing to aid me!"

Her heart plummeted. But not before she felt him pierce it. "Is that what this has been about? What it has been about from the beginning? My surrender?"

He wheeled away from her, presenting his back. "The riddle. You said I must find another way to defeat my enemy. I'm looking for it is all."

Bile rose in her throat. He had never found her beautiful. Desirable. All along, it had always been about him and his all-consuming quest to break the family curse. He'd used her. Used his looks and his sensual allure against her. She felt like such a fool. Her heart had begun to soften toward him. That was a mistake.

"I hate you," she said, then stormed from the room.

Jackson knew he should go after her. He'd been angry when he'd said those words to her. Frustrated. *I hate you.* Never had a woman said that to him. Well, he deserved it. He'd turned seduction into something cold and calculating when it had never been that for him before. The truth was, he was not the great lover, after all. He'd never had to put forth much effort. For one thing, he chose the kind of women who'd pleasure him one hour and another man the next. What his coin couldn't buy him his scent could get him easily enough.

He moved to a chair and sat. He'd not done so well with Lady Anne Baldwin, either. He thought because she had spent time with him, laughed at his clever jokes, and seemed genuinely pleased to see him at whatever social functions he chased after her at she had fallen under his spell. He had fallen under hers. She was so gentle and beautiful and well mannered. Nothing like the whores he spent too much time with. He had almost gotten up the nerve to declare himself to her when she told him quite lovingly one eve that she thought of him as the brother she had never had. It had broken his heart, but he'd never told her.

Now he'd done damage with words much more hateful. Not that Lucinda had given her heart to him, but she deserved more than what he'd done and said to her tonight. And while he was being honest with himself, Lucinda was not just a means to an end. She might have been in the beginning, but he saw her much differently now than he had then. And he desired her. He was still hard with wanting her. She was his wife, for however much longer, and he'd treated her worse than the whores whose beds he once had frequented too often. For the drug they gave him. Belonging.

Lucinda was like him even though they were worlds apart. Maybe for once, she had wanted to belong, too. In this house, in a society that would once not give her a second glance. He ran a hand through his hair. Should he go to her? Apologize? Could he even do so without wanting to kiss her again? Wanting to touch her? Make sweet gentle love to her? No, not tonight, he decided. He still had the taste and scent of her on him, and no matter how hard he tried not to want her, he did. Instead, the great lover would go to bed. Alone. Again.

Chapter Seventeen

Lucinda wanted to hide in her room during breakfast, but she would not allow herself. It was a coward's way, and she'd never been a coward. She was humiliated and embarrassed that she'd allowed Jackson to get so far into his game of seduction last night. If she could cast a curse on him, she surely would. One that would shrivel that impressive member he seemed so fond of sharing with any and all into a little nub that wouldn't scratch a flea's back. But of course she could not. She'd settle for other forms of punishment.

Jackson stood when she entered the dining room. She fought down a blush when her gaze landed upon the table. He pulled a chair out for her. She gave him a dirty look but sat. Hawkins bustled about lifting warming covers and dishing out food on their plates. Neither Lucinda nor Jackson spoke a word to the other until after Hawkins had finished and bustled out again.

"About last night," Jackson immediately began. "I—"

"What about it?" Lucinda cut him off.

"I wanted to apologize," he continued.

"I hardly recall last night," she went on. "I'd rather not talk of it."

"But I feel moved to," he insisted.

"I know perfectly well what part moves you the most," she said drily. "I said I would rather not discuss it. We can discuss your displeasure with me over our bargain. I have remembered something. I thought you might be opposed, but since it seems nothing is too distasteful if it means freeing yourself from the curse, I've decided we should probably give it a try. It will involve a whip and a great deal of pain. Are you up for that?"

He stared into her eyes, his expression void of amusement. "Are you serious, or simply out for blood?"

"Both," she answered honestly. "It's been done for centuries. You whip the demon from the afflicted one's body. You drive it out with pain."

His gaze never wavered. "And if it doesn't work, at least one of us will feel better afterward."

She smiled. "Exactly."

Lifting a hand to his high collar, Jackson tugged. She tried not to look at his hands. He was much too good with them. "Maybe as a last resort," he agreed.

Lucinda pouted her lips. "I thought we might give it a go after breakfast. It's a jolly good day for blood sport."

Jackson cocked his head to one side. "Where did you learn to talk like that? You sound like a proper snob."

"The duchess," she informed him. And then she remembered she was supposed to talk to Jackson about the party. She planned to tell him she had no intention of going, to please refuse the invitation so her grace would leave her alone. Now, Lucinda reconsidered. Jackson had humiliated her last night. Perhaps she could humiliate him in turn. Maybe she would black out her teeth and carry a cauldron of boiled toad heads around with her on one arm.

"She wants us to attend a party with her this coming weekend," Lucinda said. "I promised her I'd ask you."

"A social function?" He laughed. "The two of us?"

Lucinda narrowed her gaze on him. "I'd like to attend."

He sobered. "In truth? Or are you only trying to punish me more?"

"Both," she answered honestly again.

Sighing, he sat back from the table. "I'll only agree to attend if you'll agree to hear my apology."

She realized the wounds he'd inflicted last night were still too raw to discuss the matter. "After the engagement you may apologize to me," she decided. "Until that time, I wish for you not to speak to me."

"But—"

"Beginning now," she added, and lifted her fork, the correct one, and went about eating her breakfast.

She obviously was not a woman to cross. But then, Jackson already knew that about her. She looked lovely, her lips still kiss swollen from last night, her cheeks flushed with anger. He wanted to kiss her again. Badly.

Instead, he picked up his fork and started in on his breakfast. He probably needed longer to decide what to say to her regarding his decision to use seduction as a means of defeating her. He wasn't sorry what happened between them last night had happened, but he was sorry for hurting her the way he had. Maybe the beast was becoming the more dominant. Maybe it had always been, because he had allowed it to be.

And maybe, just maybe, he really was a self-absorbed, whoremongering bastard like everyone thought he was. No longer a drunkard at least. But no longer content with the life he'd made for himself, either.

"Lucinda," he began.

She held up her fork. "Not a word or I will fork you.

Not to be confused with a term I believe you were going to use in regard to what you planned to do to me last night, before you decided upon the gentler-sounding word 'seduce.' "

Jackson closed his mouth.

Lucinda's knees shook beneath her gown. She wished she had not pushed Jackson about attending a ball with the duchess. Lucinda wished she were back at the town house with Sebastian, singing to him and playing with him. Her stomach was tied in knots.

"Almost finished, my lady." Her grace's abigail dressed Lucinda's hair. She sat very still while the woman took hot irons to her hair and arranged soft baby's breath into the curls. Her gown had been laid out on the bed to be slipped on once her hair had been dressed.

The dowager had sent her coach earlier to collect Lucinda, the arrangement being Jackson was to arrive early in the evening to escort them to the ball. All of Lucinda's rigorous training seemed to have vanished from her head. Any time she tried to recall proper forms of address, when to curtsy and when to nod, what was proper to discuss and what wasn't, she got a headache.

This was a mistake. Lucinda's strong intuition told her so. She had no business trying to pass herself off as a lady. She was not a lady. She was a commoner, a witch from a small village who'd spent her whole life being ridiculed by those of a much lower station than the society she would brush skirts with tonight. Lucinda had thought to punish Jackson by insisting that they attend. What a fool she was.

Jackson had an understanding of these people. He might be shunned by them, but he also had been raised in a way so that at least he could blend in among them. Lucinda would never blend in.

"All right, my lady, time for the gown."

Her stomach rolling around, Lucinda allowed the maid to help her out of her chair. The woman then tightened Lucinda's corset strings to the point that she couldn't breathe and helped her slip into her gown. It was a lovely creation. The gown was made of emerald silk, shot through with gold thread. The bodice hugged her slim waist, made slimmer now by her corset, displaying a fair amount of her cream-colored skin but not so much as to be considered vulgar. The skirt billowed out and called for three petticoats. The short puffed sleeves rested just on the edges of her shoulders, and Lucinda pulled on a pair of long white gloves.

The duchess entered just as the maid was buttoning up the last buttons on the back of Lucinda's gown. The older woman gasped softy.

"Oh, my dear, you are a vision."

A little of Lucinda's tenseness faded over the woman's compliment. She smiled. "Do you think I'll pass muster?"

"You'll pass and then some," the dowager assured her. The woman strolled farther into the room. Lucinda noticed the black box in her hand. "Jackson is downstairs. He sent this up, said you might wish to wear them."

Upon opening the box, it was Lucinda's turn to gasp. Inside was a lovely diamond necklace and dangling earrings that matched.

"I recognize those," the duchess said softly. "They belonged to his dear mother. How thoughtful of Jackson to present them to you to wear this evening."

The jewelry, although beautiful, only served to remind Lucinda of how different her and Jackson's lives had been. Lucinda's mother never owned a piece of fine jewelry in her life, certainly never diamonds. With trembling hands, Lucinda lifted the beautiful necklace from the velvet case. The dowager helped her secure the piece; then Lucinda clasped the earrings upon her ears.

"Perfect," the duchess announced. "You look like a fairy princess, Lucinda. I can't wait to see the look on Jackson's face when you walk down the stairs. Let me go first," she whispered excitedly, again reminding Lucinda of the young girl she must have been. "Give me a moment, then come down. Geoffrey has our wraps by the door."

The dowager, looking splendid herself in a gown made of rose brocade, hurried from the room. Lucinda went to stand before a full-length mirror. She didn't recognize the woman staring back at her. Her hair was piled upon her head in an arrangement of attractive curls. Diamonds glittered around her neck and called further attention to the long, slim column of her throat.

Lucinda took as deep a breath as her corset would allow, turned from the mirror, snatched up a small silk purse that matched her gown, and went to meet Jackson and the duchess downstairs.

Jackson's collar was already bothering him. Although he dressed for the most part like any other gentleman, he'd not been this turned out in some time. He wore white-tie, of course, and his finest black silk coat tailored for him by Weston's on Conduit Street. He and Hawkins had argued over Jackson's choice of footwear. He had wanted to wear his high polished black boots, but Hawkins had insisted Jackson wear black pumps and the traditional white stockings. He detested the fashion. He found it feminine and not to his more masculine taste.

Glancing toward the dowager and noting the necklace of rubies she wore, he was thankful he'd thought to bring Lucinda his mother's diamonds. They'd been given to him upon her death, she'd said because as a small boy he had always been fascinated by anything that glittered.

Jackson was just brushing imaginary lint from his coat, for it had to be imaginary, because Hawkins would never allow him to go out with lint on his clothes, when he felt Her Grace nudge him in the ribs. He glanced at her and she nodded toward the stairs.

When he looked up, Jackson felt as if he'd suddenly been kicked in the gut. Never, not ever in his whole life, had he seen a more beautiful woman than the one poised at the top of the stairs. He must have walked to the banister, for he felt the polished wood beneath his hand as he stared up at Lucinda.

Her hair shone like molten copper. The emerald gown she wore showed her splendid figure and matched the color of her eyes. She was a vision. When she didn't take another step, he held out his hand to her.

Slowly, she descended the stairs until finally her gloved hand slid into his. He clasped her slender fingers and pulled her down the last step and into his arms.

"You are beyond words," he said softly.

She smiled up at him. "You are prettier," she teased.

"You make a most striking couple," the dowager said, reminding Jackson she stood watching them.

The dowager's presence was probably a good thing. Jackson was tempted to sweep Lucinda up in his arms, carry her upstairs, and undo her perfection.

"Shall we go?" he asked instead.

Lucinda took a deep breath, which lifted her breasts delightfully above the neckline of her gown. "I suppose we should."

"Our wraps, Geoffrey," the duchess demanded.

Chapter Eighteen

Lucinda's head was spinning. After the first initial strained silence that came with announcing them, it seemed as if everything that followed had happened at whirlwind speed. Introductions were made. Lucinda hoped she curtsied when she should have and extended her hand when she should have; mostly she followed the dowager's lead. Jackson was nervous. Lucinda knew him well enough now to sense his discomfort.

"What do you think so far, Lucinda?"

She glanced at him from the corner of her eye, much too busy taking in the grandeur before her. "I've never seen a more vulgar display of wealth. To be honest, it rather sickens me."

He laughed. "I suppose it is a lot to take in. Even for one born into it." He took her hand in his. "Do you hate it?"

His touch was both comforting and disturbing. Tiny shock waves of pleasure raced up her arm.

"Not nearly as much as I should," she answered. "It's not as if I've ever belonged anywhere. I would feel just as uncomfortable at a village fair."

He opened his mouth to say something, but they were interrupted.

"Jackson Wulf, is it really you?"

They both turned at the young lady's inquiry. Lucinda didn't know where to look first, at the beautiful young woman's face, which positively beamed, or at Jackson's, which almost drained of color.

"Lady Anne," he said, dropping Lucinda's hand. "It's been a long time."

The young woman's smile grew brighter, if that was possible. "I haven't seen you since I returned to London. You look marvelous."

Jackson stepped forward, took the young woman's hand, and planted a chaste kiss there. "And you are just as beautiful as I remember."

Lucinda swore she felt the hair on the back of her neck rise. She had a strange desire to arch her back and hiss at the beautiful young woman.

The young lady glanced in her direction. "I heard you had married."

As if Jackson suddenly remembered he did indeed have a wife, he released the young woman's hand and turned toward Lucinda. "Yes, Lady Anne, let me present my wife, Lucinda."

Prepared to hate the woman immediately, Lucinda was surprised when the young woman took her hands and gave them a warm squeeze. "You are the luckiest woman," Lady Anne said. "And the most beautiful I have ever seen. I should have known Jackson would find a woman to share his life who is nothing less than perfection. We became quite close when we were both abroad last year," she explained. "I love him madly."

Lucinda didn't have the slightest notion of how to respond. Lady Anne was a beauty in her own right, with the softest brown eyes, like a doe. She emitted a genuinely warm feeling, and the color around her was soft. There was no venom here, no jealousy, except maybe on Lucinda's part.

"I won't stay and ruin your intimacy," the young woman teased them. "I had to say hello to Jackson. And I have been dying to meet you, Lucinda."

"Your aunt is scowling," Jackson said to the young woman. "You should go before she comes and drags you away."

Lady Anne rolled her eyes. "She knows that I would never give anyone the cut. She also knows I choose my own friends. Perhaps your lovely wife would allow me the pleasure of dancing with you later." Turning to Lucinda, she said, "I am sure you are aware that Jackson is the most splendid dancer."

Lucinda was not aware, nor did she know how to dance. Not the polite, stiff movements she'd witnessed of the couples dancing here tonight. She danced for the moon with a primitive rhythm sounding in her head. Now she not only felt inept and out of place, but she couldn't swear that she wasn't jealous of Lady Anne.

The young woman took her hand and squeezed again, then gave Jackson a quick peck on the cheek before taking herself off. From the corner of her eye, Lucinda watched Jackson stare after Lady Anne. In a brief flash of emotion, Lucinda saw something in his eyes that confirmed a suspicion that had surfaced. A quick glimpse of pain and longing. She knew then. This was the woman who had stolen his heart and brought the curse down upon him. The woman he loved.

The realization hit Lucinda harder than she would have thought, certainly harder than she would have wished. "She's lovely," she found herself admitting.

Jackson turned to look at her. "Yes," he agreed, which for some reason only added to the cross mood she felt coming over her.

"And very sweet," he added. "Any other woman would be crucified tonight for approaching two outcasts such as us, but she won't be, because it is her nature to embrace everyone. She doesn't know how to be a snob."

"She's the one," Lucinda said.

"She *was* the one," he corrected. "That was a long time ago."

Lucinda forgot they were at a party. It was as if everything and everyone faded into the background and her total focus was on Jackson. "She said she loved you madly."

He brushed a hand through his hair, which she was glad he didn't wear pulled back away from his face. She liked it brushing his shoulders. "She told me the same thing over a year ago in Paris," he said. "Only then she added that she loved me like the brother she had never had."

Her heart both broke for him and did a little jump for joy. She placed a hand on his arm. "I'm sorry."

Jackson shrugged off her concern. "It's all right. I'm over her." Even as he made the declaration, his gaze strayed across the room to where the young lady now stood conversing with a rather sour-faced woman Lucinda suspected was the aunt Jackson had mentioned.

Now Lucinda's heart plummeted again. It was still there in his eyes, the heartbreak, even if he failed to acknowledge his feelings.

"Do you want to dance?" he suddenly asked Lucinda. "These affairs are terribly boring unless one takes the initiative to enjoy oneself."

"I don't know how," Lucinda admitted. "And I won't embarrass either of us by attempting to learn at such an event."

Jackson nodded. They stood quietly for a time. The dowager, ever the watchful hen, conversed with a group of older women not far from them.

"Why don't you ask Lady Anne to dance?" Lucinda finally suggested, some inner pride warring with jealousy and even deeper feelings she cared not to examine at the moment. "She said she wanted to dance with you."

"I would not hurt your feelings," Jackson said.

He had already, but that was beside the point. "I could care less," she assured him. "One of us should have a good time."

He stared into her eyes for a moment. Perhaps she had managed to wound him, as well. He shrugged. "Maybe you will enjoy the dowager's company more than mine."

So saying, Jackson took her arm and steered her toward the duchess. Once the older woman had infiltrated Lucinda into her small group, Jackson disappeared into the crowd. Lucinda tried to listen to the boring conversation taking place among the older women, but her gaze kept straying around the room in search of a tall blond man dressed in black and easily the handsomest man present this evening.

"Pardon us, ladies," she heard the duchess say. "I must have a private word with my young charge."

After the duchess took her arm and led her from the group, the woman leaned close and made a soft snoring sound that had Lucinda giggling.

"Dreadfully boring," the dowager confided to Lucinda. "Where has Jackson gotten off to? I hope not the rum punch table."

"Jackson no longer drinks," Lucinda took a measure of pride in saying to the duchess.

"I told you if a woman got him off the liquor and away from the brothels he'd make a good husband," the dowager said, obviously pleased by Lucinda's news.

That was when Lucinda finally spotted Jackson and her pleasure diminished. He was dancing with Lady Anne, just as she'd told him to do.

A moment later, the duchess sighed. "I had hoped he wouldn't see her, that they might accidentally miss each other in passing."

"You know about Jackson's feelings for her?" Lucinda asked.

The lady nodded. "I'm afraid it was common gossip when Lady Anne returned to London. Jackson, of course, didn't know because he doesn't mix with this crowd. Lady Anne is too naïve to know that behind her back, everyone was whispering that Jackson Wulf was in love with her. I suppose the younger set all thought it was what she deserved for befriending him as she did. The talk soon died down and now I fear it will be revived again."

Would it? Lucinda watched them move together. Lady Anne hadn't been merely kind about Jackson's abilities. He moved with a grace and skill no man on the floor could match. Lady Anne was laughing up at him as they passed. Lucinda couldn't bear to look at them. Emotions she'd never dealt with were rolling around inside of her. She suddenly couldn't breathe with the throng of society pressed in close around her.

"I have to get out," she said to the duchess, and turned to make her escape. Lucinda ran into a man in her haste. Embarrassed she'd nearly knocked him backward, she glanced up to apologize. Her heart slammed against her chest and she froze.

"I was just coming to demand that Her Grace give me an introduction," the man said. "And perhaps to be so bold as to ask you to dance."

Words would not form in Lucinda's throat.

"Lord Cantley," the dowager drawled drily. "I have not seen you in London for years. How is your dear wife?"

The man did not look away from Lucinda to address the dowager. "In the country with the children," he answered. "She has long preferred the peace of the country over the fast pace of London during the season."

"May I present Lady Jackson Wulf." The dowager did her duty, if Lucinda could sense she did so reluctantly.

Lord Cantley reached down, took Lucinda's hand in his, and brought it to his lips. She nearly snatched it away. It took all of her willpower, still peppered with a great deal of shock, to allow the contact.

Lord Cantley inclined his head. "Lady. You look familiar to me. Have we met before?"

"I doubt so," the duchess answered, which Lucinda was grateful for, since she still hadn't found her voice. "The lady has been hidden away at her parent's estate in the country most of her life. I believe her marriage to young Jackson was arranged years ago."

It was a bold-faced lie, but Lucinda was glad that the lady had concocted it. Was Lord Cantley playing with her? Or did he really not recognize her in her finery? For certain, he would never expect to see her at such an affair. She wondered if he even knew her name. He'd always referred to her as the red-haired witch.

His gaze dipped to the neckline of Lucinda's gown and her skin started to crawl. "I must apologize, but I do not dance," Lucinda finally managed, and she tried as hard as she could to inflict her voice with a proper English accent and the proper amount of snobbery. "I am just on my way to the refreshment tables," she added, hoping to make a clean break of it.

The man took her arm. "Allow me to escort you, then. Unless of course your husband would count it too familiar. Did you say his name is Wulf?"

Still dazed, Lucinda allowed Lord Cantley to draw her away from the duchess. Did the villagers of Whit Hurch know Jackson's name? Would it be simple for the man to put two and two together and arrive at the correct conclusion? She had to ask Jackson, that was, if he could tear himself away from Lady Anne in order for her to do so. Other than make a spectacle, Lucinda had little choice but to accompany Lord Cantley to the next room and the tables of refreshments set up there.

Moving through the crowd did not allow them to speak to each other, which Lucinda was grateful for. What she would do when they reached the less crowded adjoining room she had no idea. If she somehow managed to escape Lord Cantley, perhaps he wouldn't give her a second thought.

If the man spent any time in London at all, she realized, he would probably realize who she was. There were the rumors about her, if he was to inquire. All Lucinda could do at the moment was hope to escape him and hope once she had he wouldn't think of her again.

The refreshment room was surprisingly sparse of people. Only a few gentlemen stood talking in one corner, close to the punch she knew had been spiced with rum.

"Could I intrude upon you to pour me a glass of punch, Lord Cantley, while I go and freshen up a bit?" Lucinda called behind her, making certain she stayed one step ahead of the man.

"I would be honored," he answered.

"I shall return momentarily." Lucinda kept moving through the refreshment room, where she hoped to find a hallway leading back to the ballroom and to Jackson. Just being near Cantley churned her stomach, both with loathing and with fear. She didn't fear so much for herself, although she never again wanted to be within touching distance of the man, but she feared for Sebastian. Lord Cantley had no scruples, no sense of honor.

Suddenly Lucinda drew up. Flustered as she was, she

had taken a wrong turn and seemed to be heading away from the music rather than toward it. She turned to retrace her steps. A figure blocked her way.

"Lord Cantley," she gasped. "I said that I would return in a moment."

He smiled at her. "I've hunted enough to know when my prey is fleeing from me. Why are you afraid of me, Lady Wulf?"

Although she was trembling, Lucinda lifted her chin in what she hoped was a confident manner. "I am not afraid. Should I be?"

Taking her off guard, he reached out and touched her cheek. Lucinda flinched and took a step back.

"Such soft skin. I think I have felt it before. A rather lot of it."

Her confidence now fading, Lucinda had to muster all her strength and control to carry on the game she played with Lord Cantley. "I am a married woman," she said. "And you go too far by pursuing me as if I have given you encouragement."

The man merely shrugged. "Some men don't need much encouragement." He took a step closer. "They see something they want, and they take it."

Or drug a woman so she can't fight back, Lucinda wanted to say. She suspected Lord Cantley was waiting for her to say something in line with her thoughts. He was trying to trick her. She lifted her chin another notch.

"You've spent too much time in the country. You have the manners of a stag in rut. Excuse me." Lucinda thought to step around him, but again he blocked her path.

"You remind me of someone. But of course she couldn't come to be here, married to a wealthy, if we both know unacceptable, family, could she? Although she was a witch, and I know well enough how easily she can cast a spell over a man."

As Lucinda feared, he knew who she was, but she had to continue to pretend otherwise. "I do not know who you are speaking of, but if you do not move from my path, I shall open my mouth and scream, and you will be called to account as to why you would try to accost a married woman, one who gave you no encouragement."

The earl suddenly seemed less sure of himself. His gaze narrowed on her face. "Only one woman could have eyes that color. What is your Christian name, Lady Wulf?"

"Lucinda."

She had not spoken her name. Jackson stood behind Lord Cantley, looking calm enough, if she knew him better. His eyes held a faint blue glow.

"Jackson," she breathed.

Lord Cantley turned to face her husband. "I was just escorting your lovely wife back to the ball," he said. "She seems to have lost her way."

"I will help her find it," Jackson assured the man.

Each man took the other's measure.

"The lady seems familiar to me," the earl went a step further. "I was merely trying to find out why, and where we might have met before."

Jackson stepped around Lord Cantley and placed himself between the man and Lucinda. "I doubt that you have had call to meet my wife before tonight. Neither of us moves among society frequently. Now, if you will excuse us."

Rather than turn to leave or move and allow Jackson and Lucinda to pass, Cantley stood firm, staring past Jackson at Lucinda. "A man doesn't forget those eyes," he said. "Or that lovely skin."

Even in her limited experience, Lucinda knew Lord Cantley had just issued an insult. A man did not suggest intimate knowledge of another man's wife to his face. Not without perhaps being run through.

"You greatly tempt me to call you out," Jackson said, his voice low and threatening. "May I ask where you hail from?"

"My country estate encompasses a good deal of land in the Midlands; the manor house sits in an area close to the village of Whit Hurch. Perhaps you and your lovely wife have been in the area before."

There was a moment of awkward silence, silence in which Lucinda was well aware that Jackson had made a connection between her and Lord Cantley.

"My wife is from Yorkshire, as am I," Jackson drawled. "Again, I must insist that you do not know her, and that you do not speak to her again."

Lord Cantley inclined his head, and Lucinda thought it was the end of the matter, if she knew it wasn't the end of the matter between her and Jackson. The man moved off down the hallway a little ways; then he turned back.

"Odd, though," he said. "That this woman I knew, and knew well, mind you, has the same first name as your wife. The same red hair. The same emerald eyes. The same delightful figure. They could be twins, the two of them." Then he left.

Jackson didn't outwardly respond, but Lucinda saw his back muscles tighten, saw his hands fist at his sides. Lord Cantley was insulting in his implied familiarity with her and he deserved a sound thrashing, but Lucinda wouldn't let Jackson make a worse spectacle of them at their first social appearance together. She stepped forward and placed a hand upon his shoulder.

"Let it go, Jackson," she said softly. "He's not worth it. And neither am I."

Jackson turned to face her, and the blue of his eyes

glowed in the dim hallway. "Did you sneak away with him?"

She was not ready to tell Jackson about Lord Cantley. About what he'd done to her or the threat he posed to them. Not yet, not now, not here. "I would like to go home," she said instead, moving past him.

He wouldn't let the matter go. "I asked you a question, Lucinda."

Now it was her turn to lash out. "If you had not been otherwise occupied, you would know what I did or did not do in your absence," she clipped.

"I only did what you bade me to do," he clipped back.

"And quite enthusiastically," she muttered, moving forward. "There's a saying about the pot calling the kettle black."

"So you take revenge by throwing your own past indiscretions in my face?"

He walked beside her now. Lucinda didn't have to glance at him to know he was still angry. "Could we deal with your petty jealousies somewhere more private? Say at home?"

Jackson didn't answer, but by the heat she felt coming off of him, the matter was far from settled. How much could she tell him? And would he even believe her story? Lucinda might tell herself it was none of his business, but that was a lie. Or would become one if Lord Cantley didn't drop the matter and dismiss her from his mind, which she felt more than certain he would not do.

Chapter Nineteen

Jackson knew his jealousy was unreasonable. He was quite taken off guard by it and struggled to deal with emotions foreign to him. Lucinda was right. It wasn't as if he didn't have far more indiscretions in his past than she ever could. But he knew her now. Knew that in order to get her into bed a man would have to steal into her heart, regardless of what she'd said to him about Sebastian's father.

Her kisses in the beginning were enough to convince Jackson that whatever past experiences she'd had with men were far fewer in number than his own experiences with women had been. She was still almost innocent in her responses when he kissed or touched her. Why did it tear him up so to think of her being with another man? She had a child. Of course she'd been with other men . . . or at least one.

The more he thought about Lord Cantley, for the duchess had told him the man had escorted Lucinda to the refreshment tables, the more Jackson's thoughts turned toward Sebastian and the resemblance between them. No common farmer had Lucinda been involved with. No, Jackson should have known her beauty could win her the attention of a man far above that simple station. The lord of the manor. An earl. She would have settled for nothing less.

Jackson's gaze cut toward her in the coach. They'd not spoken a word to each other since seeing the dowager home. Lucinda had acted uncaring if he danced with Lady Anne. So he had, he supposed, angry over Lucinda's lack of caring what he did with other women. But as he'd danced with Anne, teased with her as he'd done so long ago, and made her laugh, all he could think about was Lucinda and why he could not charm her or make her laugh.

Lucinda didn't care for him. Not the way he suddenly realized he'd come to care for her. Perhaps now that the earl had seen her in a fine gown, moving easily among higher society, he'd want her back. Lucinda had said Sebastian's father had a wife. Perhaps then he hadn't been inclined to simply make Lucinda his mistress and care for her and the child, but tonight might have changed his mind.

The coach lumbered up in front of the town house. Jackson allowed the footman to get the door and help Lucinda out; then he bounded out behind her. Hawkins had the door for them, taking wraps before Jackson dismissed him and followed Lucinda upstairs. Jackson waited, standing at the door, while she checked on Sebastian to make sure that the babe was asleep and all was well.

Lucinda lingered overlong, staring down at the large cradle. Jackson wondered if possibly seeing the child's father again had made her regret her decision to flee him so quickly and tie her life with Jackson's instead.

The thought caused a pain in his chest. His heart. Maybe he'd known that he would someday lose her, but he hadn't thought he'd lose Sebastian as well. In that moment with the possibility looming before him, Jackson realized he did not want to lose the babe. He realized he did not want to lose Lucinda, either.

The realization so startled him that his anger at her vanished. Jackson walked to his room, went inside, and closed the door. He moved toward the liquor cabinet out of habit. His mouth watered for a drink to steady his suddenly frayed nerves and perhaps to drown his sorrows. When he'd stopped drinking, he'd never had the bottles and glasses removed. What test of strength was there in resisting something that wasn't there?

He resisted the urge now, both to pour himself a drink and to storm into Lucinda's room and demand answers from her. The curse cut into his thoughts. The bargain between them. All it took to release them both from their obligations to each other was breaking it. Of course he would keep his promise as far as Sebastian was concerned, provided Lucinda didn't change her mind about that. It occurred to Jackson that Lucinda, now that she'd seen her lover again and also knew he was still interested in her, might simply take the babe and slip away. But no, Jackson knew her well enough to know she would insist on fulfilling her end of their bargain.

The marriage. He'd never worried overmuch about it. Perhaps he should. If he never slept with Lucinda, an annulment might be purchased just as easily as the license to marry had been. A divorce was out of the question. Lucinda could not marry her lover. But Jackson, he might one day marry again if the curse was broken for him and his brothers. The thought held little appeal to him at the moment. He already had a wife. A wife who did not wish to stay with him.

The liquor cabinet called to him again. He resisted. Instead, he removed his coat, his stock and tie, tossing all

upon a nearby chair. He stretched out on the bed, staring
up at the ceiling, hands behind his head. What he really
wanted to do was go into Lucinda's room, take her in his
arms, and make love to her. Let her know his thoughts tonight were not on Lady Anne or what life they might have
had together if he were not cursed but of Lucinda and
how to ever convince her that all she was to him was not
simply tied up in a curse.

Lucinda lay awake. The expected confrontation with
Jackson had not come. Why? That he seemed jealous of
Lord Cantley had brought her a certain amount of satisfaction . . . of hope. If in his heart he still longed for the
beautiful Lady Anne, why would he even bother to be
jealous? Simply out of pride? He could not bed Lucinda,
so he wanted no other man to do so, either? But then that
would make his confession of thinking seducing her
might break his curse, and pursuing her for only that purpose, false.

   She needed to break the curse, for it would clear up
any confusion about what Jackson Wulf did or did not
want from her. At the same time, it would end her ties to
Sebastian. She was torn. Torn between a bargain and her
heart. Torn, if she was being honest with herself, not only
about leaving her son but also about leaving Jackson. And
while she was being honest, could she not admit that
there were many things she found agreeable about her
husband? Not just his face or his fine body. He had protected her at the inn. He had not taken full advantage of a
situation many of his station would have already taken
advantage of. He was good with Sebastian. He seemed to
care about her son.

   Did she love Jackson? That she would even ask herself
that question mentally startled Lucinda. Love, at least between a man and a woman, was something she thought

would never be hers. Not with her background. She knew by her reaction to seeing Jackson and Lady Anne together that she was not immune to feelings for him, even if she couldn't quite bring herself to admit to possibly being in love with him.

Since honesty was her current course, she also had to admit that Jackson and Lady Anne made a striking pair . . . a much more suited pair. Might Lady Anne's affections for Jackson grow beyond the bounds of sisterly love if Lucinda was out of the way? Would the lady be a good mother to Sebastian? Although it was hard to picture the scene without nearly breaking into tears, Lucinda knew in her heart that Lady Anne would be a good mother. The lady was nothing but goodness and positive light.

And therefore very hard for Lucinda to dislike.

The door creaked and Lucinda sat with a start. Jackson entered her room. Had he finally come to question her about Lord Cantley? She wasn't ready to tell Jackson all. But lying to him might put not only Sebastian in danger but Jackson as well.

He moved to the bed and looked down at her. "This new plan you have to break the curse. What does it involve besides a whip and a great deal of pain?"

She blinked up at him in the darkness. This was not the inquiry she thought he'd come to make. The fact that it took precedence over his earlier anger suggested he'd been lying awake thinking the same as her. He'd weighed what was most important to him. Perhaps seeing Lady Anne again had made him more determined. Lucinda fought down the despair that suddenly gripped her.

"You must prove to be stronger than the beast within you," she answered. "The man must endure what the beast cannot."

"What you're saying is that you must beat it out of me, correct?"

She suppressed a shudder. "Correct."

"I'll spend the week preparing myself, and come week's end you will perform the ritual. It must be late, when no one is about."

Lucinda suddenly wished the idea had not come to her. No matter how angry she had been at Jackson for trying to seduce her with only his own selfish reasons in mind, she would not wish this upon him. "All right," she finally agreed. "That will give me time to prepare the salves to heal your wounds."

The horror of it hung between them. Lucinda would need the week to mentally prepare to perform a ritual she'd never thought herself capable of. Jackson turned toward the door. She thought the conversation had ended, but he paused.

"One thing. The man I saw you with tonight. Is he Sebastian's father?"

His question wasn't that simple. But her answer was. "Yes," she admitted. "His name is Lord Cantley," she went on. "He is a cousin of the king."

Jackson shook his head. He laughed softly, although she couldn't say it was a genuine sound of humor. "And I thought I had done right by giving him my name. He has royal blood running through his veins."

Which was why he was a threat to the future of England, Lucinda wanted to add. She must tell Jackson all, she realized. Hiding her secrets from him was now a dangerous game. "I wish to explain."

He held up a hand. "Not now. My mind must be free of dark thoughts of you and him in order to prepare myself for the coming ritual. Breaking the curse must take precedence over everything else."

What he said was true. His mind must be clear, his body strong, in order to withstand the ritual. Could she go one more week without telling him the whole of her and

Sebastian's situation? Could she go for a week with him thinking the wrong thing about her relationship with Lord Cantley? Perhaps the earl would leave them alone. Perhaps he'd already forgotten about her. She prayed so.

"You are right. We will not speak of it yet."

"Good night, Lucinda."

He had never been in her room when he hadn't at least made a suggestive remark to her. She found his coldness now toward her heartbreaking. And she wasn't so certain she should leave Jackson without knowing what she had thus far missed with a man regarding intimacy. If anyone could show her how it should be done, she suspected it was this man.

"Good night," she said softly. "I hope you don't think too badly of me."

He shrugged. "You said yourself that would be a bit like the pot calling the kettle black."

When he retraced his steps to the bed, her heart suddenly leaped.

"I did not give you my apology for what I said to you the other night, for what I've done to you. I ask your forgiveness, Lucinda. Once this is all behind us and you . . . you are gone, please do not think too badly of me, either."

Before she could respond, he wheeled away and left her room, closing the door softly after him. Tears welled up in Lucinda's eyes. He had not asked her to stay. He accepted that she would leave. Of course she had accepted it from the very beginning, never once allowing herself to believe otherwise. But somewhere deep inside of her she had hoped. She had dreamed. She should have known better.

Lucinda lay back down against the mattress, her head resting upon her pillow, tears streaming down her face. She had made a bargain with him. Her word was all she had to give. Her word and her heart, her only son. She would allow Jackson this week to prepare for the ritual. She would mentally prepare for it herself, and then she had to tell him everything and pray that he would still keep his word regarding Sebastian. Lucinda could not protect her son, not the way Jackson could. Nor could she provide for Sebastian. She would do well to provide for herself.

She dared not think about the week's end. She dared not think of taking a whip to Jackson's flesh, of driving the beast from him, or of all that would happen were she to succeed . . . or fail, for that matter.

Chapter Twenty

Two days passed and nothing happened. Lucinda was almost afraid to hope it would be the end of Lord Cantley for them. She did not go out for fear that he might be lying in wait for her. She slept with one ear trained on the room next door, and any slight noise from Sebastian had her up and into his room to make certain her son was all right. Her nerves were stretched to the snapping point. And while she fretted and feared, Jackson prepared. She watched him now, working a horse in the enclosure outside the stables.

Lucinda sat on a blanket with Sebastian on the grounds, shaded by the hedge that separated one property from another, although the property next door held only the blackened ground where a house had once stood. Hawkins had told Lucinda that Rosalind Wulf had once lived in the house and that she'd lost her stepmother and her stepbrother in the fire. Lucinda sometimes had bad feelings about places, and the burnt ground next door was one of them. Something bad had happened there.

"Excuse me."

Startled, Lucinda jumped. A lovely young woman approached from the path leading from the house. At first Lucinda thought it was Lady Anne, but then she saw the young woman's blond curls as they bounced beneath her hat.

"Pardon my intrusion, but I am Lady Amelia Sinclair. I'm a friend of Rosalind's," she further identified herself.

Lucinda snatched up Sebastian and rose. Her nervousness increased. What did the young woman want?

A little out of breath, Lady Amelia reached Lucinda's side and immediately swept off her bonnet and seated herself on the blanket. "It's dreadfully hot today," she complained, fanning her face with her bonnet. "I heard you and the younger Wulf were in residence and I have to admit, I'm as curious as a cat. On a whim, I decided to drop over and meet you. I know it's terribly rude to do so, but my mother is not fond of my friendship with Rosalind. I must often go behind her back when an opportunity presents itself."

Lucinda had never met anyone so straightforward . . . or, she supposed, according to etiquette, so rude. "I am Lucinda," she introduced herself. "And yonder with the horse is Jackson."

The young woman stretched her neck, shading her eyes with her hat. "Oh yes, he has their look, all right," she said. "Handsome as sin, it would seem . . . all of them."

Lucinda suddenly felt awkward standing. She settled back upon the blanket. "This is my son, Sebastian."

The young woman smiled at the baby, her expression soft for a moment. "He's a beautiful babe," she said, then cocked her head. "He doesn't have much of the Wulf look, though. Not with that dark hair."

"No," Lucinda agreed, not offering more. "You are a friend of Lady Rosalind's?"

"Oh yes," Amelia assured her. "We're thick as thieves. I do so miss her and wish she'd come home from her honeymoon, but then, if I were honeymooning with Armond Wulf, I wouldn't be in any hurry to return, either." The young lady's smile was devilish. "I thought I should introduce myself to you since Rosalind and I are friends, and I am certain we will be, as well."

Having a friend was still an odd notion to Lucinda. She immediately took to Amelia Sinclair, however. The young woman seemed straightforward and uninhibited. It was a nice change from the stuffiness Lucinda had witnessed at her first "social" affair. Since Lucinda didn't have much in common with the young woman, she asked if she'd perhaps attended the same affair.

"Oh no," Amelia answered, looking a little down in the mouth. "I am engaged to be married now. I'm not required to attend the bulk of the parties anymore. I am off 'the marriage market,' as they call it, and my fiancé doesn't really enjoy the social scene. He prefers country living, or so he has informed me."

Although Lucinda had rarely given thought to women and men and their compatibility, she immediately sensed this was not a good match. Amelia Sinclair seemed too full of fun and life to be confined to country living. Lucinda knew enough about etiquette now to know it wasn't something she should mention. The two women sat in comfortable silence for a time, allowing Sebastian to charm them with his cooes and smiles.

Lucinda thought Amelia was about to make her excuses and leave when she glanced toward the enclosure and saw that Jackson was walking toward them. He drew his sleeve across his brow. Oh Lord, he was sweating. That didn't bode well for an introduction to Amelia Sinclair.

"Do you know my husband?" Lucinda ventured. "Have you met him before perhaps through Lady Rosalind?"

Having taken notice of Jackson moving toward them, the young lady was rude enough not to take her eyes from him even though she'd been addressed by someone else. "No, I've never met this one," she commented. "I do know Armond, of course, and I have once caught a glimpse of Gabriel, in the flesh. And what flesh it was," she seemed to add unconsciously.

"Who do we have here?" Jackson swaggered toward them with his inherent panther grace, looking good enough to eat in tight black trousers, knee-high boots, and an open frilled shirt.

Lady Amelia immediately stood for the introductions. Before Lucinda could provide them, the young lady introduced herself. "I am Lady Amelia Sinclair, a personal friend of your sister-in-law." The young woman held out her hand.

Jackson took her hand and kissed it gently, causing the young woman to visibly shudder in the afternoon heat.

"Pleased to make your acquaintance, Lady Amelia," he said, flashing his dimples, which, in Lucinda's opinion, he had no need to do. The young lady was already slack jawed and under his spell.

Scooping up Sebastian, Lucinda rose from the blanket. She moved forward and thrust the babe into Jackson's arms. "Would you mind taking Sebastian back to the house?" she asked. "It has grown too warm outdoors for him, and you do need to go inside and clean up. *You're all sweaty*," she emphasized. "I believe the young woman was about to make her excuses, and I will see her to her carriage."

"Yes, I am sweaty," Jackson agreed, looking not in the least contrite about what he was doing to the poor young woman. "That is why I stopped my business with the horse," he explained to Lucinda. "It was a pleasure to meet you, Lady Amelia."

The young woman couldn't even respond. She merely nodded. Jackson winked at Lucinda, which she didn't find in the least amusing, and took himself and Sebastian off toward the house. Only when he'd moved off a ways did the young lady seem to snap out of her lethargic state.

"Oh my," she whispered. "I think the heat has gotten to me." She bent, scooped up her hat, and began fanning herself profusely.

"Yes, the heat," Lucinda muttered. "Would you like to come inside for refreshments?" it occurred to her to ask.

"No thank you," Amelia answered, still looking somewhat dazed. "I should be getting home. I have to bribe my driver and my chaperone to be silent about my visits, and I fear the longer I keep them waiting, the more my allowance dwindles."

"I'll walk you up the path," Lucinda said, bending to grab up the blanket she'd brought out with her to spread on the ground. She then took Amelia's arm and steered her along the path toward the house and the circular drive where Amelia's carriage no doubt sat in wait for her.

"It was wonderful to meet you," Lucinda said dutifully. "Perhaps we will see one another again before . . ." She let the sentence trail. She couldn't very well say *before I am forced to leave.*

"If not out among society, at my wedding," Amelia said, misinterpreting Lucinda's near mistake. "Whether Mother likes it or not, I will have my friends invited. I'll be sure to have you and your husband added to the guest list."

Lucinda, the witch with no last name, invited to a society wedding? It was almost too much to comprehend. She walked the young woman to the drive, watched her hurry to the coach and scurry inside, then walked to the front door. Hawkins opened it before she got there and she smiled at him, then went upstairs to make certain Jackson had transferred Sebastian to his nurse.

He was just coming out of the nursery. "You behaved very badly with Lady Amelia," she immediately scolded. "You should be—"

"Whipped?" he broke in, raising a dark brow. "Don't worry; you'll have your chance."

She didn't want to think about that. She didn't like the sudden distance between them. She didn't like the lies between them. Once, she felt uncomfortable when he made suggestive remarks and tried to seduce her. Now, she wanted very badly to hear him tease her again, to have him look at her with warm desire in his eyes instead of cold aloofness. She'd envied Amelia Sinclair earlier. Envied the feel of his mouth against her hand, the teasing glance he settled upon her. Lucinda realized he hadn't washed yet. That scent was on him.

"You should wash," she said.

He stepped closer, backing her against the wall, placing one hand against the wall beside her head. "Am I bothering you?"

She swallowed with difficulty. The fire crept in then, a little ball that formed in her belly and spread heat outward, to every part of her. He looked so good. He smelled so good. His mouth, it was so close, so distracting. She couldn't think. Couldn't speak. Couldn't breathe.

"I . . ." That was all she could manage. Her mind and her mouth wouldn't work, but her hands did. She was suddenly touching him, her hand trailing up his chest to his neck, around the back of his head, her fingers twining into his hair. She pulled him closer and there it was, that spark she wanted. The flame that lit his dark eyes and turned them to blue fire.

"Damn you," he said huskily, and then he kissed her.

It wasn't a gentle kiss. Nor was it brutal. Something in between and entirely suited to her needs. And since when did she have needs when it came to a man? Since the first moment she saw him. His tongue probed her and all thoughts fled. She matched the swordplay. Then he pressed against her, his desire evident in his snug-fitting trousers. She pressed back. He broke from her lips with a groan, taking her hand and pulling her into the closest room, which was hers. His hands were suddenly in her hair, holding her head still while he ravaged her mouth. Then he was backing her toward the bed.

Lucinda knew his intention and for the first time felt no moment of panic. No sudden urge to bolt, only an acceptance of the way it was and the way it should be. He was a man. She was a woman. He was right. This was inevitable.

They fell upon the bed together, mouths locked, hands roving. She pulled his shirt from his trousers while he set to work at the buttons at the front of her day frock. His hands shook, his fingers clumsy in his hurry. His sudden awkwardness excited her more than his past leisurely seductions. She would help him, she decided, burning for the feel of his hands and his mouth against her skin, against her aching breasts. Suddenly his fingers closed over hers. He surrendered her mouth, breathing heavily, his forehead pressed against hers, and then he looked into her eyes.

"No," he said. "Not like this." He rolled off of her and stood, staring down at her.

Lucinda could hardly catch her own breath. Was he refusing her? Perhaps he thought she was still unwilling. "But I want—"

"You want the scent of me on you," he broke in. "That is all you want." His gaze roamed her, his eyes still aglow with passion. "Once, that was enough for me. It's not anymore."

Disbelieving, she watched him turn away and walk from the room. She heard the sound of his boots moving down the hallway to his own room, then his door closing.

She was still on fire, burning for him, aching for him, not his scent, him. She started to rise and go after him. It wasn't the sweet seduction he was so skilled at that had broken through her defenses but the man who teased her, the man who held her son in his arms late at night and spoke softly to him. The man who would walk away from her complete surrender, because he wanted more.

But to what end would such a confession bring her? She was not a lady, not like the one he had first given his heart to. Not like the one who, for all Lucinda knew, still held his heart. Jackson might want her in his bed, but he did not want her in his life. Was that enough for her, as well?

A moment ago, when passion had ruled her head, it had been enough. Now, she wasn't certain. Should she take what he would give her before she left him? Or would that make leaving even harder? Lucinda didn't know, but she supposed she should be grateful Jackson had given her the time to decide. Although time, Lucinda knew well enough, was running out.

Chapter Twenty-one

It was by chance that Lucinda first noticed it—a carriage that passed more than once in front of the town house as she stared brooding out her window. She might not have noticed at all except for the crest on the side of the coach. She had seen it before. A dragon. It was the Cantley coat of arms. Coincidence? She didn't believe so. Not for a moment.

She had to tell Jackson everything. He couldn't go on believing that she had feelings for Lord Cantley other than loathing and fear. He had to understand that Sebastian was in danger from the man. That possibly they were all in danger. But it was the day—the one Jackson had been mentally and physically preparing for all week. The day Lucinda had been trying to prepare for as well.

Jackson's mind had to be clear of worry, his body strong. Could baring her soul to him wait just one more day? And what about tonight? If Lucinda managed to exorcise the beast from Jackson, she would have to stand by her promise to leave him. If Lucinda failed Jackson again, she would have to worry about not only Lord Cantley's threat but also the threat of Jackson himself when the moon ruled him in only a week's time. He would have to take himself off somewhere, and she would be left alone with Sebastian, defenseless.

The dilemma twisted her stomach with worry as the day wore on. Add to all the ordeal ahead, and by nightfall Lucinda was jumping at shadows. It worried her also to leave Sebastian alone in the house, but she couldn't very well take him out with her and Jackson, not with what they had planned. Instead, Lucinda had placed a magic circle around Sebastian's cradle. She'd told the nurse to keep an ear trained for trouble. Martha's eyes had rounded with curiosity, but Lucinda couldn't tell her the whole of the situation when she hadn't even told Jackson yet.

The only solution seemed to be to get the exorcism behind them as quickly as possible and, whatever happened, tell Jackson of Lord Cantley's threat. Then decisions could be made. Action could be taken. Finally, as the shadows grew longer, a soft knock sounded upon her door.

Lucinda opened the door to see Jackson standing there. Their eyes met. "It's time, Lucinda," he said softly so not to wake the nurse and Sebastian. "Come."

He held out his hand and she took it, somehow reassured by the warm strength she felt flowing through him. They went downstairs and crept like thieves through the house, using the back entrance. She was surprised to see Hawkins stationed there. As they slipped out, he said nothing but took up a position at the unguarded door.

"What did you tell him?" she wondered once they were outside, heading toward the path to the stables.

"To guard the door," Jackson answered. "Beyond that, it is it not his place to ask. For all he knows, we're going for a midnight ride, or a midnight tryst. I didn't want to leave the door unguarded, though, not in London, where thieves roam the night in search of any unlocked door or window left cracked."

She at least took a measure of comfort that Hawkins would be guarding the house. Now, to focus upon the task at hand. Her mind shied away from it. Lucinda didn't allow herself to think as Jackson led her through the darkness. His eyes were much more suited than hers for roaming the night. He led her to the tall enclosure where he worked the horses.

The walls were high enough to hide them, but yet it was open and far enough from the stables to, she hoped, not raise any alarms, with either the man in charge for the night or the horses. Lucinda gasped softly when she saw what Jackson had fashioned in the middle of the enclosure.

It was a scaffold of sorts, with thick leather straps tied overhead. Straps about the size of a man's wrists. Two lanterns sat on each side and he bent to light them, soon casting an eerie glow around the enclosure. In the glow, she saw the whip leaning against one of the scaffold poles. Lucinda shuddered.

Jackson retrieved the whip and walked toward her. When she stood with her arms at her sides, he lifted her hand and molded the whip into it. He reached beneath his shirt and brought a pistol from the waistband of his trousers.

"Do you know how to use one of these?"

Oh, aye, her mother had taught her at an early age. Lucinda had hunted at times for them, when coin was too sparse to afford much and no one cared if the village witch and her child starved to death during winter.

"Yes," she answered.

"Good." He shoved it into the pocket of her skirt. "If this doesn't go well. If I come at you. Shoot me."

Her knees nearly buckled. Shoot him? How could she shoot him when she . . . when she cared for him? "Are you sure, Jackson?" she asked. "Are you certain you don't want to wait and see if I can think of another way?"

"I'm tired of waiting," he answered, staring down into her eyes. "It's time to end it once and for all."

She wondered if there were double meanings to his words. Then she had trouble thinking at all when he began to strip from his clothing. He pulled his shirt over his head and threw it on the ground. His boots followed; then he reached for the fastenings on his trousers.

"Must you take off everything?" she asked breathlessly.

He paused. "You're just going to cut them to ribbons anyway," he said. "And if the beast emerges the winner, there will be nothing left of them."

"The beast cannot win," she reminded him. "You mustn't allow it."

He nodded but still unfastened his trousers and shucked them down his long, muscular legs.

Lucinda didn't attempt to avert her gaze. How could she when he was so perfect in face and form? So beautiful with the glow from the lanterns dancing across his tawny skin? He walked barefoot and naked to the scaffold. She watched as he slipped his hand through one leather strap, using his other hand to tighten the bonds.

"You'll have to secure the other," he said over his shoulder.

Fighting down repulsion over what she must do to him, Lucinda laid the whip on the ground and walked to where he stood. She wasn't as tall as he and had to stand on her tiptoes to reach his wrist, forcing her body against his in her efforts to pull the binding tight. She bumped against him several times during the process. It didn't help her nerves.

Once she secured him, she stepped back and looked up at him. "Are you sure, Jackson?" she asked again.

"Yes."

"Positive, because we can—"

"Do it, Lucinda," he growled. "I want to be free!"

Free of the beast? Or free of her? In all likelihood, free of the both of them. She took a deep breath and stepped away from him, walking around behind him to where she had laid the whip. With trembling hands, she bent and retrieved the object meant to purge him. She'd seen what a whip could do to a man's back before. Lord Cantley's overseers were not kind men and used the whip often to encourage the workers in the fields. Lucinda had tended many a torn and bloody back.

Staring now at Jackson's smooth, unmarked skin, Lucinda wished she had never in her anger mentioned this ritual to him. He was already tensed for the blow and she brought the whip down, letting it uncurl like a snake on the ground. She couldn't force herself to bring it back up, to hurl it at him and let it slice into his skin.

"What are you waiting for?" he asked through clenched teeth. "Begin."

"I don't think I can," she whispered.

"Of course you can," he growled at her. "Now is your chance to take revenge for all I've done to you."

Lucinda tried to summon feelings of revenge. She could not. "You gave me a home and your name. You have given me fine clothes to wear and provided safety and care for my son."

"I wanted to kill you in the beginning," he reminded her. "I almost got both of our throats slit on our wedding night. I tried to seduce you as a way of defeating you."

"You protected me from those men at the tavern," she argued. "You could have taken advantage of me later that night when the brandy had gone to my head. You did not."

"I wanted to," he shot back. "I undressed you, and all the while I couldn't think of anything but having you. I still can't think of anything but having you. It has become an obsession. Thrash it out of me."

"You're lying," she called. "You could have had me already. You know that. You walked away."

"I walked away from a bitch in heat!" he yelled. "In heat from the smell of me. That is all it's ever been for me. The women. It was never me they wanted; it was the scent. You're not any different!"

Lucinda drew back and sent the whip slicing through the air before she could stop herself. How dare he say that she was no different! She'd been different all of her life. She had been on the outside looking in. She had been hungry and whispered about. She had been drugged and molested and given a child. A child a man wanted to kill because of the mark he bore.

The whip landed with a crack upon Jackson's back. He automatically jerked. His breath hissed between his lips. Stunned by what she had done, Lucinda could only stand and stare at the red welt that suddenly appeared upon his smooth skin.

"That's more like it," he said. "Witch," he added harshly.

He would not bait her again. Lucinda understood his game now. If understanding dawned one thrash too late. Lucinda threw the whip down as if it burned her hand. She walked to him and went around to face him.

"I cannot do this," she said. "I thought I could, but such cruelty, no matter how much has been dealt to me in my life, is not in my nature."

"Lucinda." His voice softened. "I would have this beast taken from me so I can find only the man I am. So that I can be only the man I am. I want it gone for my brothers as well, so that they can also only be men. Do not take this chance from me."

"And her?" she had to ask. "Do you want it gone for her sake, as well?"

His brow furrowed. "Her?"

"Lady Anne," Lucinda said impatiently. "If you are only a man, and if I am out of the way, you are free to pursue her."

"If I wanted her that badly," he said, "I could have used my scent on her long ago. That part of my life is over, Lucinda."

Her heart lurched. Few words had ever sounded sweeter to Lucinda, but still, he had not said he had feelings for her. He had not asked her to stay. But then, he, too, suffered from a misconception about her relationship with the earl.

"It wasn't what you think," she said. "Lord Cantley—"

"You call, my love?"

Again Lucinda's heart lurched, but for a different reason. Knowing the blood must have drained from her face, she stepped to the side of Jackson and saw Lord Cantley and two of his henchmen standing inside the enclosure.

"What strange tastes your husband has," Lord Cantley drawled, taking in the odd scene before him. He lifted a brow. "Or was all this your idea?"

"What are you doing here?" she managed to gasp, though her heart was now pounding so hard and loud inside of her chest she thought it might break free of her body.

"You know what I'm doing here." He turned to one of his men. "Go to the house and get the child."

"No!" Lucinda cried, rushing forward while digging for the pistol in her pocket. She couldn't lift the weapon from the deep folds of her gown before Lord Cantley was upon her.

She gasped in pain when he forced the weapon from

her hand and the pistol fell to the dirt. Lord Cantley grabbed her, putting his hands around her neck.

"What is happening?" Jackson's shout split the night.

Lucinda saw him struggling with his bonds, but to no avail, since they were secured tightly to hold him in place. Lord Cantley dragged her around to where they were both facing Jackson.

"What little game are you and the witch playing?" Lord Cantley asked. "She never wanted to play games with me. If she had, I wouldn't have had to drug her with one of her own potions to take my pleasure of her."

Jackson had been struggling, but suddenly he stopped. "You did what to her?" he demanded.

"She didn't tell you?" Lord Cantley pulled Lucinda closer against him. "Then maybe she didn't mind so much after all."

Lucinda struggled, but his cruel fingers dug into her throat.

"Take your hands off of her!" Jackson demanded.

The earl laughed. "I've had them on her before," he taunted Jackson. "All over her. Of course she was unconscious and the thrill was dampened by her lack of response. I've been thinking a lot about that. Wondering what it would be like to have her again, when she's awake and fully conscious of what I'm doing to her. What do you say, Lucinda? Shall we have another go around?"

She stomped on his foot. He cussed and loosened his grip. She almost managed to twist away before he grabbed a handful of her long hair and pulled her back.

"You see now why I took the easier route of drugging her," he said to Jackson. "She's a spitfire. I knew that about her, but I wasn't expecting her to be virgin. That was a rather nice surprise. The babe. Now that wasn't a nice surprise."

"You leave him alone," Lucinda bit out, still struggling

despite the man having his hands around her throat again, cutting off her air supply.

"He has my mark, doesn't he? Otherwise you wouldn't have taken him and run. How did you get this man to marry you? I hope you didn't cuckold him into believing he sired the brat."

Jackson was enraged . . . and helpless. Lucinda should have told him the truth, but why did the earl care about Sebastian? Then Jackson remembered Lucinda saying the man was a cousin of the king. Royal blood. A bastard someday upon the throne. The mark to prove his heritage. Now a lot of things made sense. Lucinda knew Jackson had come to kill her that day in the cottage, but she thought he'd been one of this man's henchmen, come to make sure the babe he'd sired never drew breath.

The man slid one hand down Lucinda's neck and fondled her breast and Jackson saw red. Now Lucinda's reactions to him made sense, as well. She'd been drugged and used by this man, and although it seemed as if it was something she might not remember, it was the lack of control that had bothered her more than the attack itself. It was being helpless and at this man's mercy. He'd kill him.

The leather bonds cut into Jackson's wrists as he struggled to free himself. Damn, he'd made them tight so he couldn't escape and turn on Lucinda if the beast's rage rose up inside of him. And it was rising now.

"Maybe we should give you what you were wanting from the witch," the man said. "Or maybe she likes this. Either way, no need for you or her to go unfulfilled."

The man nodded in the direction behind Jackson. The whip suddenly whistled through the air and sliced into his back. Jackson jerked with the sting of it.

"No," he heard Lucinda gasp. "Please, don't hurt him. I did lie to him. He is the innocent caught in the middle.

Do what you will to me, but leave him alone. And my child, please do not hurt him."

"See how prettily she begs?" the man asked Jackson. "I didn't think she had it in her. Prideful woman, especially for being a witch. Turned up her nose at me. But she's not so haughty now, is she?"

Lord Cantley ran his tongue up the side of Lucinda's face. Jackson's rage grew stronger. He let it come, welcomed it. The whip whistled again, but he hardly felt the pain, so focused was he on Lucinda and the man who dared to touch her, dared to threaten both the woman and the child under Jackson's protection. Again the lash fell, only bringing the beast that much closer to the surface.

"Take me with you," he heard Lucinda plead again. "I'll do whatever you want, be whatever you want, if you will just leave him and the child alone!"

"You'll do that anyway!" the man spit back at her. "The child cannot live. You know that." The man glanced up at Jackson again. "I'll give her back to you when I'm finished with her, if there is anything left of either of you."

Jackson's strength grew with his rage. He yanked as hard as he could at the leather bonds around his wrists, pulling one hand free. The pain was in his stomach now, not in his back where the lashes had stung and cut. The smell of his own blood only drew the beast closer to the surface. Lord Cantley's face paled and he took a step back, dragging Lucinda along with him.

"What spell have you cast upon him, witch?"

"One that will be your death," Jackson answered the man, his voice low and gravelly. He felt the fangs lengthen in his mouth, flashed them in the eerie glow of the lantern light.

"Your pistol, man!" Lord Cantley shouted. "Draw it and shoot him!"

"You cannot kill it!" Lucinda hissed. "The beast that he becomes is beyond death. Run now, while you still can!"

Claws had jutted from Jackson's free hand. He used them to rip at his bonds, tried to maintain his human thoughts even as he felt the beast rush up to take him. He heard the sound of running feet behind him.

"Coward!" Lord Cantley shouted, Jackson could only assume at the man who'd been wielding the whip.

Jackson's thoughts were becoming harder to form, to hold on to. He'd almost gotten his bound wrist free. He felt the fur sprouting out from beneath his skin, felt his bones expanding and retracting, rearranging themselves for the change.

"Good God, he's a monster!"

Those were the last words he heard with the coherent thoughts of a man.

Chapter Twenty-two

Lucinda watched in fascinated horror as the change came upon Jackson. She smelled the cold sweat of Lord Cantley's fear now. He shoved her away from him.

"This isn't over," he assured her; then he ran like the coward he was.

She stood frozen for a moment, mesmerized by the sight of Jackson, still half man, half beast, struggling to free himself from his bonds. Then she remembered Sebastian. With a cry, she ran for the house. She stumbled in the darkness but kept on the path. A tall shape suddenly loomed before her.

"Didn't count on that bugger guarding the door," the man grumbled. "Gave me a good blow to the head and shoved me outside. Wait; you're not supposed to be roaming free," the man suddenly realized.

"Let me pass," Lucinda warned him. "Your master has run like the coward he is. If you're smart, you'll do the same."

"Lord Cantley said we was to take you with us. You

and the babe." He reached forward and made a grab for Lucinda.

She stumbled back, fell over a rock, and landed hard on her rump. The man chuckled over her clumsiness and stepped toward her.

"Come along quiet now," he warned. "I ain't above hitting a woman if I have to."

The man bent toward her, but before he could grab her, a dark shape leaped from behind Lucinda and knocked the man backward. She heard growling, saw the glowing blue eyes of the beast, and then heard the man scream. His screams gurgled in his throat and Lucinda struggled up, ran past the fallen man and the dark shape tearing out his throat. She rushed to the house, hurried inside, and nearly met with the butt of Hawkins's pistol.

"Lady Lucinda," Hawkins breathed. "I thought you were the intruder come back."

Lucinda quickly closed the door and threw home the locks. Her hands trembled. "Sebastian?"

"Fine, my lady," Hawkins assured her. "No one has gotten into the house except the one I pistol-whipped and threw out."

She tried to slow her racing heart and catch her breath.

"Lord Jackson?" Hawkins inquired. "Where is he?"

What to say? *Out yonder tearing out a man's throat?* Lucinda shuddered. "He took off in pursuit of the thieves," she lied.

"Perhaps I should go and help him," Hawkins suggested.

"No!" Lucinda wished she hadn't snapped the word. "I mean, he said to tell you to stay in the house and guard us until he returns."

Hawkins frowned. "Very well. You look pale. May I get you something, my lady?"

"Brandy," she rasped. "A good strong glass of brandy."

Hawkins inclined his head and went to fetch her drink. The back entrance was in the kitchen. Lucinda moved to a sturdy table where the servants ate their meals and seated herself. She was still trembling when Hawkins returned with a glass of amber liquid. She tipped it up and drank it all.

"What shall we do now, Lady Lucinda?" Hawkins inquired.

She nodded to a seat across from her. "We wait."

Hawkins had nodded off and Lucinda had trouble keeping her eyes open by the time she heard a soft rap on the back door. She rose and went to the door, pressing her ear against it. "Jackson?" she called.

"Yes, let me in," came his reply.

She struggled with the heavy locks and eased the door open. He stepped inside, dressed in the clothes he'd worn earlier, bloody and ragged looking.

"Are you all right?" she whispered, her heart pounding.

He nodded, although she took note of the haunted look in his eyes.

"Lord Jackson." Hawkins came awake with the relieved words. The steward quickly rose from the table and hurried toward him. "You're bleeding."

"It's not serious," Jackson assured the man. "But bring fresh water and bandages up to my room. Lucinda can help me up the stairs."

So saying, Jackson draped an arm around her neck and allowed her to help him through the house and up the stairs. Once in his room, he removed his shirt. Lucinda sucked in her breath at the sight of his bloody back. He had four bleeding lashes and one welt, the one she'd delivered in anger but without the obvious strength of the other four.

"Let me fetch my ointments." She hurried to her own room to snatch up the medicine she had made for him in advance. When she returned, Hawkins was there with the basin of clean water and bandages.

"May I assist you, Lord Jackson?"

"No, Hawkins, Lucinda has a skill with these matters. Find your bed. It's been a long night."

"You don't wish me to stand guard for the rest of the night, Lord Jackson?"

"The night is nearly gone," he answered, and Lucinda noticed he would not rise from the bed where he sat, his back shielded from Hawkins's sight. "They won't be coming back. Not for a while leastwise. Go to bed, Hawkins."

"As you wish," the man said, then quit the room.

Lucinda went to the basin, took clean cloths, and rinsed them in the cool water. She sat next to Jackson on the bed, and he turned to give her access. The ugly marks on his smooth back nearly made her sick. Yes, she had doctored such wounds before, but before they had always belonged to someone she was not emotionally tied to. This was much more difficult. He didn't flinch as she cleaned the wounds. They sat in silence, but she knew the silence wouldn't last long.

Finally, he said, "You lied to me."

Lucinda chose her words carefully. "I simply did not tell you the whole truth," she defended herself. "I thought if you knew Sebastian's father was intent on killing him, and that the man had ties to the king, you would not let us stay. You would not keep your promise to look after him."

"By keeping your secrets, you put us all in danger, Lucinda. Tonight might have turned out much worse than it did."

Tears pricked her eyes. He was right. She should have told him the moment he questioned her about Lord Cantley. "I knew your mind needed to be clear for the ritual. I planned to tell you after our attempt, regardless of what happened."

He turned to her, holding up his hands in front of her face. "There is blood on my hands," he said. "There is dirt beneath my fingernails from burying what was left of the man I killed for you."

Bile rose in her throat and she glanced away from him. "Will you put us out now?"

He rose from the bed and went to the basin, dipping his hands in the water to cleanse them before he picked up a strong bar of soap and scrubbed. "Leave you and Sebastian to fend for yourselves against a man who has the king's ear? A man who would murder his own son and misuse the child's mother?" He turned to look at her. "You have lived beneath this roof with me for long enough to know me better than that. It stings sharper than the whip that you do not."

Bowing her head, she could not argue with him. A moment later, she felt the soft touch of his fingers against her chin. He lifted her face to look up at him.

"But maybe I gave you no reasons to trust me. Maybe you were wiser not to. You should have told me about Lord Cantley. You should have told me what he did to you."

"Would you have believed me?" she asked. "In the beginning, would you have trusted my word any more than I could have trusted yours? I have been called whore all of my life, even though I was pure when Lord Cantley drugged me with a potion I had brought for his laboring wife. Why should I have believed for one moment that I could confide in you and you would hear my words and count them as truth?"

His hand moved up her face, where he cupped her cheek. "I knew the first moment I kissed you, you were no whore, Lucinda. A whore takes greedily of her pleasure, and yet you would deny yourself, and me the pleasure of teaching you the joy to be found in a man's touch."

"I was afraid," she admitted. "The loss of control I felt stealing over me. A feeling of helplessness against my own body's betrayal. I do not remember what Lord Cantley did to me while I lay unconscious and defenseless against him. But my mind provides details that are probably worse than they were."

"I should have killed him tonight," Jackson said. He dropped his hand from her cheek and walked back to the basin. A clean pitcher of water sat on the table. Jackson went to the window, opened it, retrieved the basin, and threw the water outside. He wiped out the basin with a clean cloth, refilled it, and went about the business of washing his face and cleaning his mouth. Lucinda rose from the bed, retrieved her liniment, and joined him, careful as she applied the salve to his raw back while he finished cleaning himself.

"What now?" she asked. "It won't end tonight. I would go if it was only me Lord Cantley wanted. But Sebastian . . ."

He turned suddenly. "You will not take him from here," he said sternly. "You cannot protect him, Lucinda. Against a powerful man you cannot even protect yourself. Neither of you will go, do you understand?"

At the passion in his voice, she nodded. "But what will we do? He said it wasn't over. He won't give up so easily, Jackson. He's a man used to having what he wants, and doing as he pleases."

Jackson ran a hand through his long hair, pulling it back from his handsome features. "I don't know. I will have to think on it."

Lucinda gasped when she saw the raw skin around his wrists where he'd fought his bonds. She smeared salve upon her fingers, lifted one wrist, and began rubbing the ointment into his frayed skin.

"The man . . ." She paused to take a breath. "What did you do with his body?"

"I buried him deep in the ground next door," he answered. "The beast did not hold me for long once it had killed him. I came to staring into the man's sightless eyes and tasting his blood in my mouth."

She shuddered. "Lord Cantley could go to the king about us," she said. "He could have us both burned at the stake."

"But he will not," Jackson said. "He'll want to take care of his dirty deeds himself. He will want to erase the proof of his indiscretions with no one the wiser."

"Maybe," Lucinda agreed, taking his other wrist in her hand to doctor. "If he doesn't, you must say that I cast a spell over you, Jackson. You have wealth and your family has lands and titles. I am no one. I—"

He placed a finger against her lips. "Why do you demean yourself, Lucinda? Why can you not see how special you are? You use your gifts for good, not evil. You save lives. You give of yourself and expect nothing in return, with, I suppose, the exception of our bargain."

His words sent warmth through her, but they also brought guilt. She glanced away from him. "I have failed in our bargain," she whispered. "Tonight, I could not drive the beast from you."

Reaching out, he brought her face around to look at him again. "It's better that we keep him for now. We may have need of him."

Her mouth dropped open. "You would remain cursed for us? A woman who deceived you and a child not of your own seed?"

"Until this business is behind us," he answered. "We

don't have much time to make plans. I have much to think about. You are tired. Go to bed."

Jackson moved to his own bed and sat. He removed his boots and she saw that the effort pained him.

"I'll need to bandage that back first," she said. "Stay put while I do it."

Moving to the table, Lucinda retrieved the bandages that Hawkins had brought up. She joined Jackson on the bed and began to carefully wrap him. She tried to be as gentle as possible. His skin was warm and smooth beneath her hands, all but his back. He would carry the scars of tonight with him always. And it was her fault. She couldn't believe he had placed the most important thing in his life, breaking his curse, aside for her and Sebastian.

Jackson thought he had no honor, but he had more than any other man she had known. He had told her she was special. And tonight Lucinda felt her own worth for the first time. Tending to him, she realized whatever curse was upon her, as well, could also be counted as a blessing. She moved around to kneel before Jackson, crisscrossing the bandages from back to chest in order to keep them in place. When she felt his eyes on her, she glanced up at him. Their eyes locked and held before he glanced away from her.

Lucinda reached up and turned his face back toward her. Maybe it was time for her to trust someone. To trust him. She leaned forward and touched her lips to his. He allowed the gentle contact for a moment before he turned his head away.

"You don't owe me anything, Lucinda," he said.

Reaching, she turned his face toward her again. "Yes, I do. More than I can ever repay you. But this is not about that."

"What is it about?" he asked.

It was about her feelings for him and allowing them recognition. But mostly it was about . . . "Letting go," she answered. "Teach me the joys so that not only the dark deeds are in my mind. Chase them away."

He looked away again. "The night's events have made you emotional. You don't know what you're asking."

"There is no scent upon you now," she said. "No reason to ask except the true one. I want you."

His gaze came back to her. He stared deep into her eyes and she saw the first spark of blue flame. "You pick an odd time to challenge my virility."

She lowered her gaze. "I didn't mean tonight. I know you are injured." Lucinda started to rise, but his hands grasped her shoulders and held her in place.

"We may not have tomorrow," he said.

Then he leaned forward and kissed her.

Chapter Twenty-three

His lips were warm and firm, his breath fresh with the mint he'd used to cleanse his mouth. Lucinda drank from him, drew from his strength, and lost herself in the wonder of his mouth. His hands slid up to her face, his fingers raking through her hair to hold her to him, which he had no reason to do. She did not want to escape.

The lamps flickered low, and again Lucinda wondered if he could somehow command the more intimate lighting . . . or if perhaps the talent was hers. His hands slid down to her shoulders again and he pulled her up off of her knees. His slight wince reminded her that he'd been injured, and she felt a stab of guilt for causing him to exert himself.

"I should go," she whispered.

"No. Stay with me."

For a moment, she could close her eyes and pretend that he meant for more than only tonight. Lucinda settled on the bed next to him. He stretched out, again wincing when his back met with the soft mattress of the bed.

"You fear the loss of control," he said. "I give it to you tonight. I am yours to command."

For him to take the passive role, she imagined, was further torture for him. Yet he would surrender his power to ease her fears. It was the strongest form of seduction.

Lucinda crawled toward him on the bed. Leaning over him, she kissed his neck. Moving lower, she tasted his skin through the crisscross of his bandages. Jackson made a low sound in his throat, but his hands remained at his sides.

She worked her way back up to his mouth, teasing him with her tongue until he met her challenge. They stayed that way for a time, kissing, until her hands began to roam. She ran her fingers down his bandaged chest to his navel and followed the intriguing line of dark hair that disappeared into the waistband of his trousers. Her hand slid lower, over the front of his trousers where she found the proof of his desire evident. She heard the slight intake of his breath, but still he did not touch her.

Her hand moved back up the rigid bulge to his waist-band, where she unfastened his trousers. Opening them allowed him to spring forth, and she again marveled at his size and his magnificence. Her hand closed around him and he jerked involuntarily, although again he did not reach for her or touch her. Touching him was a lesson in contradiction. Hardness covered by velvet skin, hot and hard in her hand. Touching him also had a strange effect on her. She wanted the feel of his hands on her, as well.

Sliding up and off of him, Lucinda unbuttoned her gown down the front. Jackson watched her fingers like a man mesmerized, only the ragged rise and fall of his chest an indication that she affected him. She shoved the gown down around her waist, then reached for the silk ribbon of her chemise and slowly pulled it free, lowering the straps off of her shoulders.

Jackson stared, his eyes glowing bright blue in the dim lighting, but he did not touch. Not until she took his hands and guided them to her aching breasts. He cupped her, moved his thumbs across her nipples until they hardened. She slid her hand through his hair to cup the back of his head, rising on her knees to straddle him before pulling his mouth to her breasts. He took her nipple in his mouth and sucked, licked, and even bit, although only tenderly. Throwing back her head, Lucinda savored the feel of his mouth moving over her breasts, tasting and teasing until the gentle throb between her legs intensified.

Her fingers still twisted in his hair, she pulled his head back to look up at her. She bent to capture his mouth, slowly sinking down to sit on top of him. His hips arched up into her, an involuntary response, she realized. The friction was not unpleasant. As their mouths worked against each other, below, the steady press of male and female parts against each other made breathing difficult. She suddenly felt on fire.

"Undress me," she whispered.

Hers to command, Jackson pulled her fully down on top of him. He used his legs to push hers together so he could shove her clothing down her body as far as his hands would reach and unfastening anything he encountered along the way. While their mouths were still joined, their tongues still entwined, his hands brushed over her bare bottom, light enough to make her shiver. Lucinda wiggled out of the clothes tangled around her hips.

She tugged at Jackson's trousers, sliding down the whole length of him in order to remove them. Once she sat at his feet, her gaze roamed him, sprawled naked before her. His beauty nearly stole her breath. Slowly, she ran her hands up his legs, his thighs, muscular and the same golden tone as the rest of him. She was at an impasse.

"I'm not sure what to do next," she said.

"What do you want, Lucinda?" he asked, his voice low and husky.

"I want you to touch me again," she answered. "The way you touched me downstairs in the dining room."

"Come here."

She crawled back up the bed and settled beside him. First, he kissed her—a long, languid kiss that had her melting against him. His hand slid down her stomach, lower to the nest of curls between her legs. From the first soft stroke of his fingers, she was his. He was gentle until she pressed harder against his fingers, arched into him.

The pressure kept building, and between breathless kisses she moaned his name. Jackson slipped his finger into her, nearly causing her to gouge his shoulders with her nails.

"You feel so hot, so tight," he said against her lips, and even the raw sound of his voice pushed her higher.

She was close to losing control, and for a moment she fought surrender, but then Lucinda remembered this was her choice, her doing. She could trust him.

"I want more," she whispered. The press of him against her leg was what she wanted. Him inside of her. How her body knew what her mind did not question. Not tonight. Not now.

"Are you sure?" he asked.

"Yes," she answered without hesitation.

He pushed her onto her back, and then he was on top of her, wedged between her legs. She braced herself for what would follow, but instead of rushing, he bent to kiss her again, slid his hand between them, and continued to stimulate her. She was sensitive, unable to control the quiver of her thighs or the way she rocked against his fin-

gers. He took her nearly to the breaking point, and then
she felt him, poised and ready at her woman's entrance.
He did not rush forward but gently eased into her, a little
at a time.

Lucinda knew much about her own body, women's
bodies in general, since she'd been called upon at such a
young age to deliver children. Normally, he would meet
with a barrier, but Lord Cantley had taken that from her.
Tears gathered in her eyes that he had stolen what had
been her right to give.

"Am I hurting you, Lucinda?" Jackson's lips touched
the tear that had escaped down her cheek.

She shook her head. "No. T-this should be my first
time."

"It is your first time," he said. "Your first time with me.
And it is my first time with you."

He kissed her, sliding deeper into her, stretching her so
that she gasped against his mouth. He was large and filled
her completely. Completely and then some. Then he began to move, and move in a way that stimulated her even
more than his fingers had done. She caught the rhythm
and moved with him, his deep groans of pleasure only an
aphrodisiac that greater fueled her passion.

They moved together, kissed, broke apart to gasp, and
kissed again when their breathing would allow it. The pressure inside of her began to build again, stronger than before. Sweat coated their bodies. His scent was on her, and
something primal rose up inside of her. She bucked harder
against him, her head thrashing against the pillow until he
captured her face with his hands and kissed her again.

When she opened her eyes and looked at him, he was
looking at her. His eyes were twin balls of blue fire, and
just the sight of them sent her spiraling out of control. Her
body arched, convulsed, and pleasure so intense it was
painful washed over her. She clung to him, her nails bit-

ing into his shoulders, her teeth biting into his neck. Then
he thrust deep, seemed to hold himself there for a second
before he suddenly pulled out of her, his body jerking, his
breath ragged as he spilled his seed outside of her womb.

She held him to her until her own shudders quieted and
he lay spent and breathing hard against her, their hearts
pounding in unison against each other. Then her hand
moved down his back and she felt the blood.

"Your back," she gasped. "I've hurt you."

He nuzzled the skin of her throat. "It's nothing," he
said. "I could die right now and die a happy man."

She smiled, feeling so very right in this man's bed,
skin against skin, heart against heart. "You must let me
bandage it again," she said, running her hands through his
silky long hair.

"No point in doing it yet." He rose on his elbows,
looked down at her, and kissed her again. "I'm just going
to break it open again."

"You're sure about that?" she asked saucily.

He was nothing but serious when he answered, "Yes."

Jackson awoke first to the sharp stinging in his back. He
tried to move only to find a woman sprawled halfway
across him. The second discovery made the first more
bearable. He lifted Lucinda's red curls from her face and
brushed them back. A sensuous smile curved her lips
while she slept. Jackson wanted her again immediately.
Then it occurred to him that she had at last surrendered to
him, and the realization made him turn inward.

He did not feel any differently than he had yesterday.
Glancing back down at Lucinda, he admitted that was not
the truth. The beast still lived inside of him, but so did
feelings of passion and of tenderness for Lucinda that
were now stronger than they'd been the day before. Yes,

there had been women in his past, too many women, but none were like her.

None had made him feel the way she had last night. As if it were his first time with a woman. No need for drink to blight the pain of his loneliness or to wonder, when he sobered, if she would have wanted him without the animal magnetism his scent put out.

She had not wanted his scent. She had wanted him. And without the liquor to dull his senses he had wanted her, more than any woman before she came into his life. Only Lucinda truly made him feel as if he belonged. And perhaps it was only a feeling of belonging to her. But it was something that had evaded him all of his life.

"What are you thinking?"

He glanced down to see her staring up at him. Jackson ran his finger down her creamy shoulder. "I'm wondering if my back will protest too much if I make love to you again this morning."

"More than your back will protest," she said. "What have you done to my body?" She tried to move and groaned.

"Not nearly as much as I'd like to do," he answered, kissing the top of her head.

"Perhaps after I've had a good long soak, and tended to your back, we can discuss the matter again."

He sighed. "All right. We have other matters to attend to as well this morning."

Her eyes met his. Like him, he supposed, she had welcomed the opportunity not to think about last night or their current dilemma. Jackson had murdered a man. To his knowledge, his first. But it had not been he who had torn the man's throat out. The beast had done that, but would the man have done any differently when Lucinda was being threatened? No, he did not believe so.

"I need to see Sebastian," she suddenly whispered. "I need to hold him."

Jackson eased her weight off of him, tantalized by the feel of her warm, soft skin, then rose from the bed. He went to his wardrobe, pulled out a pair of clean trousers, and slipped them on. For Lucinda's sake, he tried not to wince every time his movements pulled at the lashes on his back. Tugging on a shirt was pure torture. Funny, he didn't remember his back bothering him nearly so much last night.

"I'll get him," he said. "Stay put."

Lucinda pulled the covers up and tucked them beneath her arms. She looked very tempting waiting in his bed. Almost too tempting to resist, but he should have a care to not only his own injuries but also the demands he'd already placed on her throughout the night. *Later,* he promised himself.

Sebastian's nurse always looked nervous when Jackson entered the room. Soon they would have no further need for her. Sebastian was growing and a bit of cereal and a transfer to goat's milk was in his near future.

"The lady wishes me to bring her son," Jackson explained to Martha. The woman nodded and stayed out of his way. Jackson walked to the cradle and smiled down at the boy. Upon seeing Jackson he grinned his toothless grin.

"Hello, little man," Jackson said, then reached down and plucked him from the cradle. It surprised him how natural he felt now while holding Sebastian. And how someone so small could tug so strongly at his heartstrings. "Your mother would like a word with you," he said to Sebastian, carrying him from the nursery and into Jackson's bedchamber.

Lucinda had her arms outstretched before he even reached the bed. "Give him to me."

Sebastian let out a little squeal of excitement upon seeing his mother. Jackson could hardly blame the boy. He handed Sebastian to Lucinda, watching as she brought the babe to her and spread kisses over his face.

"Ah, to be young again," Jackson said, smiling at her when she glanced up at him.

She giggled. It was delightful. His dark thoughts could no longer be held at bay, and he sat upon the bed, watching as Lucinda played with Sebastian. "We cannot deal with Lord Cantley here in London," he said. "He is too well protected."

Little Sebastian's fingers curled around her finger, she glanced up at Jackson. "Should we flee?"

"I don't like to think of it as running but rather leading him away."

"To where?" she asked. "The country estate?"

He shook his head. "I will not bring this business to Armond and Rosalind's door."

"But he's your brother," she argued. "He could help us."

"And we could very well get them killed, as well," he explained. "Besides, the curse comes upon me soon. He does not know. I would rather him not know, at least for now."

"Has this to do with your pride?" she asked.

It was a good question, and Jackson thought long and hard about it before he answered. "You and Sebastian are my responsibility, Lucinda. I need you to trust me. I need you to have faith in me, so that I can have faith in myself."

She glanced down at her son. Jackson needed her to trust in him so desperately. To believe in him. But could she when her life and her son's life were in jeopardy?

When she glanced back up at Jackson, her eyes softened. "All right, Jackson. I will trust in you. Together, we will come up with a plan."

Chapter Twenty-four

Once Lucinda had a long bath and short nap, she returned to Jackson's room with needle and thread. "While we talk of plans, I am going to stitch your back," she said. "Otherwise I fear the slashes will never heal."

She took note of his hip tub still sitting in the center of the room. His hair was damp and he'd obviously removed his bandages before his bath, since his chest was bare. Her heart did a sudden lurch at the sight of him. Her thoughts were not at all in line with his continued healing. Lucinda climbed onto the bed and patted the mattress. "Sit here."

"If you want to get me into bed again all you need do is say so, Lucinda," he teased.

"Now, none of your nonsense," she scolded, but she couldn't hide her smile. He sat and her smile faded. The ugly lashes oozed blood. "Have you been stitched before?" she asked.

"Not that I recall," he answered. "But then, there is a large portion of my life I don't recall much of over the past year."

"It will hurt," she warned him.

"I would think it might be better to lie to your patients in a situation such as this one," he suggested.

She smiled again. "All right, it won't hurt at all."

"Too late," he muttered.

Lucinda had chosen her smallest needle, she hoped to make the scars less noticeable, but it would also call for using more force to push it through the skin. She took a deep breath and started. "We should discuss our plan now," she said. "It will help take your mind off of what I am doing."

"My plan is to lead Lord Cantley from London and kill him," he said matter-of-factly.

She felt no sympathy for Lord Cantley, he was a cruel man and a threat to her son, but she wished further killing and Jackson putting his life in jeopardy could be avoided. She didn't know how. Certainly she'd tried to cast spells to make Lord Cantley forget her when she'd been hiding in the woods. They hadn't worked. Lucinda wasn't nearly as skilled as her mother had been, yet Lucinda's healing abilities were stronger.

"He won't come after you alone," Lucinda assured him. "I will have to come along as bait."

"No," Jackson argued. "I want you and Sebastian somewhere safe when I deal with him."

"He won't follow you if you're alone," she insisted. "It's me and Sebastian he's after. Mostly Sebastian," she added. "I won't put him in danger, though."

"No," Jackson agreed. "And as much as I hate it, you're probably right about him not coming after me alone."

Silence settled between them as she stitched. Lucinda knew that Jackson would feel the needle more if she didn't keep him distracted. "We have to fool him in some way," she continued. "Make him believe a lie."

"I suppose we could pretend we're fleeing to the country estate," he said. "We could use a doll in place of Sebastian and instruct Hawkins and the nurse to take him somewhere safe. I'm guessing Lord Cantley will send some of his henchmen to accost us on the road. He'll want us brought to his country manor, or somewhere close, to deal with us."

"I don't think it's a good idea to allow them to accost us," Lucinda spoke up. "What if Lord Cantley simply instructs them to kill us on sight?"

"Once they realize Sebastian is not with us, they'll have to have at least one of us to torture his location from," Jackson said. "You would be the likely one chosen."

"Perhaps not," she said. "They would assume you would care less." Lucinda had almost finished with his back. The gouges were long but not as deep as she first thought them to be. It occurred to her to ask Jackson what she'd wondered the night they attended the ball with the dowager.

"Do the people of Whit Hurch know who you are?" she asked. "Did you introduce yourself to them by name?"

"No, not my real one," he answered. "I was trying to get information about you in a subtle manner, and thought giving them my name would only raise their suspicions about me. My family is not unheard of even in the small villages. Why do you ask?"

"I worried about that when I first saw Lord Cantley at the ball," she said. "I was afraid if he knew you had once been snooping around Whit Hurch, he would put two and two together and realize I was in fact who he thought me to be. Of course now it doesn't matter. He knows who I am, and who you are."

"But he still doesn't know exactly what I am," Jackson

said. "He didn't stay long enough to see the transformation."

"He saw enough to be leery," she assured him. Finished with her stitching, Lucinda rose from the bed, went to the table where her healing salve and more bandages sat, and scooped them up before returning. "I still don't like the idea of us allowing Lord Cantley to capture us. Neither of us will come to any good at his hands."

"I don't intend to be captured," Jackson said. "And there is no way in hell I would allow that man to get his hands on you again, Lucinda."

Lucinda opened the jar of salve and began coating Jackson's wounds. Her hands shook slightly at just the thought of Lord Cantley touching her. Not now, not after she knew what it was to be with a man she desired. And desired above all others. Once Jackson's back was coated, she began bandaging him again.

"When do we leave?"

"This afternoon," he answered. "If we don't look as if we are making haste, Lord Cantley will find it suspicious. Best to force him into action quickly. Pack a small bag, one with clothes easy for riding. We'll take to the woods again. Keep that in mind."

"My old things," she decided. Which brought to mind her old life. In a sense, if they did manage to draw Lord Cantley away from London, and to escape the henchmen he might send after them, she would be returning to what she'd known before Jackson came into her life. The feelings that realization stirred in her told her something else. She did not want to go back. Not ever. But there wasn't time now to figure out if last night had changed more between them than a bargain once made. A bargain she had not kept. A bargain he had forsaken for the time being . . . for her and for Sebastian.

Having finished bandaging Jackson, she thought to move off the bed, but he turned and blocked her escape. "It's an uncertain future we have ahead of us," he said. "I would love you again in case the option is not there later."

She nearly melted at the heat in his eyes, but her practical mind would not see her work undone. "Not until you're better healed," she said. "It is not a good time for you to be fleeing a man bent on killing my son, or breaking your back open pleasing a woman, Jackson."

He frowned and she thought it was because she would deny him, but he said, "Can't he be *our* son, Lucinda? He took my heart the moment I first held him and heard his cry of life. I have vowed to you to watch over him, to feed him, clothe him, and protect him. Doesn't that make me his father?"

She couldn't stop the rush of tears that moistened her eyes. If she didn't love Jackson before this moment, she loved him now. She would always love him. "Yes," she answered. "To me, you are his father."

He looked well pleased with her answer, and then he leaned forward and kissed her. How convincing he could be, she decided a moment later when she nearly melted into him and his tongue dipped into her mouth, setting her blood on fire. It took a great deal of effort to break from the kiss and push him away.

"Your back," she reminded, then smiled at his frown. "Besides, if we are to leave shortly, there is much to be done. Get me safely to the woods that surround Whit Hurch and we will discuss the matter further."

"Sounds like a bribe," he said, still frowning. "I'll hold you to that promise," he assured her.

Teasing faded as the task ahead settled over them. Jackson rose, grabbed up his shirt, and slipped it over his broad shoulders. "You'd best go and tell the nurse a measure of what is happening. I'll have a talk with Hawkins."

For a moment, she wanted to return to their teasing and forget they had trouble waiting for them around the next corner. But she could not, and nodding, she went to do what he instructed, her mind reeling with sudden worry. Maybe she should have let him make love to her again, his stitches be damned. Maybe there would not be another chance. She closed her eyes and tried to see into her future, but there was only darkness.

Jackson and Lucinda made a great show of packing to leave the London town house throughout the day. Empty trunks were loaded on the coach in front of the house so that anyone who passed would see that a trip was under way. Inside the house, Jackson and Lucinda were giving Hawkins and Martha last-minute orders.

Lucinda held Sebastian to her, placing soft kisses on his head and looking as if she would break into tears at any moment. Jackson hated separating them, but it was for Sebastian's safety that he must.

"Do you understand what you are to do?" Jackson asked Hawkins.

The steward nodded. "Tonight, under cover of darkness, I am to take Martha and young Sebastian to her sister's home on the east side. Tomorrow at first light, I am to hire an unobtrusive hack to take us all to the country estate."

Jackson took the steward's arm and led him a short distance away. "And?" he prompted quietly.

Hawkins would not meet his gaze. "And if you and your lady do not return to us at the country estate, I am to ask Lord and Lady Wulf to raise the boy as they would their own."

"Good," Jackson said. "And if only Lucinda returns?"

"She is to have all the honors and privileges of being your wife. As your firstborn, Sebastian will be your heir."

"You will make that understood?"

"Most certainly," Hawkins assured him.

Jackson patted him upon the shoulder. "Good man." He turned back toward the women. "Lucinda, it is time for us to go."

She seemed to draw on her strength, reluctantly handing Sebastian back to Martha. "Take good care of him," she said.

The wet nurse nodded.

Earlier, Jackson had sent Hawkins into the heart of London to purchase a doll. Lucinda now held the doll. Wrapped in Sebastian's blankets, the doll could easily pass for the real thing at a distance. Jackson walked to the nurse, placed a kiss on Sebastian's head, then took Lucinda's arm, escorting her to the door.

Hawkins followed them, as it would look odd if the steward did not come outside to see them off. Jackson glanced up at the coach driver.

"Remember your instructions," Jackson said. "At the fist sign of trouble, you are to stop the coach, climb down, and make for any safe ground you can find."

Thomas nodded. "Aye, but you know I don't mind fighting at your side," he added.

"We discussed that already," Jackson reminded him. "It is not an option."

The footman, a young man who also knew his instructions, got the door. As Jackson handed Lucinda up into the coach, he said to the young man, "Keep your eyes trained behind you. You're too young to take a ball in the back." Then Jackson climbed up into the coach beside Lucinda, allowing the footman to secure the door. The coach lurched forward. Jackson drew the drapes down, immediately tugging at his high stock and loosening his cravat. He removed his jacket, reached for his valise, and withdrew two pistols, which he laid on the seat beside him.

Taking her cue from him, Lucinda opened her valise and removed one of the coarser gowns she'd brought with her to London. Having her undress was the worst distraction, but he kept his ears trained for trouble. He doubted that Lord Cantley would try anything until they left the city but wouldn't underestimate the man.

Not long afterward, Lucinda sat across from Jackson, her long red hair down around her shoulders, wearing a simple work frock that had seen better days. She reminded him again of the witch he'd gone searching for months past. She was beautiful, had an earthy look that appealed to him. She had a lusty nature in bed that also appealed to him. She wasn't a woman he would ever grow tired of or bored with.

"Stop looking at me that way," she said softly, a smile tugging at her full lips. "Your mind should be on other matters."

"Am I so obvious?" he asked.

Her gaze slid over him and focused on the front of his trousers. "Yes," she answered. "You are very obvious."

Now that Lucinda had dressed, Jackson rolled up the drape next to his window. The summer coach didn't have paned glass in the windows, so that air could move freely through the coach. He stuck his head out the window, watching the city fade behind them. It would soon be dark. He hoped if Lord Cantley sent henchmen after them or even came himself, they would strike before night fell. It would be to Jackson's benefit if they did not, due to his superior eyesight in the dark, but it would not be an advantage for the coachman and the footman.

The idea had no more formed than a ball went racing past Jackson's face. He quickly ducked his head back inside the coach and glanced at Lucinda, saw her face blanch; then, as Thomas had been instructed, the coach was suddenly slowing to a stop.

"Get down on the floor," Jackson said to Lucinda. "Cover your head with your hands."

He waited until she obeyed; then, scooping up his pistols, he kicked the coach door open with his booted foot and lunged outside. Jackson rolled on the ground, tried to ignore the protest in his back, and came up, training the pistols on the four horsemen bearing down on the coach. He took aim at the man in the lead, pulled the trigger, and watched him fall from the saddle. A bullet kicked up dust next to Jackson's right foot. He took aim with the second pistol, and squeezed the trigger and another rider fell.

Jackson's odds were looking better, until he heard the thunder of hooves approaching from the other direction. He wheeled around. Four more riders headed toward the coach. Without Thomas on top, the coach horses started to rear and jiggled the coach.

"Run, Jackson!"

He glanced at the coach. Lucinda had crawled to the door. She saw what was happening.

"There are too many!" she shouted. "Go while you have the chance! Run!"

"I won't leave you here with them!" he shouted back, quickly reloading his pistols. Jackson took aim at the four riders approaching now from the front of the coach, managing to drop one of the riders.

"They won't kill me!" Lucinda tried. "Not if I'm the only one left with the knowledge of where Sebastian is! Go now, Jackson, and you can help me escape later. Stay and you won't be alive to help me!"

Another bullet whizzed past, grazing his left arm. Jackson jerked with the sting.

"Jackson!" Lucinda screamed. "Please!"

He had sworn to her that he would not let this happen—that he would not let her be taken. Jackson had no choice. If he grabbed Lucinda and they both tried to run, she might get shot in the cross fire. She was right. They wouldn't harm her. Lord Cantley would have issued strict instructions to bring her to him if she was captured.

"He will not touch you again!" Jackson swore to her; then he ran. Two riders broke off to give chase, but the roads were lined with forests and Jackson made much easier progress through the thick foliage than a horse and rider could. He let his instincts guide him, ran faster, he knew, than a normal man could even imagine. His eyesight sharpened, and ahead he saw paths no horse could take, paths perhaps no mortal man could see through the thick forest. He took them, winding his way ever farther from the coach, from Lucinda, and feeling the man inside of him slip away and the beast rise up to save him.

Chapter Twenty-five

Lucinda sat on a log close to the fire. There were five men stirring around the camp. She didn't recognize any of them from Whit Hurch. These looked like rough thugs whom Lord Cantley might have hired from the London docks. They obviously knew little about her, except that she was to be taken to Lord Cantley. She and the child, which they had already discovered was not a child but a doll.

She shivered when she felt their eyes on her. What lady riding in a grand coach dressed as she dressed? They were curious, and worse, they were interested in her as a woman. They stared at her lustfully, if, so far, none had dared to touch her.

"What do you think he wants with her?" one of the men spoke up.

"None of our business," another grumbled. "He just said to bring her and the child to him and not to touch either of them. Said we won't get the rest of our coin if we don't do exactly as he says."

"We ain't got the child," another said. "Think he won't pay us as much?"

"Shut up," the grumbler instructed. "We had nothing to do with the child not being in the coach. He'll have to take that up with yonder lovely. We'll get our coin, or he won't get the woman."

"Right," another piped up. "He doesn't pay, he doesn't get her . . . then we can have her."

"Don't see why we can't have her anyway," the man across from her whined. "She's got a brat. She ain't no virgin maid. No difference in a woman being had by one man or one hundred after that. It's all the same."

"Shut up," the grumbler snarled again. "Don't be putting ideas in the others' heads. With the coin we make for bringing this one to him, we can have a hundred just like her."

The whiner stood, moving to stand before Lucinda. He took a lock of her hair between his fingers. "Not like this one," he argued. "Look at that pale skin, those eyes that shoot daggers at me for daring to touch her. Her hair is like the sun."

Lucinda jerked back when the man's dirty hand came close to her face. "I am a witch," she spit. "Did he tell you that?"

The man before her took a step back. "A witch?" He glanced at the grumbler, who Lucinda realized was the leader of sorts of the ragtag group. "You didn't say nothing about her being a witch!"

The grumbler was suddenly on his feet. He marched over, grabbed the whiner by the scruff of his shirt, and shoved him away. "She's lying. If she was a witch she wouldn't be in this predicament, now, would she? She'd turn us all to toads and go about her merry way."

Lucinda wished in that moment that her powers could

be used for something other than good. Could she cast a spell over these men? Could she turn them into toads? She closed her eyes for a moment, but all she heard was her mother's voice.

In this hard life, evil will call to you. Resist the urge to become its handmaiden, or you will be lost to the dark side. Once you are lost, you will never find your way back to the light. Do not go there, Lucinda. Promise me, your gifts will only be used for goodness, for love, for healing.

Lucinda had promised. Where was Jackson? He had escaped; she'd seen that with her own eyes, relieved when two riders had returned to report they had lost him in the forest. He would come for her. She had to be patient.

"You still resemble a man to me, although you do have a toadyish look about you," the leader teased the other man. "Leave her alone," he said with less teasing. "You will not spoil the stew by stirring a pot better left alone."

The whiner glanced broodingly toward her but moved away and took his seat, staring into the fire. Lucinda released her breath slowly. She was safe, at least for the moment. Not long after, the leader ordered bedrolls laid out. One man was ordered to guard the camp while the others slept. Lucinda was shoved down upon a dirty blanket, the leader taking a position not far from her.

She tried to close her eyes and sleep, but it would not come to her. Jackson was somewhere out in the darkness. Had he managed to track them? When would he come? Soon, she hoped, very soon. Lucinda lay awake for a time, listening to the crackle of the fire, the night sounds, the light snoring of the men. In the distance, a twig snapped. Perhaps the man posted to guard the camp moving about. So intent on listening for the distant sound, Lucinda didn't hear the closer danger. A hand was suddenly clamped over her mouth. The whiner knelt over her. He brought his hand up and the glint of a knife flashed.

"Ssshhh," he whispered. "Make no sound, or I'll cut you up."

Her heart slammed against her chest. His scent gagged her, that and his dirty hand pressed hard against her mouth. He made no bones about what he wanted, laying the knife down in order to shove her frock up around her knees. She struggled, but quick as a cat, he had the knife up and pressed against her cheek.

"Don't fight me and I won't cut you," he whispered. "No one has to be the wiser about what we do together tonight."

Slicing her up seemed more appealing to Lucinda than what he had in mind. So deciding, she prepared to bite him and scream her head off when he yanked his hand back from her mouth. She prepared herself for the move, but she was not prepared for what leaped from the darkness onto the man's back. The man toppled sideways, frantically trying to get the beast off of his back.

The leader came awake quickly. "What the bloody hell," he croaked, jumping to his feet. One look at the man being torn apart by a wolf and he grabbed for his pistol. Lucinda glanced down, saw the knife lying on the ground, and hurriedly bent to retrieve it. She didn't think as the man took aim. She merely reacted. Lunging forward, she buried the knife into the leader's chest. His eyes widened. He glanced at the knife protruding from his chest and stumbled back. The man collapsed.

The other men came awake, obviously confused by what was taking place. Lucinda knew if she didn't run now, she might not have a chance later. She was torn, torn between trying to help Jackson—and it was Jackson, she knew—and escaping while she had the chance. The whiner now lay motionless. The wolf turned on the next man closest. Lucinda had to trust in Jackson. He'd asked that of her, been so desperate for her to believe in him.

With a cry, she ran into the woods. She didn't get far before she stumbled and fell, landing on top of a man. The guard. His eyes stared sightlessly up at the stars, his neck bloody and torn. She nearly screamed. Scrambling up, she took off again. Behind her, she did hear a scream. A man's scream.

She ran as fast as her feet would carry her, although she had no idea in which direction she was running and often tree and bush branches tore at her clothing and scratched her face. She ran from her captors, but deep inside she knew that she also ran from Jackson. He said he did not know his own mind when the beast took him. Yet the beast knew to follow the scent of men, or her scent. The beast knew to attack the man who was trying to force himself upon Lucinda, or was it just that the man was moving about while the others were still?

Farther and farther she ran. Pain stitched her side, her breathing was ragged, and thirst made her mouth dry, but she dared not stop, dared not rest. The light of dawn was a blessed sight. Only when the sky lightened from gray to blue did she stop to rest. Lucinda collapsed on a soft bed of pine needles. She raised her hand to brush her hair from her face, and then in the light of day she saw the blood staining her hands. She rolled over and retched. She had killed a man. *One who would have killed Jackson,* she reminded herself. But good Lord, what if the wolf had simply been a wolf?

She was borrowing trouble and she knew it. No ordinary wolf attacked a group of men, not while a fire still burned in their camp. It was Jackson. He had called upon the power of the beast, and it had come to him. When she saw him again, if she saw him again, would it be as a man or as a beast? Would she run gladly into his arms or run as fast as she could away from him?

The sound of a stream gurgling in the distance reached

her as she sat, struggling with her thoughts and her guilt over killing a man. Lucinda rose and moved toward the sound. It was farther than she thought, and she was already drenched in perspiration when she reached the babbling brook. She knelt and washed the blood from her hands first. Only after she was certain the blood had been carried downstream did she bend and cup water into her mouth. The cool brook refreshed her immediately, and scooping handfuls, she washed her face and neck.

Her stomach grumbled and she wished she hadn't stubbornly refused food when the men had eaten earlier last night. It had been foolish. How quickly she had forgotten what it was like to be hungry, to accept any meal offered for fear of where her next one might come from. But she had lived that life, she reminded herself, and she had survived. She would survive now, as well.

Lucinda scavenged through the forest in search of berries. If need be, she could also dig for roots. She refused to allow the dark thoughts flitting around in her head to light. Thoughts of Jackson at the camp last night and if he'd managed to survive. She hadn't heard the sound of shots while she ran away, but she imagined all the men were armed with knives. He could have been gravely injured or even killed. No, she wouldn't let herself go there.

She could try to look into her future, to see if Jackson was still there, but what if all she saw was the darkness again? The darkness had unnerved her. Had it meant she had no future? Had it simply meant her future was undecided at that time? Perhaps it meant her future was up to her and not to be predetermined.

So deciding, Lucinda took a moment to get her bearings. She must find the road again. Perhaps she could find a coach or a cart to take her to Wulfglen. She could only imagine what Jackson's brother and sister-in-law would think if she arrived looking as she did. There was no help for it. Taking a moment to judge the sun's position in the sky, Lucinda headed west, where she hoped she would eventually meet with the road again.

She walked well into the afternoon before she felt it. A presence. As if eyes were watching her in the forest. Lucinda stopped. A twig snapped behind her and she wheeled around. She saw nothing at first. As her gaze scanned the shadows, she focused on one tall shape that seemed to have sustenance. It was a man. He stepped into the sunlight and the sun caught his blond hair, forming a halo around his head.

"Jackson," she whispered. Lucinda ran to him and into his arms. He buried his face in her hair.

"Thank God for that scent," he said. "It was the honeysuckle that I followed."

Lucinda clung to him for a moment, reveling in the solid feel of him against her. She pulled back to look at him. He wore coarse clothing and carried a pack. His hair was damp and she assumed he had paused at the brook to clean himself the same as she had done.

"Are you all right, Jackson?" she asked, examining him for cuts or bullet holes.

"I am uninjured," he assured her, although she noted that his eyes held the same haunted look they had when he'd killed one of Lord Cantley's henchmen in London.

"Those men?" she prompted.

"Will not come looking for us," was all he said.

She reached up and touched his cheek. "You were only protecting me, Jackson. Even when the beast rules you, it seems to know that I am in danger and act on my behalf."

"Does it?" He glanced away from her. "Or would you have fallen victim to him, too, if you had not fled?"

It was a question she could not answer. She did not

know, but soon the full moon would be upon him and he would not be able to control the beast from rising. Then Lucinda supposed she would have no choice but to learn the answer.

"We need to go," Jackson said. "Find the road and get you back to London. It's closer than Wulfglen. I want you safe and out of the way."

"There's no time for that," she said. "If we are to make the woods surrounding Whit Hurch by the full moon, we cannot take time for you to see me back to London. I'll have to go with you, Jackson."

"Damn! I will not have you at his mercy, or at mine!"

His outburst startled Lucinda, but she stood her ground. "We have no choice. Not unless you want to miss this opportunity. Lord Cantley has returned to his manor home. I heard the men say that I was to be taken to his hunting lodge there in the woods."

Jackson's jaw was so tense she thought he might crack his teeth. "I cannot be trusted, Lucinda. Not while the beast rules my head. How can I know that you will be safe from me?"

They were wasting time. Lucinda had to give him some type of hope. "Perhaps I can come up with a spell, one that will let you think like a man, even in your wolf form."

His dark eyes searched her face. "Do you think that is possible?"

"I will try," she promised. "Now, we need to go. We'll never make Whit Hurch in time by foot. We must find the road and, hopefully, a ride."

"My scent frightened off the men's horses, or we would have one," he muttered darkly.

Since he had not budged, Lucinda took off in a westerly direction. "We'll get nowhere standing still." She walked for a few paces before he settled into step beside her. Lucinda eyed the pack on his back. "I don't suppose you have food in there. I'm starving."

He hefted the pack in front of him, dug inside, brought out a loaf of stale bread, tore off a large chunk, and handed it to her. Nothing had tasted as good to her in a long time.

They found the road before nightfall. It was deserted. They walked for a good long while before they heard the jangle of harnesses. Turning around, they saw a caravan of brightly painted wagons drawing near.

"What are they?" Jackson wondered.

"Gypsies," Lucinda answered. "Or a traveling troupe. Maybe they will give us a ride."

Jackson was thankful for the coarse clothing that both he and Lucinda wore. He was also glad that Lucinda had the idea to rub mud over his skin before the group drew close enough for the horses to catch his scent. He was dirty, he was tired, and he was worried about bringing Lucinda along with him to Whit Hurch, but at least they were both inside of a wagon. Lucinda rested upon a cot and he sat on the floor because he was too dirty to foul someone's bed.

The group was not a band of gypsies but a traveling band of entertainers. They were an odd-looking lot, but then, who was he to cast stones or to complain? Later tonight, when the group made camp, he would have to steal a couple of horses. Jackson didn't like that, stealing, killing; he was better off when he'd simply been a drunkard and a womanizer.

Glancing across the wagon at Lucinda's sleeping form, he admitted that he had not been better off. Before he met her, he'd had no purpose, no ambition, and no future. Lucinda had helped him find purpose and ambition, but what of the future? She had not asked to stay with him. Not once. Did she so easily accept the bargain they had once made, even now, when everything between them had changed? Or had nothing changed for her?

The wagons slowed, distracting his thoughts. They bounced and swayed, and he knew they had left the road. In all probability, the entertainers would find a place in the woods to circle and rest for the night. The mud on his skin itched and he smelled bad. What he wouldn't give for a nice hot bath. But he would have to wear the mud, either that or frighten the horses, and he couldn't very well steal two of them later if he couldn't get close enough to catch them.

Crawling across the floor to where Lucinda slept, he nudged her gently. "Wake up, Lucinda. The wagons are stopping."

"Already?" she asked sleepily. A moment later, she sat up, shoving her heavy hair back from her face. "How long have I slept?"

"Not long enough," he assured her. "We've only been traveling an hour or more. We'll have to move on later to-night after I steal two of their horses."

"Steal their horses?" She frowned at him in the darkness. "Not a very nice way to repay them for taking us in off the road."

"It can't be helped," he said. "I have no coin with me. Nothing of value to trade for them. We have to keep moving, Lucinda. We don't have much time."

She reached out and touched his shoulder, spreading warmth to the spot. "I suppose you're right. Let me look at your back while we have the chance."

"You can't see it anyway," he said. "The stitches did not survive the transformation. I'll heal on my own."

The door was suddenly opened. The tall man with the purple birthmark covering half of his face stuck his head inside. He'd introduced himself as Philip.

"We'll have a fire and food on in a short time. You're welcome to sup with us and spend the night."

"Thank you," Jackson said. "You are most kind."

"We've had our share of hard times, too," Philip said. "Come out and join us. Try not to stare," he added with a smile that flashed white in the darkness.

Jackson took Lucinda's hand and led her from the wagon. A fire blazed and two women, one tall and stout, the other he first thought to be a small child but was in fact a midget, had made a spit. The women now loaded the spit with wild fowl and two skinned rabbits. Jackson's mouth nearly watered.

"We hunted this morning," Philip explained. " 'Tis best that way so when night comes we have a meal to cook quickly."

The man had a booming voice. Jackson assumed since he was in the lead wagon of the group, he was in charge of the troupe. "We've found a stream over yonder," the man said, nodding. "Feel free to clean up before the meal."

Jackson didn't miss Philip's nose crinkling slightly as he stared at his mud-caked face. It was embarrassing to be so dirty, and yet Jackson had wanted to keep the mud to coat his scent from the horses.

"Thank you, we will wash up," Lucinda said, dragging Jackson along with her.

"I wanted to keep the mud," he said as they moved off from the camp. "It might make stealing a couple of horses easier later tonight."

"You cannot go to a meal looking like that," Lucinda argued. "It is rude even for my class."

He glanced at her. "Do you really think I see any boundaries between us now? Look at me, Lucinda. I have crossed the lines of what was even acceptable to me at one time."

She surprised him by laughing at him. "Even with the mud, and the clothes, I imagine if you started snapping orders, all would follow your commands without thought to your appearance."

They reached the brook and bent before it. Jackson pulled off his shirt, cupping his hands in the water to wash the mud from his face and neck. The cool water felt like heaven against his itching skin. Lucinda washed, then came around behind him to look at his back.

"It could be worse," she muttered. "But it's still not a pretty sight."

Jackson rose and turned to face her, holding his shirt draped over one arm. He reached forward and brushed a lock of hair from her eyes. "I'm sorry, Lucinda. I vowed that I would not let you be captured, and yet you were. You are my responsibility, and I have failed you."

She surprised him by turning her back to him. "You also rescued me," she pointed out. "It matters naught in what form you did it. I know when you agreed to my terms of the bargain you had no idea that your responsibilities would include risking your life to save me and Sebastian from a man bent on destroying us. What I have endured is little compared to what you have been forced to endure."

Had he somehow managed to hurt her feelings? Her words were stiff, her back even stiffer. Jackson started to ask her, but Lucinda walked away from him toward the camp.

"We should return," she called. "We'll figure out what to do about the horses later."

Jackson pulled his shirt over his head and followed her.

Chapter Twenty-six

Responsibility? Was that all Lucinda was to Jackson? She tried to tamp down her hurt that his feelings did not run as deeply as hers. He had never promised her anything else but what was agreed upon in their bargain. Making love with him was perhaps a mistake on her part. Lucinda couldn't seem to separate the physical act from the deeper emotional feelings that had led her into his arms and into his bed. Now, her feelings only seemed stronger.

Leaving Sebastian, she had known, would be the most difficult thing she would ever be faced with doing in her life, but she had not counted on feeling just as torn inside about leaving Jackson.

"There are our guests!" Philip called upon seeing her and Jackson returning. "Come and sit by the fire; the food will be ready soon."

The rest of the troupe members had gathered around the fire. Lucinda was as busy studying them as they seemed to be examining her. There was a man with a hump on his back, the stout woman she'd seen fixing the spit, an older man who should have gone with them to the stream to clean up, the midget woman, and now Lucinda saw a midget man as well and a young girl, strikingly beautiful amid the strangeness surrounding her.

Lucinda seated herself on a log that had been pulled near the fire. The smell of roasting meat set her stomach to grumbling. Jackson sat next to her. All eyes turned to him and seemed to stay there. The young girl's mouth dropped open. Curious, Lucinda glanced at Jackson. He looked handsome to be sure, with his hair pushed back from his face and his attractive features now scrubbed and clean.

"He looks like Sterling," the young girl whispered. "He is almost the image of him."

Jackson suddenly tensed beside her. "What did you just say?"

"Sorry to be rude and stare," Philip apologized. "We're quite used to things being the other way around. But you do favor him so."

"Did you say 'Sterling'?" Jackson repeated, now rising from the log.

"The beast tamer," the young girl supplied. "Sterling. You favor him."

Suddenly Jackson sat back down. The color had drained from his face. "You know where he is?"

Philip moved to stand in front of them. "Not at the moment. But he has been traveling with us for many years. His wife, Elise, is great with child and he did not want her to have the babe on the road. We left them in Liverpool."

"His wife? A child?"

Lucinda remembered the family portrait in the front parlor. "Your youngest brother," she suddenly understood.

"Brother?" Philip boomed. "Well, then that explains the resemblance."

"Sterling is like family to us," the stout woman said. "Both him and his sweet wife, Elise. That makes you family, as well."

Jackson was clearly overwhelmed. "We did not even know if he was still alive," he finally managed. "I haven't seen him for ten years or more."

"Oh, he's alive and well," the stout woman assured Jackson. "Said his traveling days were over, though. With the babe and all, I think he decided perhaps it was time to go home. He never told us much about his past, never even what his last name was. The child is a boy, I can tell you. I have the gift of sight, you know."

The man who needed a bath chuckled and leaned forward, swatting the woman on the bottom. "Now, Sarah, don't be putting on like a gypsy fortune-teller to these young folks. They are, as you said, close to kin."

The woman put her hands on her hips. "It is a boy, I tell you. Saw it in my mind plain as day. A good strapping fellow, too."

"Excuse me." Jackson rose and stumbled away from the camp.

Lucinda rose, as well. "Forgive him," she said. "I think he's had a bit of a shock."

Hurrying after Jackson, she found him pacing not far from the camp. "I can't believe it," he said. "To know he is safe, alive, soon to be a father, it is a shock."

She went to him, placing a hand against his chest to stop his pacing. "A good one, though, I would think."

"Yes," he agreed. "Married and to be a father? What of the curse? Does this woman, Elise, hold his heart?"

"These are not things you can find out at the moment," she said. "Just be glad in your heart to know your brother is alive, and at least you have an inkling of where to find him."

"Yes," he agreed. "I will find him." Suddenly he reached forward and pulled Lucinda close. "Sterling is alive!"

She laughed at his joy, and for a moment, as he stared

down at her, smiling, she saw him before the curse had taken him. Before the liquor had consumed him. Before the women had given him solace. He was so breathtakingly pure and beautiful. She couldn't help but rise on her tiptoes and kiss him. Their mouths lingered against each other. He nudged her lips apart with his tongue.

Lucinda opened to him, allowing him inside, allowing him to sweep her away from the moment. She surrendered fully to sensation. And when emotion rose inside of her, she did not fight it, or the loss of control she felt stealing over her.

"We should go back and share the meal," he said against her lips, and it was odd that he was being the practical one when all she wanted to do was lose herself to him and the darkness.

"Yes, we should," she agreed breathlessly. He stepped away from her and she could think clearly again. Jackson took her hand, and together they returned to camp. They were accepted fully by the strange group, and as they sat and ate, different entertainers would regale them with humorous stories about Sterling, the beast tamer, and Jackson would laugh and again she would see the boy in him.

The great cats that once traveled with the caravan had been sold to a wealthy merchant who thought to make them into pets, Jackson and Lucinda learned. Without Sterling, it had seemed pointless to keep them. Jackson had deeper questions about his brother, she could tell, but he would not ask them. Instead they laughed, they ate, and as the night grew darker she knew Jackson's mind could not be distracted from their own quest and their own troubles.

Philip offered them the use of his wagon for the night, but Jackson declined, saying they would bed down next to the fire. The task at hand now taxed him more than it had before, she understood. Stealing from strangers was one thing; stealing from people who claimed to consider him their kin was another. As the group went to their wagons for the night, Jackson rose from beside the fire.

"Stay here," he said to her before he set off for Philip's wagon.

Jackson couldn't steal from these fine people. His conscience wouldn't allow him, no matter how desperate he was to end Lord Cantley's threat toward Lucinda and Sebastian. He would have to be honest.

He knocked softly upon Philip's wagon. The door opened and the man with the birthmark over half of his face stood looking down at Jackson.

"I have a dilemma," Jackson admitted. "I need two of your horses. I am not a thief, but I had planned to take them from you once everyone had settled in tonight and gone to sleep."

Philip scratched his chin. "But now you cannot steal from family?"

"Yes," Jackson admitted.

The troupe leader stepped down from the wagon. He patted Jackson on the shoulder. "I knew from the moment I met Sterling that he did not come from a common background. It took him a long time to learn what you have yet to learn. Most people have no need to steal from others. All they need do is humble themselves enough to ask for what they do not have."

The man was right. The thought of simply asking had never occurred to Jackson until he learned of his brother's affiliation with these people. "Humility is a lesson I am still struggling with," he admitted.

Philip laughed and clapped him on the back. "Come, we'll find Taylor and send you and your pretty wife on your way."

"I don't know when I can return the horses to you, or even how to find you. Where are you going?"

The man shrugged. "Wherever the wind takes us. We will meet again someday."

Jackson had never met people such as these. He understood why his brother would stay with them for so many years. Jackson was half-tempted to fetch Sebastian, grab Lucinda, and go along with the caravans. It would be a simple life far from the danger that now plagued them. But that was something the old Jackson might have done. Now he knew he must face his problems head-on and deal with them.

"You'll need food," Philip said as they walked the length of the wagons. "I'll have Sarah Dobbs fix you up a pack."

"You are very kind," Jackson said. "All of you."

The man laughed. "Not to all. We have our share of troubles. There is always trouble, it seems, when a Wulf is about."

"Sterling told you his full name then?"

His eyes sliding toward Jackson, the man smiled. "No."

Chapter Twenty-seven

Lucinda nearly slumped from the saddle in exhaustion by the time Jackson stopped the horses to rest. Due to his superior eyesight in the darkness, they had covered good ground with him leading her horse. The sun was just rising when he stopped deep in the woods, the sound of the gurgling brook they followed further lulling her into a need for sleep.

Jackson dismounted, then came around and helped her from her horse. He looked as bone weary as she felt.

"First we'll wash up and have a bite to eat; then we sleep for a few hours."

She nodded and proceeded toward the stream while he saw to the horses. The water was chilly in this part of the woods, the tall trees not allowing much for the sunshine above to reach the ground. The water revived her when she washed her face and hands, but she longed for a nice hot bath and her scented soaps. Jackson joined her a few minutes later.

He removed his shirt and washed as best he could. His back had scabbed over and looked to be healing . . . probably healing much faster than normal. She knew animals ofttimes healed faster than humans and wondered if the beast within him had something to do with his ability. A moment later Jackson pulled his shirt back over his head, rose, offered her his hand, and led her back to the camp.

He had spread blankets on the ground, unsaddled the horses, and tethered them in an area where the grass was more plentiful. She sank gratefully onto her blanket, dug in the pack sent along with them, removing a bit of bread and cheese and two apples.

Jackson dropped down beside her. She feared if she didn't get him to eat, and quickly, he'd be asleep before she could set the food out.

"How much further?" she asked, having no sense of direction herself, since he'd led her horse through much of the night and she'd dozed on and off in the saddle.

"Another night's ride, I'm thinking," he answered. "Do you miss Whit Hurch?" he suddenly asked.

What to tell him? That she never wanted to go back to the village or her former life again? That it had been a lonely life, would be lonelier yet without him and Sebastian? Lucinda would not make Jackson ask her to stay with him out of guilt. No matter what else had happened between them and what had happened inside of her, they still had a bargain.

"I suppose I could return there . . . if Lord Cantley were gone," she said. "If not, there are many such places for me to go."

He watched her while he lifted the apple and took a bite. "And how will you live?"

She shrugged. "As I have always lived. From the coin of selling potions and spells or delivering babes. From what I can kill or grow with my own two hands."

"It sounds like a hard life."

Lucinda pinched off a piece of bread, added a thin

slice of cheese, and took a bite. She waited until she had chewed and swallowed to respond. "Most live a hard life. Few are privileged enough to be born into wealth. It is hard, but it is simple at times, too. A person can't miss what they've never known." And so in a way, she was now cursed, too.

"And what of Sebastian?"

She glanced away, feeling the sudden prick of tears burning her eyes. "Sebastian will be better off with you and all you can give him."

"A mother's love is worth its weight in gold."

"And he will always have mine," she said softly. "You must make certain that he understands that. I only want what is best for him."

"And if the curse cannot be broken? Am I still what is best for him, Lucinda?"

"Your family—"

"Are all cursed, as well," he interrupted. "There are things not even the Wulf fortune can buy."

She turned back to him. "We will find a way to break the curse," she promised, although she still wasn't certain how. "And we will stop Lord Cantley's threat, by whatever means becomes necessary. Then Sebastian will have all that I wish him to have in life. Then I will be happy. I will be content, no matter what turns my own life may take after that."

He said nothing but took another bite of his apple, looking off into the distance. For a second, she thought his eyes watered, but then, he was exhausted; her eyes were watering from lack of sleep, as well. They finished the slight meal in silence. Jackson stretched out, turning on his side away from her. She thought he was asleep in seconds.

Lucinda gathered the food and put it back in the pack. Jackson had made sure he laid the pistol the troupe leader had given to him on one corner of the blanket, within easy reach of him. She lay down beside him, staring up through the trees at the blue sky. How easily she lied these days. To Jackson and to herself.

She did want what was best for Sebastian. But she couldn't tell Jackson that she also wanted what was best for her. To be with her son. To be with the man she loved. He had made love to her, but he had never said that he did love her. And she wouldn't force him to speak a lie. She had forced his hand in marriage. She had forced her way into his life. She would not take anything else from him that he wouldn't willingly give.

As her eyes drifted closed, she thought of spells and magic potions. How tempting it would be to try to cast another spell on Jackson. One that would make him love her for eternity. One that would bind them together for life. But again, it would be a spell. She would never know if he truly loved her or if he loved her because she had commanded that he do so. Once, she had thought such requests for love spells and potions were silly. Now she understood how desperately a woman might want a man to love her who did not.

Gradually, the slight breeze and the sounds of insects buzzing in the woods lulled her to sleep. She awoke a short time later, snuggled up next to Jackson. She glanced up at him. He lay on his back, and she wondered if he was uncomfortable, considering his healing lashes. One arm was flung over his eyes; the other was pinned under her neck. His lips were slightly parted. How tempting they looked.

Awareness of him stirred with the breeze that tugged playfully at his hair. He was sensual, even when asleep. She ran her hand up his chest. Jackson shifted, laying the arm he had shielding his eyes by his side. His lashes were long and dark and thick against his high cheekbones. She couldn't help herself. Rising up on one elbow, she bent down and pressed her lips against his.

His eyes opened slowly. She drowned in their dark depths for a moment; then, lowering her lashes, she found his mouth again. His hand slid up to cup the back of her head. Slowly, his tongue crept into her mouth . . . almost reluctantly. Lucinda decided she had mistaken his response. Jackson Wulf reluctant to kiss a woman? Never.

She realized a moment later, however, that she seemed to be the one doing most of the kissing. She teased him with her tongue, nibbled on his bottom lip, even climbed halfway on top of him and rubbed her body against his in order to draw more response from him. He might have hidden the fact he was affected at all, had it not been for the quickness of his breathing and the definite bulge in his trousers.

Lucinda broke from his lips to kiss his neck. He made a sound in his throat, but it was as if he tried to bite it back. Suddenly he threw her weight off of him and was looming over her. His eyes now had the faint glow of blue to them.

Would he ravage her? Here, in the open? Beneath the tall trees, the sun peeking down at them through their branches? She hoped so. Her body was now aware of what he could offer her. Aware and desirous to have its needs fed. He stared down at her for a moment longer, as if a silent battle took place within him.

"We must go," he suddenly said, his voice low and husky. "We've slept too long as it is."

Shocked, she watched him rise, scoop up his pistol, and head out to where he'd tethered the horses. She simply lay there for a moment. He had rejected her advances. Her face started to burn with embarrassment and, she supposed, a good dose of anger, as well. Had he tired of her already? They'd only had one night together. But then, considering the type of women Jackson was used to consorting with, perhaps that was all any woman had ever spent with him.

Lucinda forced herself to rise, to bend and begin rolling the blankets. Her hands shook and she was glad Jackson had busied himself saddling the horses so he wouldn't see how he'd affected her. She couldn't very well demand he make love to her . . . although for the time being, he was her husband. If a husband could demand such rights, why couldn't a wife? She had to make a lifetime of memories with him in such a short span of time. He had denied them a perfectly good opportunity to be together when there was a possibility of them never being together again.

Her heart broke, just as she'd known it would if she ever gave it to him. Damn the man. Why couldn't he have left her heart untouched? Her body ignorant? Her opinion of him unchanged? Because he was a master at seduction, she furiously reminded herself. She stood no chance against him from the beginning. He had led and she had followed, then and now, for he was still leading and she was still following.

"Hurry, Lucinda," she heard him call at her back. "We'll lose what light we have left."

In her anger, her embarrassment, she might have purposely dawdled to annoy him, but the situation was too grave to let her hurt feelings delay them on their journey. She would have to push aside his rejection of her and set her thoughts to making the woods that surrounded Whit Hurch as soon as possible. Lucinda didn't want to think about what would happen once they reached their destination. Nor did she want to see into a future that held only darkness.

Grabbing up the blankets and the pack of food, she walked to where Jackson had just finished readying the horses. One rolled blanket went behind her saddle, the other behind his. Lucinda was in charge of the food. Jackson helped her mount. When he stood close to her, his hands on her waist to help her up into the saddle, she stared at him. He wouldn't look at her. She placed a hand upon his shoulder. He nearly flinched, as if her touch pained him.

Suddenly she thought she knew what might trouble him. "How is your back? Do you feel feverish?" She placed a hand against his forehead, but it was cool and dry.

"I'm fine," he bit out. "Let's be off."

He nearly hefted her up and over the other side of the horse. Jackson did not know his own strength at times. She righted herself; then he went around to mount his horse. They rode from a place that might have held special memories for her but instead only held the bitter disappointment of his rejection.

Trailing along behind him, she wished for the first time she knew something of seduction. Deception, yes, she supposed she was good enough at that, but how to make a man want her? Odd that she thought of such things when she'd spent most of her life avoiding men's advances. It was something to think about leastwise, since Jackson didn't seem inclined to converse with her. And it was more pleasant to think about than where they were headed and what might happen once they arrived.

Jackson felt Lucinda's eyes boring into his back often during their ride through the woods. He'd confused her. Her expression had been stunned when he'd resisted her charms. He hadn't denied her because he couldn't perform for her. One kiss and she brought him to full arousal. No, it wasn't as if he hadn't wanted to accommodate her and ease his own need for her, as well. It had been what she'd said earlier to him.

Lucinda would be happy and content without him, as long as she knew Sebastian was well taken care of. Her honesty had wounded him—had, in fact, broken his heart. Good God, he was in love with her. And for once, Jackson wanted a woman's love in return. For once, he wanted the act of making love to be just that. Since when did he have any morals? Since when did a woman make her sexual wishes known to him and he not drop his trousers in record time to meet those wishes?

Since the first day he met Lucinda, he realized. The brave witch struggling to give birth to a child already damned. Coming to know her had deepened Jackson's love, but it had first come upon him the moment he looked into her deep green eyes. He would die for her. He would die for Sebastian. Was her love for him too much to ask? Too much to hope for? She had surrendered her body, and the old Jackson would have counted that as enough. But he was no longer the man who first went in search of a witch.

He had fallen in love before. It had led to nothing but heartbreak then, too, and a curse. Where would it lead him this time? Down a road toward Whit Hurch to either kill or be killed? To fulfill the promise of a bargain made and nothing more? Perhaps he could live with his curse if it kept Lucinda tied to him by her precious bargain. But what of his brothers? Could he selfishly sacrifice their future happiness for his own?

And would he want Lucinda to stay with him out of duty alone? No. Jackson wanted her to stay with him because she loved him. Because she wanted to make a life with him. Him, her, Sebastian, and, if Jackson could break his curse, children made between the two of them. He could not be selfish, even though he knew he was by nature. He supposed he thought being cursed allowed him that indulgence. Now it did not.

"Will we ride all night again?" Lucinda called to him.

It wasn't fair to push her as he did. She wasn't used to riding great distances on horseback. Night had already fallen, and he thought they had made good time. He didn't want to dally too long on their journey lest Lord Cantley become suspicious that his men had not done as he'd instructed. Jackson wanted the element of surprise on his side.

"We will stop for the night shortly," he called back to her. "I want to get a little closer to Whit Hurch."

She did not complain. Any other woman would have. Lucinda had lived a hard life. She was probably more suited to traveling and living in the woods than he was. At least the man in him. If his life had been cursed, he realized, it had also been blessed. He'd like to give her all that she had been denied. All that they had both been denied.

They traveled a little farther, moving in toward the stream they followed. They could at least have the comfort of washing the dust from their bodies before they caught a few hours' sleep. He would hunt in the morning. They needed fresh meat to sustain them. The night was warm, the stars out in brilliant display when they could see them through the trees. They would make faster time on the road, but Jackson dared not take it. Especially at night.

The sound of the gurgling stream became clearer and he finally pulled his horse to a stop in an open area where the horses could graze. Jackson dismounted and went around to help Lucinda down. She looked as if she was asleep in the saddle. He reached up, took ahold of her, and pulled her down into his arms. She came awake with a start.

"We're going to rest for a while," he said. "The stream is just there." He nodded. "We'll clean up before we have something to eat."

Still dazed from sleep, she turned toward the stream and stumbled toward the gurgling sound. Jackson saw to the horses before he joined her. She sat scooping water into her hands, washing her face and neck.

"We should have brought Hawkins," she muttered when Jackson bent beside her. "He'd have made sure we had hot baths and hot meals even in this wilderness."

Jackson laughed. She was probably right. He pulled his shirt over his head to wash. Scooping up water, he washed his face, tempted to dunk his whole head in the water. Beside him, Lucinda muttered something again, then suddenly stood, going for the buttons on her frock.

"What are you doing?" he asked, disturbed that his heart lurched, not to mention other parts of his body, just at the sight of her unbuttoning her frock.

"I'm getting in," she said. "I want all of me to feel clean."

"You cannot," he blurted, and then when she lifted a brow he added, "Someone might see you." Mainly him, he was thinking.

She laughed. "Out here? There's no one about but me and you, Jackson. You can keep watch over me if you think someone might come upon us."

Having unbuttoned the frock, she slid it down her shoulders and over her hips until it fell to the ground. His growing problem grew worse. She stood now in nothing but shift and stockings. It took effort, but he glanced away from the sight of her. He cursed his unusually good hearing a moment later when he heard the rustle of silk, even the sound her stockings made against her skin as she rolled them down. He swallowed loudly and tried to look anywhere but at her. A moment later he heard a small splashing sound.

"The water is a little chilly," she said. "But not as bad as I thought it would be."

Jackson took to cleaning his teeth as best he could, trying to keep his eyes off of her. She made a loud sighing noise that drew his gaze toward her even though he tried to fight against looking.

"It feels very refreshing once you get used to it," she said.

His breath caught in his throat. She lay in the shallow water, positioned on her elbows, her head bent back so her hair floated on the surface. The moon's glow outlined her upthrust breasts, the inward slope of her stomach, the gentle flare of her hips, and the smooth line of her thighs. She looked like a pagan sacrifice being offered up to the gods.

"Wouldn't you like to join me?"

Even in the darkness, he caught the spark of mischief in her eyes. It hadn't been an innocent invitation. "Then who will watch out for you?" he asked. "No, I'd better stay right where I am."

"Suit yourself," she said with a shrug that made her breasts jiggle in a most tantalizing way. "But I believe we are very alone in the woods tonight. I don't think we would be disturbed."

Disturbed at what? He tore his gaze from her and scooped up more water, cooling the back of his neck. "I'd better keep watch just the same," he mumbled.

The little sighs and moans she made while bathing nearly drove him to madness. He couldn't be sure, but he thought she might be trying to purposely seduce him. Most of his life he'd been on the giving end of seduction, not the receiving end. Jackson wasn't sure what to do about it. Resisting temptation had never been his strong suit. But then, he was learning, wasn't he? He hadn't had a drink since the day he decided to give up liquor. He hadn't been with another woman since before he met Lucinda. He could resist. If he set his mind to it, he could do anything.

"I didn't think to bring anything to dry off with," Lucinda suddenly said. "Will you fetch me my blanket?"

Any excuse to get away from her was met with enthusiasm. Jackson bounded to his feet and returned to where their supplies and saddles sat on the ground. He snatched up Lucinda's blanket and returned to the stream. He didn't expect her to be waiting for him. She stood wet and naked now on the bank. His damnable eyesight in the dark he'd always counted as blessing; now it was a curse. His hands shook as he quickly unfolded the blanket and just as quickly wrapped it around her.

She snuggled against his warmth. The blanket dropped lower and her cool, wet skin met with his overheated flesh. The result was jolting. Jackson sucked in his breath and reached down, pulling the blanket up around her.

"I wouldn't want you to catch a chill," he explained.

"You're nice and warm," she countered, snuggling closer to him again.

He had to bite back a groan when she pressed against him. Her womanly curves were more enticing than any drink had ever been to him. She was more enticing than any woman he'd known before her. But he wanted more than her body. He wanted her heart . . . her soul, and she would not surrender either to him. Jackson was tired of settling for whatever he could have, instead of what he truly wanted. He'd been doing so for far too long as it stood.

With effort, he stepped away from her. Bending, he retrieved her clothing. "We should return to make our camp and get some sleep," he clipped. He'd barely straightened from his task when he saw her stomp away, her spine straight, head held high, and, if he wasn't mistaken, seething with impotent anger.

At least he doubted if she'd try to seduce him again tonight. Or he hoped so. His resolve was weakening.

Chapter Twenty-eight

Lucinda had stepped on something and her foot stung like the dickens. She'd limped to the saddle and packs, removed Jackson's blanket, spread it on the ground, and now sat trying to see the bottom of her foot in the darkness. Jackson, she noted, took his sweet time to join her. He tossed her clothing on the blanket.

"What's wrong with your foot?"

"I stepped on something," she answered, perhaps more snappishly than she intended. It was doubly embarrassing to have tried to seduce him, to have failed, and for him to know she was angry about it. "I can't see what I've done."

He knelt down at her feet. "I can. Let me have a look."

Even the touch of his hands on her foot made her pulses leap. He bent close. "It's not bleeding. You probably just stepped on a rock and bruised it."

Jackson was looking at her foot one moment, and then his gaze seemed to be traveling up her leg. Lucinda realized her leg all the way up to her hip was exposed outside the blanket. She started to cover up, but he seemed somewhat mesmerized, so she halted her first instinct. As if his hands had no choice but to follow his eyes, they moved slowly up her leg, past her calf, her knee, to her thigh. Lucinda realized she was holding her breath.

For a moment, he seemed to gather himself. She thought he would pull his hands away, so she let go of the blanket she clutched around her shoulders. His gaze ran up her body to her face. Blue flared in his eyes.

"Are you trying to kill me?"

Feeling brave, she answered, "I'm only trying to seduce you, and obviously not doing a good job of it."

He drew in a shaky breath. "I want more than you will give me."

Lucinda was confused. "There is more? I mean, more than we've already done together?"

He ran a hand through his hair. "Well, yes, but that wasn't—"

"What else is there?" she interrupted. Lucinda wanted to experience everything with him before the chance was taken from her. "Show me."

She thought he would refuse, felt him pulling back, and, pride be damned, she would not let him reject her again. He wanted her. His eyes told her that in the darkness. She reached forward and hooked a hand around the back of his neck. Past shame, she leaned forward and touched her lips to his. "Do not deny me," she whispered. "Share with me, your wife, what you so willingly have shared with too many others."

His shoulders tensed. It wasn't the most romantic thing to have said to him, but why would he deny her what he had so willingly given to the women in his past? What did they have that had enticed him into their beds that she did not? He kissed her then, rather roughly, and she knew she had wounded him with her words.

"You want me to treat you like a whore?" he broke from her to ask, his voice a raspy whisper. "So be it."

She might have soothed the sting of her words with an admission of wanting to share everything with him so she could hold those memories dear when they were parted, but he was obviously finished talking. He kissed her again, forcing her back on the blanket, his body moving on top of her. She couldn't say that he continued to kiss her roughly, but it was different.

Emotion . . . that was what was missing. Certainly he was skilled at the onslaught, and she tried and failed to keep from responding to anything that felt so calculated. Instead of calling him to account, she kissed him back with all the passion inside her, pounding at whatever defenses he had thrown up around his feelings.

He moaned into her mouth, the first sign that she had managed to penetrate his barriers. She clutched at his shirt, hoping to remove yet another barrier between them, but he slid down her body to her breasts, holding her arms pinned at her sides while he teased her nipples into tight pebbles of sensation. She squirmed beneath him, but he kept her a willing prisoner.

Just when she thought she could stand no more, he moved lower, running his tongue down the indentation of her stomach. The combined silky brush of his hair and feel of his mouth against her skin made the throbbing between her legs intensify. She was no longer so innocent that she didn't understand what she hungered for. But she was still innocent enough to be shocked when he moved lower, positioned himself between her legs, and used his tongue to stroke where before only his fingers had gone.

Her arms no longer pinned at her sides, she clutched two handfuls of his long hair, thinking to pull him back up to her lips. He could not be dissuaded from his intentions, and after a few skillful strokes of his tongue Lucinda found that she didn't want to deter him. Her blood turned to fire, her bones to liquid. He cast a spell and she was helpless against him. She couldn't think beyond sensation, the building force that seemed to swell inside of her.

She couldn't stand for him to continue; she couldn't stand for him to stop. Still clutching handfuls of his hair, she did the only thing she could do . . . ride the storm brewing inside of her.

The tide rose, higher and higher; she moved her hips because she could not control her body's response to his magic. She burst apart, twitching and moaning, whispering incoherencies that were a mix of modern and ancient words. Still he drove her on until she thought she might die of pleasure, until she tugged harder on his hair and pulled him back up to her. He kissed her and she tasted herself on his lips. Then she realized that he was still fully dressed and she lay naked and limp beneath him.

He rolled to the side and sat, tugging off his shirt. While she lay dazed and content, he stripped off the rest of his clothing. She fully expected him to take his pleasure of her, so when he mounted and entered her she wasn't surprised, only rather shocked by the force of his thrust. It made her gasp and brought her out of her lethargic state. She'd barely had time to recover when he rolled onto his back and pulled her on top of him.

The position brought him deeper inside of her, and again she gasped. He placed his hands on her hips and guided her movements. He was deeper than she would have ever imagined he'd fit, and still swollen and sensitive, she caught his rhythm and felt her pleasure building again. She rode him, and somewhere in the far recesses of her mind she remembered being with him this way. The visions that had flashed through her mind the night they had gone to the stables and he had been among the horses again. This was the same. She had been seeing into her future.

Beneath her, his eyes glowed like blue fire. Moonlight

flickered over his handsome face, showing her he wasn't as in control as he had once been. She felt her own power rise inside of her, and she pushed him, rode him, forced him to shed all control and lose himself to her and to this one moment in time.

Jackson felt his control slipping away. He'd told her once that surrendering control was part of making love. He had lied to her. For never had he given up his control to a woman before. He gave it up now. Lost inside of her, he let her take him. Pleasure rose, unbearable pleasure, undeniable love for this woman, a combination that he had never experienced at the same time. It stripped his soul bare, left him open and vulnerable to his emotions. It was upon his tongue to tell her then, to admit his love for her, but the tide rose higher and all he could do was follow her into the murky depths of heaven and hell.

She was close to finding her own release. Her small gasps and moans pounded at him like the waves crashing upon a rocky shoreline. He could not remain passive beneath her and he rose up to meet her, to push her over the edge with him. Her muscles constricted around him and he was lost. The sound of her cry of release shattered whatever grasp he had managed to maintain upon sanity. His hands tightened upon her hips to pull her up and off of him as the first tremors of release took him. Then the unthinkable happened.

Along with the intense pleasure came the pain. It robbed him of rational thought. He arched up into her, releasing his seed as the combined forces of ecstasy and the knife-sharp pain of the curse both took him. He might have called out her name; he might have howled. And somewhere in the madness, he knew he had to get away from her . . . now!

◆ ◆ ◆

Something was wrong. As Lucinda drowned in pleasure made even sweeter by Jackson's surrender to her, the realization that he had not pulled away from her as he'd done before to spill his seed registered . . . along with the way his body jerked and shuddered beyond what it had normally done before. In the moonlight she glanced down at his features, twisted in both ecstasy and seemingly agony. His shout of release had sounded almost inhuman.

"Get away from me," he ground out. "The pistol, Lucinda! Get the pistol!"

She froze, nearly rendered incompetent by the still-fading spasms of release. Then she saw the fangs. Fate was unkind, no, cruel, in fact, to force her into action when her bones had dissolved to liquid and all she wanted to do was collapse on top of him. She did not have that option. Lucinda pulled away from him, rolling to the side, grabbing the blanket she had discarded earlier before wrapping it around her. She rose on shaky legs.

"The pistol!" he growled again. "Use it if you must."

Still dazed, she stumbled to their packs and found the pistol. She stared down at the cold weapon in her hands. Then she glanced up at the sky. The moon was full. Time had run out for them, for Jackson. Now he was at the mercy of the moon. And she was at the mercy of the wolf.

Lucinda knew she should run, but where? Into the woods? The horses in a grassy meadow not far away began to neigh nervously. Lucinda ran to release them lest the wolf harm the horses. Jackson said he did not know what he did as the beast. Lucinda could not know, either. She spoke in soothing tones to the animals, pulling up their tethers, which was no easy task to do while holding a pistol and clutching at the blanket wrapped around her. She had no choice but to lay the pistol aside. As soon as she released the horses they shied and ran. It couldn't be helped.

She crawled along the ground in search of the pistol.

In the darkness, the weapon was hard to see. She thought she caught a gleam from the moonlight's reflection on the barrel and crawled in that direction. She was brought up short by a low growl. Glancing up, Lucinda found herself nose to snout with the beast.

The wolf's eyes glowed blue in the darkness. She swallowed down the lump in her throat but remained as still as possible. The wolf sniffed at her hair. She expected it to go for her throat at any moment. Instead, it sat back on its haunches, staring at her.

"Jackson," she whispered. "Can you hear me?"

It wasn't as if she expected the beast to speak, but Lucinda expected some type of response. The wolf simply sat, continuing to stare at her. Her gaze strayed to the place where she'd thought she'd seen the pistol. It wasn't that far, almost within an arm's length. She scooted closer to the weapon, afraid the wolf would leap at her any moment. The animal remained where it was, and finally her hand met with the weapon. Slowly, she brought the pistol to her, then steadied it in her hands.

"Go away, Jackson," she warned softly. "I'm not certain I can shoot you if you do attack me."

The wolf did not do as she instructed. It did not move or growl but simply sat staring at her. Lucinda couldn't sit naked in the meadow all night. She wanted to return to camp.

"I'm going to move," she said, but again had to wonder why she bothered trying to speak to the beast. It was obvious the wolf did not understand her words. "Don't make me shoot you, Jackson," she said again. "I know you think I would probably enjoy that, but you would be wrong. You see, I've fallen in love with you. I love you even now, when you sit in front of me with the eyes of a wolf. So take pity upon the fool I have become. I forgot it was only a bargain between us."

Other than to cock its head to one side, the beast simply continued to stare at her. Slowly, Lucinda rose from the ground. She took a moment to slow her racing heart; then she began to walk back toward camp. The wolf simply watched her go, but she wondered as she walked if at any moment it would jump on her from behind. She made the camp and squatted down among the saddles and the supplies. Her clothes were still on the blanket she and Jackson had made love upon, and she clutched the edge of the blanket and drew it to her until she could reach them.

The wolf made an appearance a moment later. Again Lucinda froze while it stared at her. After a moment, it began to pace around the camp, stopping at times as if it was listening, sniffing at the air before it would continue in a circular motion around the camp. Lucinda dressed with slow, measured movements. She huddled behind the saddles, using them as a barrier, her back resting against a tree. The pistol was still in her hand, but she doubted that she could use it against the wolf, who also happened to be the man she loved. Still, one often didn't know what one was capable of unless put to the test. She hoped Jackson didn't force her into finding out.

After watching the beast for a good twenty minutes, Lucinda realized that what it seemed to be doing was guarding her. She swore its circular pacing, its pauses to listen and sniff the air, were the actions of a beast bent on protecting, rather than harming. She could put her suspicions to the test. If she was brave enough, she could rise and approach the beast. Lucinda could then see how it reacted to her when confronted. But then if it did not act as she hoped, either she or Jackson would end up dead this night.

Why test the fates? Lucinda decided. Instead, she settled back against the tree, her hand wrapped around the pistol, her eyes following the lazy pattern the beast made around the campsite. She watched, and she waited, and she prayed she would not have to make a choice between saving her life and ending Jackson's.

Chapter Twenty-nine

Jackson watched Lucinda sleep. He supposed he was lucky last night that he'd been naked when the change took him, or he'd be without clothing this morning. He was luckier that Lucinda was still alive and seemingly no worse for wear. She slept sitting up against a tree, the pistol clutched loosely in her hands.

When he'd awoken as a man this morning, he'd been curled into a ball a short distance from her, shivering in the morning chill. The horses were missing, he'd noticed right away. He'd have to go in search of them soon. His stomach grumbled, and he knew he'd have to hunt as well. They needed fresh meat. The curse was upon him now. Lucinda wasn't safe with him. She wasn't safe if he left her behind. She wasn't safe if he sent her down the road back toward London.

If they pushed onward, they might make Whit Hurch by nightfall. Perhaps she could stay with a friend until Jackson finished his business with Lord Cantley. Then she'd be safe from Jackson and from the lord of the manor. Jackson would discuss the matter with her when she woke. Wanting to give her more time to rest, he reached for the pistol in her hand, thinking to ease it from her grip in order to hunt with it. She came awake so quickly she startled him, pointing the pistol directly in his face.

He eased his hands back. They stared at each other for a moment before she lowered the pistol. Tears gathered in her eyes.

"I was afraid," she whispered. "So afraid I would have to shoot you."

Her words were only a reminder that the life he offered her was no life at all. Not while the curse still ruled him. He thought he could give her all that she deserved, but she deserved more than this. Fear of him. Fear of what she might be forced to do in order to protect herself. He understood now why his father had taken his own life. Jackson felt the same fear his father must have known at one time. Fear of hurting someone he loved more than life itself.

"I'm sorry," Jackson said. "Sorry to put you through this. I should have never allowed you to come with me. I should have come up with another plan. I've put you in danger, not only from Lord Cantley, but from me."

Her tear-filled eyes softened. She reached out and touched his cheek. "You did not harm me," she said. "In fact, you seemed intent upon protecting me. Do you remember any of it?"

He shook his head. "No."

"I don't think you would hurt me, even while the beast rules you. I think it somehow senses who I am."

"But we don't know that for certain," he bit out. He hated putting her in such a predicament. Hated now, more than ever, the curse that rested upon his head. "You must never trust me while I am in wolf form, Lucinda. Promise me you won't."

For a moment she chewed her tempting lower lip. "Perhaps it is you who must trust yourself, Jackson. In either form."

He laughed at her in answer, although it was not a heartfelt response. "I can hardly be trusted as a man, much less a beast that has no human thought to guide it. Have you forgotten who I am, Lucinda? Have you forgotten what kind of man you married?"

Her eyes were still misty and soft upon him. "You are no longer that man, Jackson. Why must you crucify yourself for a curse that was not your doing? For sins that are now in the past? You must forgive yourself. Only then can you move forward and become all that you can be."

She was wise, but his own self-loathing had been a part of him for a long time. It wasn't so simple to let it go. Loving her only made his sins more glaring in the light of day. She made everything new, and yet she also made the past seem somehow even uglier. He could never be pure again. Lucinda hadn't been a virgin, but she had still been pure. What had happened to her was not her fault. He'd gone willingly, even gladly, into debauchery. Good Lord, he'd slept with more than one woman at the same time, in the same bed.

His face and form made a mockery of what lay beneath his skin. What he had tried so hard to hide behind a charming mask. The beast had hidden inside of him, and he supposed he thought nothing he could become would be worse than that. He was wrong.

"I need to find the horses," he said. "And I need the pistol. I will hunt for us. The day will be long to Whit Hurch and we need more sustenance than bread and cheese."

Lucinda handed him the pistol. He rose and tucked it into the waistband of his crude trousers. "Build a small fire. I'll be back with food shortly."

◆ ◆ ◆

Lucinda watched him walk away. When she tried to rise, her aching muscles protested. Sleeping all night in a sitting position, along with making love with Jackson, had made her stiff and sore. She moved toward the stream first. She would clean up as best she could before building a fire. The water was chilly and helped revive her. She gathered kindling for the fire while her mind raced with remembrances from last night. The good and the bad.

She refused to think about the fact that Jackson had spilled his seed inside of her. No use borrowing trouble when they both had plenty to worry about as it was. Perhaps it was only courage spawned by the light of day, but Lucinda believed she could trust Jackson not to harm her while he was in wolf form. She was certain that on some level both man and beast were still connected even when the change took place.

She would talk to him about it later. Time had run out, and now they must do all they could to survive the ordeal ahead. Having gathered enough kindling, she returned to their camp and, digging flints from the pack, started a small blaze. In the distance, she heard shots. Jackson hunting, or so she hoped. Once Lucinda stacked some small branches on the fire, she took their water skins to the stream and filled them.

Upon returning to camp, she used a pine comb to wrest the tangles from her hair, pulled it back, and secured it with a piece of lace from her shift. There was little else to do but wait. She missed Sebastian and just the thought of never seeing him again broke her heart and brought tears to her eyes. She prayed that Hawkins had gotten her son safely away from London.

A horse nickered and Lucinda turned to see Jackson heading toward her, both horses in tow and a skinned rabbit dangling from one hand. He looked very much the young farmer coming in from the fields or from a day of hunting. Lucinda smiled in spite of their dire straits. In that moment she realized it wasn't so much her old life she hated but the fact that she had been alone. An outcast. How different her life might have been had she been born anyone, or anything, but what she was. And how different Jackson's life would have been, as well, with no family curse to haunt him.

Lucinda rose and went out to greet him. She took the rabbit, having already prepared a makeshift spit to roast whatever Jackson might bring back. He saw to the horses while she roasted the meat. Soon the smell had her stomach grumbling.

"Smells good." Jackson settled on a log she'd pulled up before the fire.

"It's almost ready," she said, turning the spit. "I didn't know you were a hunter."

He shrugged. "All gentlemen learn to hunt, if usually only for sport. I happen to be an excellent shot, probably due to my eyesight. We Wulfs have an advantage there."

"You have a great many advantages," she said. "Would you count your abilities as a curse if you could think like a man while the beast ruled you?"

Jackson placed his arms on his knees and leaned forward. "I suppose not, except for being at the mercy of the moon. I would have to schedule my life around it, but again, it wouldn't be so awful if I could know my own mind while running around as a wolf."

Lucinda moved the spit so that the roasted meat could cool enough for them to eat. She wiped her hands on her worn frock and joined him on the log.

"I've been thinking about that while you were gone. I believe the two of you are still connected even when the beast takes your form. Are you sure you have never remembered anything of the nights you run as the wolf?"

He sat silently for a time, as if thinking. "Honeysuckle," he finally said.

"What?"

His face turned toward her. "Last night, I remember thinking, *Honeysuckle.* And I remember hearing the sound of your voice."

Her heart lurched. Lucinda touched his hand. "You sniffed me. You caught the scent of my hair. You knew it was me, Jackson. I feel certain about it."

"I wish I could feel as certain," he said. "This is a dangerous game we are playing with Lord Cantley. When we get to the village, I want you to seek shelter with one of your friends. You are to stay there until I come for you. And if I do not come for you—"

She placed a finger against his lips. "Of course you will come for me. I trust you."

What she did not tell him was that she had no friends to seek shelter with among the villagers. Better if he thought she was safe and out of the way. Lucinda wasn't the type to stand by and wait to learn the outcome of her life, and his, anyway. Perhaps that was the reason she had never tried to see too far into her future. She believed the future could be changed. That there were paths that led to different outcomes.

"You must try hard to remember your thoughts last night. The fact that you can recall anything while you were the wolf is a good sign."

Now that the meat had cooled somewhat, she tore off a chunk and handed it to him. Retrieving the pack, she took out what bread and cheese remained. They ate in silence, and Lucinda suspected Jackson was doing exactly as she'd suggested. Trying to recall more than only the smell of honeysuckle and the sound of her voice. She nearly choked on her food a moment later. Suddenly she recalled what she had said to him. What she had admitted. She'd told him she loved him. What if he remembered that?

Chapter Thirty

They made the woods surrounding Whit Hurch before nightfall. Jackson had pushed them relentlessly, but he wanted Lucinda tucked safely away somewhere before the change took him again tonight. During their ride, he'd been thinking about what Lucinda said. If he could learn to control his thoughts while in wolf form, then perhaps he could learn to live with his curse. And if he could control his thoughts, then surely his brothers could learn to do the same.

It wasn't as good as breaking the curse altogether, but at least it was something. Jackson couldn't accompany Lucinda into the village. The villagers would remember him. He would see her safely to the outskirts of Whit Hurch. He'd been thinking today, also, of how best to deal with Lord Cantley.

Although Jackson's first instinct was simply to kill the man outright for daring to touch Lucinda, for threatening to harm Sebastian, he would try to talk to him first. If Lord Cantley understood that Jackson would care for the child, raise him as his own, and no one need be the wiser about his bloodline, maybe he would leave them all alone. It was worth a try, even if, deep down, Jackson wanted to strangle the man for forcing himself upon Lucinda.

"You had best go no farther. The village is just there, beyond the curve in the road."

Jackson drew his horse up. Lucinda did likewise beside him. "You'll be all right there, in the village? You have friends who will hide you?"

She glanced away from him. "Of course," she answered. "I grew up there. Lived the whole of my life there with my mother until she passed on."

"The lodge. How do I find it?"

She pointed east. "Keep to the woods in that direction. You'll come across it. If he's there, you'll smell the smoke from his fire. Be careful."

He glanced at her, but she still stared off into the distance, although he saw that her eyes were moist. How he loved her. Perhaps he should tell her, now, while he had the chance, in case the chance was lost to him forever.

"Lucinda—" he began.

"Don't speak to me of good-byes," she interrupted. "I refuse to believe that I will not see you again."

"Can you look into my future?" he asked.

Turning to glance at him, she said, "I do not want to. Not into yours, or into mine. I believe we all make our own futures." She nudged her horse forward.

With a sinking feeling Jackson watched her go. Seeing her ride away from him was like watching her leave him. Would she? Once this business was finished. Would she ride away from him for good? "Meet me here in two nights' time," he called. "I cannot come into the village to find you."

He saw the slight nod of her head. Jackson watched her until she disappeared around the curve of the road. At least he would not have to worry about her, hidden safely in the village while he tended to business with Lord Cantley. Jackson crossed the road, moving into the trees, headed east.

Lucinda gave him time to make it into the woods before she crossed the road just after the turn. The village was, in fact, a little farther up, but she needed to wait at a vantage point where Jackson could not see her follow him. The turn in the road suited just such a purpose. He would have argued had she insisted upon going with him. And she would have had to tell him that she had no friends. That she'd been an outcast among these people her whole life.

The battle Jackson fought was for her and Sebastian. She couldn't let Jackson go alone, although she wasn't certain what she could do to help him. While she picked her way through the forest, careful to keep what she hoped was enough distance between her and Jackson that he didn't spy her, she went over chants in her mind. There had to be some way to help Jackson keep his human thoughts while in an inhuman form.

Two lines from the poem kept coming back to haunt her: *I found no way to break it, no potion, chant, or deed.* Then how? There had to be a way. If only she could discover the secret for breaking the curse. Then she would have fulfilled her bargain. She loved Jackson so, and he had sacrificed much for her. There had to be a way. And she would find it.

Glancing up through the trees, Lucinda saw that night was fast falling. She steered her horse toward the cottage she'd once lived in for months. The cottage where she'd first met Jackson Wulf and where her son had come into the world. The villagers had burned it that night, but maybe enough was left for her to at least find some shelter. Even now she smelled the scorched scent of the cottage. She found it as she imagined she would, nearly burned to the ground.

How had Jackson managed to escape, even in wolf form? Lucinda dismounted and tied her horse to a nearby branch. Her legs were stiff from being in the saddle most of the day, and walking about was painful, if welcome. The cottage was now little more than ash with a few beams lying on the ground. She'd find no shelter here. She started to turn away when she noticed a hole in the ground near what would have once been part of a wall. Enough debris covered it on one side that she could crawl inside and be out of view. Then she knew how Jackson had escaped. He'd dug his way out.

Since she'd sent the packs with Jackson, for he needed what food they had and he had wrongly assumed she'd be fed by her friends, there was little else to do but go to bed. Lucinda returned to the horse, unsaddled him, and tethered him where the grass had not been singed. Taking her blanket with her, she crawled down inside of the hole. There wasn't much room, but the ground held the warmth from the sunshine, and snuggling with her blanket, she soon drifted off to sleep.

Something woke her a while later. For a moment, her tight confines stole the air from her lungs and made her panic. Buried alive, that was how she felt. She started to scramble up the hole, but the sight of two glowing eyes in the darkness above made her freeze in place. A low growl sounded in the silence.

"Jackson," she said softly. "Jackson, it is me; Lucinda. You must hear my words and understand them. You must remember them tomorrow when you are a man again." Since the wolf ceased its growling upon hearing her voice, she added for good measure, "And you must not be angry with me."

The wolf did not growl again, nor did it leave. Lucinda wasn't certain she should scramble from the hole. The wolf seemed to want her to stay put. While she had the opportunity, she decided to use it to help Jackson retain his human thoughts. Though she would have preferred to make a circle, to light candles and pay homage to the four directions, she made do with what she had, which was nothing but her voice. She closed her eyes and began the chant.

"Hear me now, both man and beast. As you are one, so will your minds, your souls, and your spirits combine. The man is the wisest; let his thoughts rule. The beast is the strongest; let him become only a tool. No longer will the moonlight cast its spell. For man and beast will from this night dwell, together, in accord; no conflict divides. A curse no longer, but a gift from both sides. Let it be, for I command it in the name of the ancient ones. In the name of my mother, whose magic is strong, in my name, whose magic is for naught but good. From my heart I ask it. For my love, I command it be so."

Slowly, Lucinda opened her eyes and glanced up at the wolf. "Go now," she said. "See what you will see, and remember it in the morning."

The beast blinked down at her; then a moment later it was gone. Exhausted from the days on the road and from the energy it took to cast the spell, Lucinda pulled her blanket around her and tried to sleep. Come morning, she would know if her spell had worked.

Jackson came awake naked and shivering. It was something he should have grown accustomed to by now, but he always felt a moment of confusion upon waking from a night spent as the wolf. He tried to gain his bearings. Suddenly a rush of memories assaulted him. The visions flashing in his head made him stagger. He reached out and braced himself against the sturdy trunk of a tree. The night rushed past him in a blur of shapes and sounds. He felt his blood singing in his veins. The thrill of being able to run through the forest on four legs. A oneness with nature, and with the world, he had never known.

His heart soared. He understood for the first time the beauty of a curse. He remembered. Good God, he remembered the night. His first response was to run and tell Lucinda. But then, Lucinda was in the village. Her image came to him, hidden in a hole, speaking to him.

Jackson straightened abruptly. Had he imagined seeing her, hearing her voice? He closed his eyes and concentrated. A moment later, he opened them, his jaw tightening. "Don't be angry my ass," he said under his breath. Glancing around, he was able to determine direction. He knew where he'd left his horse, his packs, and his clothes. He also knew where Lucinda was hiding.

He found his horse a short time later. Jackson hurriedly dressed, shoved the pistol in his waistband, saddled his horse, and grabbed the packs. He set out in the direction of where he thought he'd come across the burnt-out cottage.

It took him longer than he planned to find the remains of the cottage. All was quiet when he rode up. Something wasn't right; he sensed it immediately. Glancing around, he did not see her horse tethered anywhere nearby.

Dismounting, he moved to the place he recalled seeing Lucinda hiding. The hole was empty, but he hadn't dreamed he'd seen her there. The scent of honeysuckle lingered in the air. Had she come to her senses and gone to the village as he'd told her to do yesterday? Knowing her as he did, Jackson didn't believe so. She was stubborn. He glanced down and froze. Footprints, and not only her smaller ones. Two sets of larger ones, as well. Lucinda had been taken.

Chapter Thirty-one

"I will ask you once more politely; then I will not be so nice. Where is the child, witch?"

Lucinda stood shivering in the great room of Lord Cantley's hunting lodge. She'd been roused rudely from her sleeping hole, dragged up and out, then brought to the hunting lodge. The horse, she realized. She should not have left him to graze in the open. Two of Lord Cantley's henchmen had obviously spotted the animal and gone snooping around the cottage, finding her sleeping. They had taken her by surprise.

"I will never tell you his whereabouts," she finally answered. "You can torture me, kill me, but you will never hear it from my lips."

The earl sighed. "I thought as much," he clipped. "What happened to the men I hired in London to bring you and the child to me?"

Lucinda looked at the floor. "Dead," she said softly. "All of them."

He sighed again. "Well, less coin I'll have to part with, and I still got at least part of the end result. You."

She knew two men were guarding the front entrance to the lodge and suspected another was posted at whatever exit there might be through the back. She was trapped.

"You are beautiful."

Startled by his soft words, she glanced up at him. He was a handsome man, she supposed, if his features were cruel, cold, and unfeeling. If his heart was black, for no man who would harm an innocent babe could be anything but the devil.

"I've thought of you often since that night when I first took you. I've thought of having you again."

"Try it and I promise you will not find me so docile," she warned him. "Only a coward would drug a woman and then misuse her."

He shrugged but moved a step closer. "I saw an opportunity to have something I wanted. I took it. As any in my station would have done."

"Do not dare to compare all of your class with your foul traits. There are decent and kind people among your higher society. I once thought that they must all be like you, but I was wrong."

"Your husband is not like me," he pointed out. "Or considered one of the nobility, although his family is wealthy. He is as much of an outcast as you are, so it does not surprise me that you would rise to his defense."

"His bloodline makes no difference to me," she said. "A man should be judged by his deeds, his heart, and not his blood. Your deeds and your heart are both dark. My son will be nothing like you."

"Your son will be dead as soon as I learn his whereabouts, and I will, Lucinda. It is only a matter of time."

Rage rose up inside of her. "I will kill you first," she promised.

Lord Cantley moved closer. "That is why I cannot let

you live," he said. "Although I would like to keep you to enjoy for a while, this will be our last tryst together."

He kept inching toward her, she noted, and she hadn't missed his indication that he meant to defile her again. She would rather die than suffer his hands on her. She formed her fingers into claws, and without waiting for his subtle advance she flew at him. Her nails raked his face before he could react. His hand flew out and slapped her, sending her stumbling back with the force.

Cantley lifted a hand to his face, drew his fingers back, and glanced at the blood. "This is what I had hoped to avoid the night I drugged you with your own potion. Now, I find it rather stimulates me."

"If you are going kill me, do it now. I won't suffer your touch." Her cheek stung where he'd slapped her, and she had to blink back tears from a natural response to pain, but she would not cower from him. "I would rather be dead."

"Yes," he agreed. "I think you would. But that is for me to decide. As I said, in due time." He used her tactics and suddenly lunged forward, throwing his arms around her.

Lucinda found herself forced up against him. He tried to kiss her and she clamped her lips together. She stomped on his foot. He cursed but did not loosen his hold upon her.

"Vixen," he ground out. "You force me to be rough with you. Remember that was your choice."

"You give me no choices," she spit back, struggling to free herself.

"But I did," he reminded, dragging her to a masculine chaise and throwing her down upon it. "Tell me where the child is and maybe I won't kill you."

"Never," she growled.

He loomed over her, and Lucinda knew he would be

upon her in earnest in a moment. Her strength was no match for his. She might prolong the attack, but she could not stop the inevitable. There was no time to throw up a protective circle. Nor did she have the candles and sacraments needed within easy reach. She would curse him if she could, but her training did not deal in those dark deeds. Her mother had made certain Lucinda only learned the white magic.

She closed her eyes and prayed to God for intervention. It came a moment later with an urgent knock upon the lodge door.

"Lord Cantley! You have a guest!"

Lucinda opened her eyes. Lord Cantley was still scowling down at her. "Enter!" he yelled.

The door opened and Jackson was shoved inside. Lucinda's heart lurched.

"Marches up cool as you please and says he'd like a word with you, my lord," the henchman said. "Bloody idiot," he muttered with a laugh.

"Well, well, you are a brave soul, or a very stupid one."

"I would like a word with you," Jackson said, and his gaze strayed toward Lucinda, noted her appearance, her position on the chaise, and no doubt the scratches on Lord Cantley's face. A spark of blue flared in Jackson's eyes before it vanished.

"I'm sure you would," Lord Cantley said. "But I'm not ignorant enough to give it to you. Not while you aren't secured, leastwise." He nodded toward the henchman.

The man stepped forward and threw his arms around Jackson from the back. Jackson jabbed his elbow into the man's gut, turned, and hit him so hard he banged into the wall.

"Guards!" Lord Cantley yelled.

The other guard came rushing through the door; then a second man appeared from an archway behind Lucinda.

She'd seen Jackson beat worse odds than these, but she sprang into action. She glanced around for anything she might use as a weapon. Next to the hearth stood an iron poker. Lucinda raced toward it, but was brought up short by Lord Cantley's hand in her hair.

"No, you don't, witch." He shoved her back onto the chaise. She landed with a jar.

Two of the guards had Jackson down on the floor, but his strength, superior, she knew, would not have him there for long. She no more thought it than the two men trying to pin Jackson down went flying. Jackson was up again in an instant. His eyes promised death as he stared at Lord Cantley; then he was moving toward the man. Lord Cantley was wise enough to back away from him.

"I tried to talk to you," Jackson said, his voice low and deadly. "Now the option has been removed. You'll die for touching her again!"

Lucinda had no doubt that Lord Cantley's demise was at hand. She saw one of the guards rise from behind Jackson. The man pulled a pistol. Her scream seemed to come from a long way off, drawn out in a motion slower than actual time. Jackson started to turn, but the man brought the pistol crashing down against his skull. Blood oozed from a gash at Jackson's temple. He stumbled toward Lord Cantley, hands outstretched as if he meant to choke him, then collapsed.

"Jackson!" Lucinda leaped up, but again Lord Cantley reached out and knocked her backward.

"Tie him up," the earl demanded. "I would have you kill him now, but I may yet torture the information I need from him." So saying, Lord Cantley moved to the hearth, where a low fire burned, snatched up the poker, and placed it in the fire. He turned and smiled at Lucinda. "Thank you for giving me the idea."

She had to do something! Lucinda scrambled off of

the chaise and tried to reach Jackson. Lord Cantley grabbed her and pulled her back. She stood with her arms pinned behind her back, watching helplessly as the guards roused themselves. Cantley issued orders to pull a chair close to the hearth and put Jackson on it. One of the guards left but returned shortly with a long length of rope. The three men lashed Jackson to the chair.

"Bring a bucket of cold water," Lord Cantley demanded. "We'll rouse him so I can get on with the interrogation." He shoved Lucinda down upon the chaise. "Now, stay put or I'll tie you up, as well." He ran his cold blue eyes over her. "I'll deal with you later."

The guard arrived with the water. At Lord Cantley's nod, the man threw water in Jackson's face. Jackson jerked, shook his head, and looked around. Lucinda knew immediately when he'd regained his senses. He struggled against his bonds.

"You may go now," Lord Cantley said to the guards. "I'll handle things from here. Back to your posts."

Two of the guards left from the front entrance; the other went through the arch obviously toward the back exit. Lucinda sat twisting her hands. She hated feeling so helpless. Jackson could probably call the wolf to him now, but to advise him to do so might make Lord Cantley quickly take his life. As if the earl knew what she was thinking, he turned to glance at her.

"And no interference from you, or I'll kill him before he can suffer one of your spells."

The man turned back to Jackson. "Now, I'll ask you nicely once: where is the child?"

"Go to hell," Jackson answered.

"I thought you might say that." Lord Cantley bent and retrieved the poker from the fire. He waved it menacingly in front of Jackson's face. "He's not of your seed. Not of your blood. Tell me where he is and there is no reason for you to die."

Jackson stared at the man. "No one need know he is not of my seed, or of my blood. Not even the child. I take what you do not want as my own. I will raise him as my own. He is no threat to you."

"He bears my mark! He will always be a threat to me and mine. If my cousin should learn I have placed a bastard in line for the throne, he'll see me and all my bloodline destroyed. He will take all that he has generously bestowed upon me, and I will not risk that for the bastard brat of a witch!" He placed the poker closer to Jackson's face. "Do you understand?"

"I will not tell you where he is," Jackson repeated.

Lord Cantley sighed. He lowered the poker and placed the iron back into the fire. Lucinda released the pent-up breath she had held. The earl turned and walked toward her.

"Not even for her?"

She tried to scoot away from him.

"Keep your hands off of her!" Jackson growled.

Lord Cantley reached out and grabbed a handful of Lucinda's hair. "You can get other brats upon her," he said, turning to glance at Jackson. "Just give me the one, and I won't force you to watch me take her, here, now, in front of your very eyes."

Jackson struggled against his bonds again. He was strong, but the ropes were thick. His eyes had started to glow. Lucinda knew the wolf was waiting, just beneath the surface of his skin. Would giving herself to Lord Cantley distract the man enough to allow Jackson to transform without his notice? She didn't think so, or by God, she would stoop to even that. If only she weren't a mere woman. If only she knew the dark magic that could aid her in rescuing both Jackson and herself. Lucinda could not cast curses or dark spells . . . but wait, there was something she had never thought of. There had been no reason to think of it, not until now.

"Don't hurt him and I will willingly give myself to you," she said.

Both Jackson's and Lord Cantley's heads snapped in her direction.

"No, Lucinda!" Jackson said. "By God you will not!"

"Will you?" Lord Cantley asked, lifting a brow. "You know I can take whatever I want from you easily enough."

"Why take what I will willingly give you?" she countered. "I was a virgin when you had me last. I've learned much since that time. I can please you."

"Lucinda!" Jackson growled again.

"I imagine you can," Lord Cantley considered. "And I imagine it would hurt him worse to see you give yourself rather than watching me take you against your will."

"You must promise to let him go afterward," she specified, knowing anything Lord Cantley agreed to would be a lie.

"Of course," he said. "He's no use to me anyway. Unless he has changed his mind about telling me where the child is."

Lucinda had to place all of her trust in Jackson in that moment. He did not know her plans. He might weaken. But no, he would not, she knew. He would never place Sebastian's life in danger. Not even for her. Jackson knew she would never forgive him if he did.

"I will not tell you," Jackson said, his voice now cold. "And if you do this for me, Lucinda, I will never forgive you!"

Lord Cantley released Lucinda's hair. "So, do we have a bargain, witch?"

Another bargain. But this was one she would not keep.

The other she would. Lucinda had the answer now. She knew how to break Jackson's curse.

"One last kiss," she said to Lord Cantley. "To soften the sting of what I do now. You will grant me that?"

The man smiled, more of a smirk really. "I don't think he'll kiss you back," he said with a laugh. "But yes, tell him good-bye."

Lucinda took a deep breath and walked past Lord Cantley. She walked to where Jackson sat. His head was bowed. When he looked up at her, his eyes glowed bright blue.

"Do not do this, Lucinda," he said, his voice raw. "He will not keep your bargain anyway."

She bent before him. "I will keep ours now, though," she said. "Let me kiss you, Jackson."

When she placed her hands on his face, he tried to jerk back from her. "Why do you torment me? I will not kiss you and then watch you give yourself to him. You do me no favors, Lucinda."

"I take from you what burdens have been given." She leaned closer, brushing his lips with hers. "I take upon myself your sins, and the sins of those before you. I take upon myself your beast."

The blue in his eyes grew brighter. "No, Lucinda," he said as dawning registered in his glowing eyes. "No!"

She leaned forward and clamped her open mouth upon his. Something spilled forward into her mouth, a presence, a spirit, that flowed from him into her. It was hot, like bright light, and it did not go without kicking and screaming. His body bucked in the chair, but she held fast to his face. She felt the spirit fill her, and still it spilled forth from his mouth to hers. It sang in her blood, invaded her thoughts with visions of nighttime, of full moons and running free.

Hotter and hotter was the light that filled her. She felt

sweat trickling down her temple. She felt the beast come inside of her, become one with her. Then it was over and Jackson sagged against her, as if she had drained him of life. She pulled away to look at him, her hand now gentle on the side of his face.

"Jackson," she whispered. "You are free."

Lucinda's voice called to him from a great distance. What had she said? *You are free?* His eyes suddenly snapped open. She was there, kneeling before him. Her eyes were glowing blue.

"Enough," Lord Cantley snapped behind her. "Come to me, Lucinda. Keep the bargain we have made."

Her lips parted, and Jackson saw the fangs. Slowly, she rose. She turned toward Lord Cantley, keeping her head bent as she walked to where he stood waiting. Jackson watched, dazed. Lord Cantley reached out and pulled Lucinda closer. The man tangled his hand in her hair and drew her head back to look up at him. He leaned forward as if to kiss her; then he froze. His eyes widened and he tried to push her away. But it was too late.

Lucinda pounced upon the man; her fingernails were now like claws, her teeth sharp as she went for his neck. Blood spurted. The man screamed. Lord Cantley's voice drowned in his own blood. Her strength was now what Jackson's had been. She held the man to her, ripped and tore at his throat until he finally ceased to struggle. She released the earl and he fell to the floor. He was dead.

Slowly, Lucinda faced Jackson. Her eyes were still bright blue, and now there was blood dripping down the side of her mouth. She ran to him, her hands clumsy with her extended nails, trying to loosen his ropes.

"Go, Lucinda," he said, glancing at the door and expecting a guard to come crashing in at any moment. "Go now, through the back!"

She shook her head, glanced around, then grabbed the hot poker from the hearth. She moved behind him and he heard the ropes singe. They busted loose a moment later. Jackson thrust them off of him and rose just as the lodge door crashed open. The guard looked at Lord Cantley, lying dead on the floor, and rushed toward Jackson. He had no time to think. Only to act.

Jackson lunged forward, grabbed the man's head, and snapped his neck. The second guard rushed in, pulling a dagger from his belt, but Jackson grabbed the man's hand, twisted it, and buried the dagger in the guard's chest.

"Run, Lucinda!" Jackson shouted. The lodge door now stood open and empty. The sound of running boots came from the rear of the lodge. Jackson pulled the knife from the dead guard's chest. He ran and jumped over the chaise, flattened himself against a wall, and when a man came running past grabbed him from behind, quickly slicing the blade across his throat. Jackson shoved him aside and turned to where Lucinda stood. Only Lucinda no longer stood there. In her place now stood a wolf. A red wolf with feminine-looking features.

"Lucinda," Jackson whispered, but the wolf darted toward the door and out. Jackson ran after it. "Lucinda!"

Chapter Thirty-two

She smelled the smoke the next morning. Lucinda knelt by a stream, staring at her reflection in the water. Jackson, she imagined, had burned the lodge and the bodies inside. Accidents were known to happen. In these woods, it wasn't the first fire that had burned a dwelling to the ground. She couldn't recall much after Lord Cantley had looked at her with such fear in his eyes, after she'd gone for his throat, tasted his blood, and killed him. She felt no remorse.

It had to be done. Lord Cantley would no longer threaten her son. Now Jackson was free to raise Sebastian without fear of the curse that once had haunted him. Lucinda had kept her bargain after all. And in doing so, she had to release Jackson from his obligation to her.

She felt the wolf inside of her, now aware of what Jackson had felt most of his life. It was strange to feel as if she shared herself with another entity, and yet for one like her it was not so strange really. A witch, why not a shape-shifter in the bargain? Lucinda imaged she'd fare much better with the curse than Jackson had.

He was not raised in her spiritual realm. She accepted things that he never could. Understood things that he never would. All had ended as it should.

But even as the thought crossed her mind, she admitted that all had not ended as she had hoped. Before, she might have managed to fit into Jackson's life, into her son's life, but now that had changed. Jackson and Sebastian now had a chance for normalcy. She wouldn't spoil that for them. She loved them both too much.

"You're not as easy to track now."

She turned to see Jackson standing behind her. Lucinda had allowed him to track her. They had to say their good-byes.

"You are well?" she asked. "Do you have injuries that must be seen to?"

He moved toward her. "No. I am well." Jackson reached her and bent down beside her, staring into her eyes. "Why, Lucinda? Why did you do what you did?"

"It was the only way," she answered. "I realized that if I could not break your curse, I could take it from you. Lord Cantley would have killed us both. I did what had to be done."

"You must give it back," he said softly. "I would not wish it upon you. We have done what we came here to do. Give it back, Lucinda."

She shook her head. "If one of us must be cursed, it must be me. We made a bargain. You must take care of Sebastian. You must give him all that I never can. I want his life to be different than mine has been. I want the best for both of you."

"At your own sacrifice?" he asked, and tears filled his dark eyes. "You would give up everything for us? For him, I understand, but not for me. Why for me, Lucinda?"

She would not tell him that she loved him. It would only cause him guilt. He should get on with his life now.

Perhaps in his future he could marry Lady Anne. Now he could have his own sons to play with Sebastian. Jackson could have the kind of life he was born to have. Lucinda would not deny him that or cause him any future guilt that he could find happiness at her expense.

"I told you," she said. "For Sebastian. Even if I were not cursed, I am still a witch, Jackson. I would have my son be raised by a normal parent. A good parent, which I know you will be to him."

"And that's all you want from me? To raise your child?"

Her own eyes grew moist. "No," she answered. "I want you to love him. I want you to love *our* child."

Jackson suddenly rose and turned his back on her. "You know that I will," he said quietly. "You know that I do love him already."

"Yes, I do know that."

"What will you do, Lucinda? Where will you go? Back to Whit Hurch?"

She would be honest with him about her village. "I will not go back there. I have no friends there, Jackson. Not one person in the village would have offered me safe haven had I gone there. I will find another village. You needn't worry about me."

"So, our bargain is met, and that is all between us?"

As much as it pained her, she would let him go. "Yes."

"You want nothing more than what you've asked?"

"Yes."

"You want me to go now? To walk away and forget you?"

Her throat closed up for a moment. "Yes," she managed to whisper.

"What of my brothers? You have only taken my curse. What of theirs?"

Lucinda didn't know. "I believe it might be each brother's destiny to end his own curse. You found a way. Perhaps they will, as well."

She saw his fists clench at his sides. "They will find it no surprise that I got a woman to do for me what none of them has been able to do for himself."

Her heart nearly broke at those words. "Don't, Jackson," she warned him. "The bargain has been met. Take the gift I give you, keep your promises to me, and go now."

Jackson fought down the anger, the pain, the dissatisfaction of how his curse had come to be broken. Passing it to another had never entered his mind. Not except in the fear that he would pass it to his sons if he ever produced any. He'd thought while he was searching for Lucinda that she must love him to do what she had done. To bear his burden. To take his sins upon herself. But she had done it for Sebastian, and if Jackson still respected her more than any other woman he had known, she had broken his heart.

He had thought his heart had already been broken, but he realized now that love when he thought he had first felt it was only the shallow emotion he was capable of feeling at that time. He did not even know what love was . . . not until now. Lucinda had taught him love. Lucinda and Sebastian. And she had taught Jackson how truly painful it was to love and not to be loved in return.

Could he walk away as she wanted him to do? Could he leave her with his curse and take everything she held most precious from her? No. He could not. Not even if that was her wish.

"You will give it back," he said.

"It means nothing to me," she said behind him. "It is

only one more way that I am different from everyone else. Go, as I told you to do. I want you to go. You gave me what I asked for, and I gave you what you asked for. We shared pleasure. It is over now."

Damn her! No whip's lash ever hurt him more than her easy dismissal of him. He wanted to tell her that he loved her, but how could he when she kept whittling at his pride? How could he give to her when she would give nothing in return? How could he be that unselfish? But he could be, Jackson realized. What was love anyway if not truthful? He turned to face her.

Their eyes met.

"I love you, Lucinda," he said.

Her face drained of color for a moment. Tears bubbled up in her eyes, but she quickly blinked them back. "You don't have to say that," she whispered. "Please don't say that."

"I have to say it if it is what I feel," he said. "Pride be damned. The whole world be damned for all I care. I love you."

She glanced away from him. "It's the spell," she said. "That's all. The spell I cast upon you that first night when you returned to the town house. It must have worked after all. It will fade," she assured him.

"I do not want it to fade," he countered. Jackson knew it was no spell that had made him fall in love with Lucinda. "I love you for who you are, Lucinda, not for any spell you could cast upon me. I love your goodness. I love your fire. I love everything about you."

Her hands shook, he noted, when she pushed her hair from her face. "You mustn't," she said. "Not now. It's too late."

Jackson didn't know if he only wanted so badly to hear her say she loved him that he heard her say the words in his head or if she had spoken to him in truth. But no, her lips had not moved, except to tremble slightly.

He closed his eyes and again he heard her voice. *I've fallen in love with you. I love you even now, when you sit before me with the eyes of a wolf. So take pity upon the fool I have become. I forgot it was only a bargain between us.*

His eyes opened and met hers. Lucinda's now glowed a soft blue.

"You love me," he said. "I remember now. I remember you telling me."

She shook her head, but he saw more than the glow in her eyes. He saw the truth.

"Why can't you tell me, Lucinda?"

"Not now," she said, and her voice sounded strange. "Not when you have your life as it should be. Not when you can give Sebastian all I wanted for him. I will not ruin it all. I will not!"

"No," he agreed. Jackson knew what was happening to her. Emotion had brought the wolf to the surface. He would take it back. "You will not ruin it all," he said, moving toward her. "You will not ruin it all by denying me the one thing I want most. You."

He pounced upon her before she could flee. She struggled and her strength surprised him. "I take upon myself your burdens," he said. "I take upon myself the sins of your past and the sins of those before you."

"No!" she shouted, but he continued.

"I take upon myself your beast!" He placed his mouth against hers and pried her lips open. The force that spilled from her mouth into his knocked him backward. Still, they were joined by the blue light, so bright he had to squint against it. He felt it flowing from her into him; then he felt it flow back out. The light grew brighter and brighter and then suddenly no light flowed from either his mouth or Lucinda's. Both of them fell backward as if a force had held them but now suddenly released them.

The blue light took form. It was a wolf. The beast looked from one to the other before it slunk off into the forest.

Jackson shook uncontrollably for a moment; then he calmed and his breathing returned to normal. Lucinda lay on the ground, motionless. He scrambled to her, lifting her in his arms.

"Lucinda?"

Slowly, her eyes opened. They were as green as the forest around them.

"It is gone," she whispered. "It has left me, and it has left you. I don't feel it in you anymore."

Jackson took a moment to collect himself. The beast was gone. "But why?"

She reached up and touched his face. "You did not need it any longer. You are whole."

He didn't understand. "Whole?"

"The weaknesses within you that kept you from being all that you can be, you have defeated. You have broken your own curse, Jackson."

Peace suddenly flowed through him. It was odd to be without the wolf, but yet he did not feel empty. He felt whole, as Lucinda said. Whole for the first time in his life. Only one thing could make him happier than he felt in that moment. He bent and kissed her.

Lucinda broke from him. "I am still a witch, Jackson," she said.

He kissed her again. "I can live with that," he said against her mouth. "Besides, you're not a very good one."

She laughed and pulled him back to her lips. They

stayed that way for a time. In each other's arms. Finally Jackson pulled away, sat, and pulled her up beside him.

"Let's go home, Lucinda," he said. "Let's go see our son."

Epilogue

The country estate was a soothing balm to Lucinda's soul. She loved the large manor house, the fields of green where horses grazed and the sun shone down upon their silky coats. It was a place where she could find solace, where she could raise her son and spend her nights in the arms of the man she loved. And Jackson, now free from his family curse, had shocked his older brother with the way he had thrown himself into the work that must be done to keep such an impressive manor home, and such a large stable of horses, running.

He came in now while she changed Sebastian. Jackson walked up behind her and rubbed his work-sweaty body against her. "I've missed you, wife," he said.

Lucinda giggled. "You just left our bed two hours ago."

Jackson nuzzled her ear, and desire shot through her. "Two hours is a long time."

"Don't get me smelly," she warned him. "I am to meet Rosalind downstairs shortly so we can plant an herb garden."

"You two get on well together," he said, but he didn't release her. "You've become as thick as thieves in short order."

Lucinda loved Rosalind, and Armond as well. She wondered when her new friend would tell her husband about the babe she carried. It would soon be too noticeable for her to hide. With Jackson's arms around her, Lucinda suddenly noticed that he clutched an envelope in one hand.

"What have you there?"

"Oh, I'd forgotten," he said, releasing her. "I brought it up for you. Our first social invitation."

He handed the envelope to her. " 'To Lord and Lady Jackson Wulf,' " she read. It was odd, but she still got a rush of pleasure to have a last name, especially his. "I was just going to change Sebastian," she said, handing the envelope back to Jackson. "I'll read it once I've finished."

Jackson stepped in front of her and reached into the cradle to tickle Sebastian. "Read it now. I'll change him."

Lucinda walked to the middle of the room and broke the seal upon the envelope. Her gaze scanned the invitation. "It's an invite to Lady Amelia Sinclair's wedding," she told Jackson. "The social event of the year, I imagine."

"Will we attend?" He glanced over his shoulder.

Although Lucinda wasn't in any hurry to return to London, she nodded. "Yes. She is a friend. Besides, Rosalind told me that Amelia is marrying the man whose property borders Wulfglen. I believe he is a friend of yours, or once was."

"Lord Robert," Jackson supplied. "Yes, we once rousted about together as boys, although he is more Armond's and Gabriel's age."

Gabriel was a sore subject these days. Lucinda knew that Jackson was worried about the whereabouts of his older brother and felt guilty that he was missing simply because he'd gone in search of Jackson. Both Armond and Jackson had already made plans to go to Liverpool soon in hopes of finding Sterling.

Much had happened for the Wulf brothers. "Do you think Gabriel is spared now?" she asked Jackson, moving to a small end table to place the invitation to Amelia Sinclair's wedding aside.

"That is what Armond and I are hoping," Jackson said, going about the business of changing Sebastian. "It seems so odd that both of us have broken our curse, and in a time frame that makes us both wonder if perhaps the curse simply wore off."

Lucinda didn't believe that for a moment, but if it gave both Armond and Jackson some peace where their brother was concerned, she saw no harm at the moment in suppressing her own opinion. "We will see," was all she said.

"Lucinda, come here."

Something in his tone alarmed her. Lucinda rushed to Jackson's side, staring down at Sebastian. The babe looked fine, kicking his small legs and obviously enjoying being naked. Lucinda placed a hand to her heart.

"You gave me a fright, Jackson," she scolded. "What is it?"

He glanced up at her, then reached down and held little Sebastian's kicking legs still. "The birthmark. Look at it, Lucinda."

She bent over the cradle and had a closer look. The dragon birthmark that had so clearly stood out upon Sebastian's leg had changed shape. It no longer resembled a dragon at all . . . but rather the shape of a wolf's head. She glanced back up at Jackson. "What does it mean?"

He pulled her close. "It means he is truly a Wulf now. And that he is no longer a threat to England's throne,"

Jackson added. "Although I wouldn't mind seeing my son rule the country."

Hearing him refer to Sebastian as his son always warmed Lucinda's heart. She could give it now, her heart, her soul, everything she had, to Jackson and to Sebastian. She wasn't afraid any longer to share herself. To be soft, and to be strong when need be. She slid her arms around Jackson.

"I love you, Jackson Wulf," she whispered up at him.

He bent and kissed her.

"That's all I need to be whole," he said.